BROKEN *promises*

I. A. DICE

ALSO BY I. A. DICE

Broken Rules

The Sound of Salvation
The Taste of Redemption

Copyright © 2022 by I. A. Dice
Second Edition

All rights reserved.
No part of this publication may be reproduced, distributed, or transmitted in any form or by any means, including photocopying, recording, or other electronic or mechanical methods, without the prior written permission of the publisher, except in the case of brief quotations embodied in critical reviews and certain other non-commercial uses permitted by copyright law.

This is a work of fiction. Names, characters, businesses, places, events, locales, and incidents are either the products of the author's imagination or used in a fictitious manner. Any resemblance to actual persons, living or dead, or actual events is purely coincidental.

Edited by: Kylie Ryan at Final Cut Editing

Connect with I. A. Dice:
Instagram
Facebook
Reader Group

To my son,
my patient little prince

BROKEN
promises

I. A. DICE

CHAPTER ONE

Dante

Vodka burns through my veins, potent enough to intoxicate a dozen people. Just not me. So far, I've drunk four bottles in forty-eight hours. Well, almost, because the fourth, half-empty, sits on the nightstand beside an overflowing ashtray. Three more are scattered across the floor, dotted with empty, screwed-up packs of cigarettes.

Forty-eight hours... two days wasted on pouring vodka down my throat, diving into memories, trying to hate *her*, and getting fucking *nowhere*. I gulp another mouthful from the crystal glass. My taste buds died after the second bottle, so I no longer feel the scorching sensation of alcohol sliding down my throat. But I do feel pain.

Not physical—mental. Though, the intensity doesn't differ much. If anything, mental pain is ten times worse than a gunshot wound. I'd know.

Alcohol is not the answer. I'm aware of that dreaded fact, but it *is* supposed to help me forget the question. I call bullshit. All that vodka, but no results.

I don't think any amount of alcohol could silence the cacophony of thoughts swirling in my mind. It hasn't even helped put me to sleep. I'm drunk and too tired to move but wide awake, nonetheless. I sit on a bare mattress, my back against the headboard.

Bedsheets, covered by a thin layer of snow, became a questionable decoration on the driveway thirty seconds after I burst in here two days ago. The walk-in closet door hangs off the top hinge; not a single dress, blouse, or sweater in sight. The dressing table I bought for her is still by the wall, although upside down, missing legs and the drawers. The mirror is cracked: smashed by my fist in a frenzied fit of rage.

Clothes, shoes, cosmetics, and even the Christmas tree she decorated flew out of the windows. *Everything* that reminded me of the petite, sassy star I fell in love with flew out of the fucking windows; everything except my mind, which can't escape her no matter how hard I try.

Trust me. I try really fucking hard.

But she's all I think about.

I hold my favorite gold revolver in one hand, spinning it around my index finger. Three turns left, three turns right, three turns left, three turns right.

Since she vanished without a trace, she's constantly on my mind. Not a second goes by that I don't imagine her smiles, kisses, or recall her voice. Her steel-gray eyes. Full lips. Every whispered *I love you.* Every tear she cried when she aimed Frank's gun at my heart outside that warehouse. Forty-eight. Hours. Ago.

I can't escape her. Memories resurface, each one like a steel-cap-boot kick to my ribs even though I'm already down, for fuck's sake. I'm not trying to pull myself up. Why should I? What is the point of my damned life now that the only person who mattered up and left?

And so, not for the first time, I toy with the revolver weighing my options. I want to forget about her for a few minutes, long enough to catch a fucking break. Erase my mind like you would a hard drive. Forget how beautiful she is, the sweet smell of her perfume, the delicate touch of her small, warm hand on my chest when she nuzzled into my side every night, falling asleep in my arms. I want to forget the bliss on her face when she whispered *I love you* but most of all, I want to forget that *I* love her. I can't stop.

I miss her so fucking much.

I miss her smiles, gestures, and that godawful attitude. I miss the peace that came with knowing she's mine. She's not. I don't think she ever was. She was a fucking illusion. An idea. A smoke screen.

My heart and mind rebel against my efforts to hate her. I can't. Not for one second. Not in the slightest. Why the hell not, though? She's not worth the hassle; she doesn't deserve me; she's an emotionally challenged teen who allowed her father to manipulate her. She played along, fulfilled his orders, betrayed my trust, gave me the world, and took it away. All of that's true. And it doesn't mean shit.

I still love her.

I would be better off if I could forget she exists, but she's so fucking deep under my skin that I'd need a new one if I tried to claw her out. I spin the fucking revolver right, left, then right again. Wouldn't it be easier to pull the trigger?

Night turns to day for the third time before I rise to face the world without her by my side. I'm not ready. I don't think I will ever be ready, but I don't have a choice.

Spades blows up my phone every hour. He came over yesterday, revved the engine on the driveway, and yelled at the top of his lungs when the maid refused to let him inside. Apparently, the Chief of police is eager to discuss the eighteen bodies we left outside of the warehouse plus a dozen more inside. Julij wants to talk business. The V brothers require a new delivery schedule.

Looks like the world keeps spinning.

I grab a hot shower, drink three shots of espresso, and force a bagel down my numb throat because a liquid diet won't keep me alive for long. The maid risks a few glances my way, her eyebrows drawn together, thoughts unvoiced. She must wonder where the hell my star is or why her stuff litters the driveway. If she utters her name, I'll fucking shoot her.

"Tidy up upstairs." I shove a cigarette between my lips, heading onto the terrace with my phone pressed to my ear.

In the distance, lake Michigan glistens in the early morning sun as if nothing fucking changed. Fresh, biting air fills my lungs, filtering through two days' worth of cigarette smoke buildup.

Spades answers before the first tone rings out as if he

resigned his time to staring at the phone until I called. "Finally," he huffs down the line, a long, annoyed exhale. "Jeremy's busting my balls, Julij's calls every hour on the hour, and the delivery from Detroit is way late. You need a chauffeur, or will you drive yourself to Delta?"

Again, the amount of alcohol in my bloodstream could intoxicate a dozen people... I'm probably in no state to operate heavy machinery. Too bad I'm all bright-eyed, bushy-tailed, fucking kinetic with vim and vigor. Talk about irony.

"Pick me up. I'll call Vince to check on the load. You tell Jeremy we'll meet him at the club in two hours. And stall Julij. I can't deal with his pompous ass today."

Delta's in dire need of refurbishment after the fire. I paid no attention to the damages when I tortured the fucker who—

Nope. Not going *there*. I inhale the freezing air and create a mental bullet-point plan of action. Damage assessment first. Then, contractors to fix the place and update a few details while there's an opportunity. Delta's too profitable to close for refurbishment, but now that there's no other choice, I can think of a few changes.

Thirty seconds on the phone with Spades redirected my thoughts away from Layla. I had zero breaks for two days, not even for one second, but now I broke free from her spell, even if only for a moment, but that's more than I managed by myself. Work is my answer. Moping in bed won't help me deal with the past. I need to do something... *anything*.

CHAPTER TWO

Dante

Empty bottles, brimful ashtrays.

Broken chairs.

Shattered glass.

Ecstasy, cocaine, confetti.

Deflated balloons.

Discarded condoms.

A stale stench of booze, cigarette smoke, and puke saturates the air. A wingback chair in the corner of the living room requires a deep clean after a blonde bimbo projectile-vomited across it, marking the wall and Nate too. She attempted a run to the bathroom but missed the mark by thirty yards.

Half a dozen crystal glasses were smashed in a game of *I'll show you just how pissed off I am. Bang!* Two dining chairs require replacing after Spades broke one on the head of a royal douchebag, then hit him with the second for good measure. My house has never been a venue for a single party before. And for a good reason. Chaos finds its way to every party regardless of where it happens, but the thought of the mess afterward stopped me from hosting for years.

Unfortunately, this year, my options were limited. The idea to host a New Year's Eve bash in the comfort of my living room was a spur-of-the-moment thing. With twenty hours to midnight, the choice of venues was limited while Delta remained closed for refurbishment. The travel ban imposed by a detective responsible for the investigation concerning Frank's death squandered the initial plan of celebrating with Julij in New York or with the V brothers in Detroit.

It was supposed to be a small gathering, my entourage, their girls, and a few acquaintances. As expected, shit hit the fan when Bianca asked permission to invite her brother and his wife. Luna wanted her sister, and Jackson called in half of fucking Chicago.

I agreed to all, including those who arrived in the middle of the night in a yellow school bus. The anarchy in my living room kept my mind in check, away from Layla. And since I sweat blood not to think about her, the party got out of hand four hours before midnight.

For the past six torturous days, I have busied myself with

tasks my people usually take care of. I work eighteen-hour days, make shit up along the way, and break my neck to stay occupied. With the whole city in the palm of my hand and the forecasted increase in profits, I decided to open another club. Spades joined me on the hunt for new premises. He hardly leaves me alone these days, volunteering as my nanny. We bought two buildings, one in the North and one in the South. While my lawyer worked overtime to finalize the transactions, I shopped for sound systems, spent hours upon hours interviewing potential employees and checked every load from Detroit.

I knock myself out, but Layla feasts on my thoughts regardless of my efforts. I freeze in the middle of a conversation because one word reminds me of her. I forget the world when I'm behind the wheel as I drive by where I once saw her or where we were together. My mind switches off to all stimuli at the most inconvenient moments.

My people don't utter her name. No one mentions the times when Layla was by my side. No one mentions the night she killed Frank, either. It truly is as if she never fucking existed... but every so often, conversations cease when I enter the room, and I just know they're talking about her. Ironically, no one has said she doesn't deserve me, that I should've killed her on the spot. Only Spades found the courage to comment on my refusal to go after her.

"You'll regret it."

Fucking Nostradamus.

Day after day, night after night, Layla infects my thoughts. There's no forgetting, no moving forward. I'm stuck, my life on hold. Where is she? Is she safe? Why did she run? Is she afraid of me? Why did she follow Frank's orders?

Questions multiply daily, but answers fail to arrive.

A knock on the door snaps me out of Layla-haze. I fling the cigarette butt over the terrace railing and make my way across the filthy house, eyes on the floor as I navigate around the broken glass and dried-up puke.

"Good morning." A young girl dressed in a white apron with a pink logo of *Pristine Clean* company on her chest bows slightly. She holds two buckets brimming with chemicals. Behind her back, another girl plays tug-of-war with a hoover stuck in the trunk of a pink hatchback.

It's New Year's Day, but the owner of the *Pristine Clean* didn't complain when I rang late last night to offer triple rates if he could get my house spotless this morning. New Year's Day morning. Cleaning used to be the maid's job, but she packed her bags three days ago.

Although *ran* might fit better in this context.

She was tired—probably scared too—of my tantrums whenever I found something of Layla's around the house. She reached her limit when I upended the table after she served pancakes with honey—Layla's favorite. Every breakfast we ate together flashed before my eyes...

I freaked the fuck out.

Not for the first time, and most definitely not the last. I lose my cool a lot lately, taking the steadfast frustration out on anyone within my reach. Good job my men handle my outbursts like pros by diligently ignoring the shit that spews out of my mouth, or I'd be left with no crew by now.

"Can we come in?" The girl steps from one foot to the other, wide eyes jumping between my face and chest.

I push the door open further to let them pass. Hoover girl, a petite blonde with melon-sized boobs, eyes me up, a confident, cheeky smile on her glossy lips. The obnoxious flirting stops when we enter the living room.

"Some party," she says, peering at me over her shoulder. "Too bad I wasn't invited. I would've made you breakfast."

Courageous little thing.

"Get busy." I glance at my wristwatch—a gift from Layla and the only thing I refuse to hurl out of the window. I hadn't noticed until she was gone, but she had it engraved. Those few words speak volumes about her feelings.

Time is limited, but love is timeless.

I wear the watch every day and graze my fingers across the letters on the back every night.

"The sooner you finish, the bigger the bonus."

They exchange tight-lipped smiles before I leave the room on a quest to swallow a handful of painkillers. Thirty minutes later, the clamorous headache eases enough to make room for Layla. Every time I blink, I see the look on her face when she stood outside the warehouse and aimed the gun at my chest while tiny rivers crept down her pale cheeks.

"I really do love you," she whispers, staring into my eyes.

"I know."

Her whole, petite body trembles, but she plucks up the courage and moves her finger to the trigger. Fear fails to arrive; there's just relief that I won't have to face the world without her.

"I'm sorry," she mouths.

"Do you want me to count down from five for you, Layla?" Frank growls. His harsh, cold tone could freeze the vast lake behind Layla's back. "We don't have all fucking night. Get it over with."

Letting all air out of her lungs, she pulls the trigger.

A loud bang rings in my ears.

Frank's lifeless body falls to the ground.

And time fucking stops.

A six-year-long war ended by his daughter.

She killed him. She murdered him in cold blood, and I've never been prouder or more betrayed.

My cell vibrates, none other than the Chief on the line, his name flashing on the screen. I rub my face, exhausted, frustrated, and furious.

So. Fucking. Furious.

"It's New Year's Day," I snap, my jaw working in circles.

"Yes indeed. Should I give you my best wishes? Of course, Dante," Jeremy says in a theatrical, sarcastic tone. "I wish us many years of successful cooperation, but to make sure it will be successful, you must suffer a little. I had the CIA on the phone. Another detective will arrive here tomorrow, and he's just *dying* to talk to you. Get your shit together and meet me at the station in an hour so I can prep you for the uncomfortable questions."

Great... just what I need. As if it's not enough that he calls ten times a day to scream his head off, scolding me over the emerging evidence that points back to me or one of my people; or that the media overindulges the topic twenty-four-seven; or that I spent six hours on Thursday at the station with the FBI's finest—detective Jones. Now the CIA is involved. The next step is the DEA knocking down my door together with a whole fucking SWAT team.

Only six days have passed since Frankie Harston took his final breath, but I'm half a million dollars lighter already, bribing people left and right to close the investigation before the ink dries on the page. The chief could send four more daughters to college for his cut. But he sure deserves a round of applause for how well he works under pressure.

I called him ten minutes after Frank's body hit the ground to make sure his team would arrive first on the scene. And what a scene that was... macabre. Enough blood to sell by the pint. Chiefs men had to eliminate hard evidence and leave meaningless clues. My sole strict order for Jeremy that night: make sure *nothing* leads back to Layla in any shape or form. I found out that she worked with Frank all along less than twenty minutes earlier, but her safety remained my priority.

Pity the fool.

"Consider it done. She was never there."

My name would appear under the *prime suspect* category regardless of the evidence. The six-year-long war wasn't as brutal as you'd expect, but not quiet either. CIA, FBI, DEA, and every other institution in this country was in the know. There's probably a room in Langley dedicated to housing thousands upon thousands of pages filled with meaningless evidence they have gathered over the years, eager to shove Frank and me behind bars. Useless effort. A wild goose chase. Not one institution found enough evidence to warrant arrest. Now, they might.

My usual meticulous conduct went to hell the night Luca sent me a picture of Layla tied up, gagged, and missing a finger. I was careless that night. Under normal circumstances, under unwritten Mafia code, when Frank's men bowed before me, they would've been allowed to join my crew. Under *normal* circumstances. Nothing about that night was normal, though.

I was too fucking fervent to adhere to the rules I lived and breathed for years. Rules I imposed on myself at an early age. I needed an outlet for my rage, and the rules ceased to matter. All those fuckers, intentionally or not, hurt the woman I love. They deserved a bullet each. Still, slaughtering thirty men sparked a lot of unnecessary heat. Jeremy's been working like a Trojan to clean the mess I made.

"I'll be there in an hour." I cut the call.

It'll take longer before the house is back to a spotless state, so I dial Rookie's number. He crawled into bed five hours ago, but someone should supervise the cleaners. A shower and sweats-to-suit wardrobe change later, I'm back downstairs, rolling the sleeves of my shirt.

The little blonde, her hair in a bun, arches her back, dents her spine and winks at me over her shoulder. Yes, because a girl in rubber gloves sprinkled with puke and a mist of sweat on her pink forehead is so fucking arousing, right?

"Stop smiling, keep scrubbing." I rake my hand through my damp hair. "You lack thirty IQ points and a lot of imagination to pique my interest, kid."

Her lips part in an inaudible *oh,* and her arms fly to her sides. "I do not lack any IQ! You better watch the way you talk to me. I'll tell my brother on you!"

A lick of fury rises up my back, vibrating at the base of my neck, between my shoulder blades, and resonates to my fingers that ball into a tight fist. "Call him right now. Tell him who you're pissing off. Believe me, barbie, I'm itching to dislocate someone's jaw. Send him my way if he has the balls to fight your battles. Although, if I were you, I wouldn't hold my breath. If he doesn't already work for me, he sure as fuck knows who I am."

She scoffs, arms akimbo. "And who may that be?"

"Dante Carrow. I'm sure it rings a bell."

Her eyes widen, then narrow a second later. "Bullshit."

"I'm paying you to clean, not to talk. Either get to work or get the fuck out of my house."

She rises from her knees, taring her gloves off. "My brother will hear about this." Head up high, she marches out of the house, slamming the door hard enough to reinstate my headache.

Fucking drama queen.

"I'm so sorry," her friend squeals. "I'm really, really sorry, Mr. Carrow. It's her first day. She's the boss's niece, so she feels entitled. Please don't send me away. I will clean the whole house, fast, I promise. It will be spotless. My boss will fire me if I don't finish, and I really need this job..." she rambles on, crumpling the yellow duster in her hands, eyes on my nose or chin, never once landing on my eyes. Hers are large, blue, and brimming with unshed tears. A mess of in-need-of-combing hair surrounds her thin, freckled face.

"What's your name?" I lean against the back of the couch.

"Grace. Grace Quincy."

"Why do you work, Grace?"

She pulls her eyebrows together, staring at my nose. It's one of the gestures diffident people use to appear confident. They chose a spot close to the eyes, like the nose or forehead, avoiding eye contact.

"I need the money..."

"Yes, I figured out that much. I'm asking *why*. How old are you? Eighteen? Nineteen? You should be in school."

"Seventeen." She drops her gaze to one of the many stains marking the floor. "School won't pay the rent or buy me groceries." She pulls on a loose thread of her apron, shoulders sagging. "Please let me finish."

If I met her before Layla, her pleas wouldn't mean shit, but post-Layla Dante mellowed a touch. A touch too fucking much. I can't dismiss Grace while she's on the brink of tears.

"You can finish," I say. "I'm about to leave now, but I'll be back in three hours. One of my men will keep an eye on you while I'm gone."

"Of course. I'll make sure the house is spotless. I promise you won't regret this." She drops to her knees, shoving her small hands into the yellow gloves discarded by the blonde.

The rumble of Rookie's Camaro infiltrates the house, adding a bit more to the growing, dull ache at the base of my skull. Fuck, this is going to be a long day...

"You look like someone ate you then threw you up," I smirk, standing in the open door, not one bit sorry that I dragged him out of bed. "Make sure the house is clean before you let the cleaner go. And get Jackson to run a background check on her for me, will you?"

Rookie narrows his bloodshot eyes. "You wanna hit that?"

"No." Fuck, no. I shudder, coming apart at the seams as the mere idea of touching another woman pins me down between hard teeth. It's way too soon to ponder the idea. Besides, Grace is a minor. Illegal. I'm far from a decent human being, but there are certain lines even I wouldn't cross. "I need a maid. I want to know who she is before I offer her the job."

I've been stabbed in the back by someone I trusted with my life recently, and *lesson learned.*

Fool me once...

CHAPTER THREE

Dante

"Where would you like to see this displayed?" The interior designer stands in the middle of the first room at Delta. He looks me up and down, blowing his longish hair out of his face. "How about the entryway? Or maybe the VIP area on the balcony?"

I arrived ten minutes ago to check the progress made by the construction crew so far. The fire damage was limited to the bar area in the first room, but I used the downtime to refresh and update the rest of the place. The crew I hired took their sweet time, charging by the hour, but it looks like we'll be back in business by Friday.

"I don't know what the fuck you're holding, and you're asking me where I want it displayed? Which one of us is the decorator here? Figure it out."

The guy steps back, setting what resembles a giant copper dildo on the floor, then combs his long, blond hair with his fingers, fucking up the hap-hazard behind the ear tuck he had going on. He's a spit-shine replica of Nick Carter of the Backstreet Boys. Though judging by how often his eyes fall to the inseam of my trousers, I'm betting his sexual orientation does not match Nick's.

"It's a sculpture. A very expensive one at that, made by a world-renowned artist. It has been a part of my personal collection for years, but I feel, given your *profession*, it belongs here."

"What exactly do you think I do for a living? This isn't a male strip club. We don't need a giant dildo here."

His eyes widen as he glances between me and the so-called sculpture. "This is not a dildo! It's a *bullet*." He clicks his tongue, pulling the *duh!* face. "A nitro express bullet, to be precise. They are mostly used—"

"In large-bore hunting rifles," I say. "Don't teach your grandma how to suck eggs." I inhale a calming breath. A glass of whiskey would work faster. A clip of my gun emptied into the ceiling even quicker, but it'd delay the re-opening. "*Why* is it here?"

"It'll make for an interesting feature and add character to the..." he scrunches his nose, "...*bland* space."

Hold me, or I'll gut the guy.

The main entrance opens behind my back before I have a chance to comprehend the gibberish and word a reply.

"Wow, someone's been busy!" Jackson's words echo in the empty space. He turns his head in all directions so fast I think his head might come off the hinges. "When are we opening?"

The decorator rolls his eyes with a sigh, mocking the hopeful note in Jackson's voice.

"I didn't ask for permission," I say, watching her plump lips.

She clicks her tongue and rolls her eyes, sending a wave of desire traveling throughout my nervous system. I've been here for ten seconds. She hadn't even opened her mouth yet, but I'm already so fucking hooked on this girl. The bartender sets a tall glass in front of her, and she holds out her money, eyes fixed on the guy.

Little Miss Independent.

I like her attitude, and I hope it's not just an act.

"Will you introduce yourself, or will you just gawk at me all night?" she clips, closing her full lips on the straw.

God, where the hell was this girl all my life?

A low blow to my ribs brings me back from Layla land.

"Did you hear me?" Jackson asks, eyeing the bullet with one eyebrow pulled into a question mark. "Man, what do you need a huge dildo for?"

Mic drop.

"It's a bullet, not a dildo," the decorator retorts.

"I don't know where you buy your bullets, but this one doesn't look like any of those I use."

I smirk under my breath when the guy turns pale at the sight of the gun tucked in the holster under Jackson's jacket. "Get this out of here." I motion at the sculpture. "Have you seen pictures of this room from before the fire?"

"I wouldn't call the previous interior design classy..." He examines his fingernails and smacks his lips before lifting his gaze to meet mine. Has he any idea how much he gets on my nerves? "I can't picture any VIPs gracing this place with their presence. No finesse, no glamor."

"You'd be surprised what kind of VIPs this club's hosted over the years. Nevertheless, this is a club for the masses, not just selected individuals. Recheck the photos and get to work. I want Delta to look exactly like it used to, and I want it ready by Friday morning."

His mouth falls open in an exaggerated manifestation of deep shock. "But that's three days away!"

"Yes, I can count. We're opening on Friday." I emphasize each word. "Now, get out of my face."

He blushes, lifts the dildo with visible strain, and leaves as instructed. Such a good boy. I light a cigarette, pointing my chin to the rolled-up papers in Jackson's hand.

"Ah, right." He smacks them into my chest. "Grace's profile. She's alright. Nothing out of the ordinary. Deceased father, an alcoholic mother, and a two-year-old brother. She's been working at the cleaning company for three months."

I know all that. She told me about the car crash her father died in and the years of her mother's downward spiral into the addiction. She also told me she's been sofa-surfing at her friends' houses for months, saving every last cent for a deposit to rent a flat. I hired her to clean my house every day, so I could get to know her better. She's punctual, well-organized, and thorough.

Layla left a massive hole in my life. The burning desire to care for someone almost fucking chokes me every day. There's something about Grace—and I pretend not to have the slightest idea what—that stops me from turning a blind eye and leaving her in the swamp she found herself in.

That *something* is vulnerability.

The same kind Layla sported: a helpless kitten aura hidden under a mask of self-sufficiency.

"So? Can I let everyone know we're opening on Friday?" Jackson wanders around the room like Delta's a museum jam-packed with exhibits. "Are the V brothers coming? Julij?"

"I'll see Julij tomorrow. Let the V brothers know, update the website, and send an invitation to the usual VIP crowd."

He signals that he understood, glaring at bare walls, pulling the faces of an art connoisseur. "Here." He points high above the ground. "It's fucking crooked."

Madhouse. One walks around the club with a dildo; the other looks for imperfections ten feet above the ground.

I leave him to deal with the workers while I drive home to offer Grace a job as my maid. She's scrubbing the kitchen sink, her dull-red hair in a bun, hands dressed in a pair of rubber gloves.

"Oh, hey. I didn't expect you back so early." She bares her teeth in a full-blown smile.

She's refreshing. Smiles for no reason and acts like cleaning my house is a godsend. As if life can't get any better.

I shrug out of my jacket and pop the two top buttons on my shirt. "We need to talk. Make yourself a cup of coffee and join me in the living room."

"Is..." she bites the inside of her cheek, no longer smiling. "Is something wrong?"

"No. Everything's fine. Don't worry."

"Um... okay. Give me two minutes." She tucks the cleaning products back into the cupboard under the sink.

I leave her be and round the bar to fetch a drink. There's no vodka left in this house, so whiskey on the rocks it is. My wristwatch shows four p.m., but with zero plans for the rest of the day, I'll start obsessing about Layla again. I need to get drunk and numb enough not to fucking care. Grace joins me at the bar a moment later, an uncertain, somewhat anxious look on her face. She cups the mug with both hands, eyes on the glass standing before me.

"Can you cook?"

"Not really. I can make simple dishes, but nothing special."

"My housekeeper left a week ago. I like you, Grace. You're eager and thorough. I want you to work for me. You'll need to learn how to cook proper meals, but an evening class should take care of that. I'll rent you an apartment, you'll get a car, and we'll find a nursery for your brother somewhere nearby."

I say I'll cover the cost of her apartment and the nursery and tell her how much she'll take home every month.

She lunges forward and wraps her arms around me tightly, weeping into my shoulder. "Thank you. You've no idea what this means to me. Thank you."

I pat her on the back, stiff all over, before I push her away. "I'm off to New York tomorrow. One of my people will sort everything out for you over the weekend."

CHAPTER FOUR

Dante

My good friend, Chief Jeremy Smith had a sudden onset of a migraine when I asked him to take care of the travel ban so I could attend Nikolaj's funeral. Truth be told, I don't care much about the deceased King of New York. Unfortunately, Julij is now my business partner, so it's in my best interest to pay my respects. Especially since I hope to befriend a few of the most influential bosses from all over the country who announced their attendance.

Julij is a newbie in this world. No one will take him seriously if he starts talking business after years of observing our world from behind his late father's back. My name, on the other hand, comes with a reputation. People know me or have at least heard of me. Thanks to the V brothers and their brilliant chemist, many also respect me.

Nikolaj was their go-to guy whenever drugs were concerned. If I can take his place in the supply chain, my network will double in size. With the whole of Chicago under my command and Frank's meddling no longer an issue, I can finally stretch my wings.

"I'm driving," Spades chirps, crossing the airport parking lot. Before taking the wheel, he locks our luggage in the trunk of a sky-blue rental Challenger. "I want to get one of these next month. Let's see how it handles."

"We're supposed to meet Julij at his house before heading to the chapel."

I pull out my phone to call my mother. We haven't talked since the face-time chat on Christmas day. She called a few times when the media reported Frank's death, but I was in no state to talk at the time. I'm not in the right frame of mind now either, but I can't put it off any longer. A face-to-face chat should go down easier than a phone call, and I am in New York, so... yeah.

She should know that Layla is no longer a part of my life. That she's not getting the daughter-in-law, she wants so badly. I grit my teeth and close my eyes briefly, straining to pull my shit together.

Twelve days have gone by since Layla's disappearance. *Twelve* days. I thought it'd get easier with time, that the hole she left behind when she took my heart with her would start to heal, but the pain isn't subsiding.

If anything, it's growing stronger.

Maddening.

I lay awake for hours at night, uncomfortable without her in my arms. That's when I try to accept what happened; learn how to hate her, and convince myself that her disappearance is a good thing. It's not working, though. Sleep comes at dawn. Two, sometimes three hours of vivid dreams. She's with me in those dreams. Happy, smiling, so beautiful I want to weep. I wake up alone, empty, numb, fucking confused, and back to square one. Back to learning how to live my life without her because any progress I made the day before vanishes after I spend a few hours holding and kissing her inside my head.

"Hey, baby," Isla says. "I'm so glad you called. I've been calling you for days. I know you must've been busy with..." She trails off, clearing her throat. "How's Layla doing?"

This is the first time anyone has spoken her name aloud since she ran away. All my senses fire up at once. I gouge my fingers into the leather seat beneath me, bridling the anger that flares inside me like King Cobra's hood. I didn't think my fuse could get any shorter, but here it is, or rather isn't. "This isn't a conversation I want to have over the phone. I'm in New York. I'll stop by the penthouse tonight."

"Oh, of course. Should Marie prepare the guest bedroom?"

"Not this time, Mom. I'll see you later."

Half an hour passes, but we're not much closer to our destination, stuck in rush-hour traffic on Fifth Avenue. Spades fiddles with every button, inspecting the car as if he teleported here from the eighteenth century and can't comprehend what witchcraft this is. More boring minutes pass while I busy myself with people-watching. And that's when I spot Layla among the crowd of nameless faces. With a concerned look on her pretty face, she walks in the opposite direction to where we're heading.

My pulse throbs everywhere; in my ears, in my veins, in my fingertips. I'm palpitating, bursting with conflicting emotions that sink their teeth into my insides, biting off big chunks.

Spades pulls away from the traffic lights, crossing a busy intersection, oblivious to the anarchy seizing my mind. I grip the seat with both hands this time, clawing at the black leather. With each tattered breath I force into my lungs, I lose more restraint.

No, it couldn't have been her.

I didn't see her.

It wasn't *her.*

No fucking way.

Even if, she doesn't deserve me. Not in the slightest. Never did. Never will. She's a ghost from the not-so-distant past, and she should stay there. I loved her, but I'm over it. I'm over *love* in general.

As far as I'm concerned, the idiotic notion is well and truly dead in the water, buried under ten feet of rubble.

She's less than a hundred yards away, still walking. A sheet of brown hair cascades down her back, swaying from left to right. I grip the seat harder, anchoring myself in place. I can't move. I need to stay where I am and let her go. She doesn't deserve me. Her betrayal is all that matters.

Jesus Christ...

Who the fuck am I kidding?

I just want to touch her.

Kiss her.

Lock her in my arms and never let go.

I want to hear her sweet whispers in my ear and see my own reflection in those mesmerizing big, gray eyes of hers.

"Stop the car," I rasp, my throat so dry even I don't understand the order. "Stop the car!" I unfasten the seatbelt, my hands shaking like those of an alcoholic with empty pockets.

Spades slams on the brakes, and I leap out of the car before the wheels stop completely. A cacophony of horns rises above natural street noise the second I take the first step, forcing one of the drivers to veer off to the side. It's a blur, a smudge of dark colors dotted with yellow cabs. Layla's the only thing I see in full HD mode. My heart races as I sprint across the busy road, not daring to spare a glance at the oncoming traffic and lose Layla out of my sight.

I brace against the hoods of different cars, bounce from one to another, and stop the drivers, pushing through the busy street. My stomach wraps itself around my spine, the rumble of horns louder and louder.

I'm thirty seconds away from seeing her pretty face, from touching her petite body and tasting those plump lips. I can almost fucking taste the sweetness of her mouth, feel the warmth of her breath and silk of her tongue. In thirty seconds, I'll have her back. My relentless attempts to hate her come to an abrupt halt, leaving no trace, no proof that I ever wondered if she's worth the trouble.

I can't hate her.

I can only love her with everything I have.

I reach the pavement, elbow my way through the crowd of pedestrians, shoving them aside, ignoring the outraged *hey's and watch-where-you're-goings.* I wasted almost two weeks, rebelling against every fiber in my body, trying to convince myself that her betrayal matters, that it can't be forgiven... what a fucking waste of nights and days.

Frank's plan might've been the sole reason we met, but Layla lost herself in me somewhere along the way. She chose *me* and killed her father... *that* matters.

The power of her feelings matters.

She proved I'm the one she wouldn't be able to live without when she sacrificed her father to protect me.

Turning right, she descends the stairs to Bryant Park subway station. I chase after her in my tailor-made suit, a pair of fifteen-hundred-dollar shoes, and a gun under my jacket. My chest heaves with effort. My heart slams against my ribs, straining to pump enough blood into my veins. Another twenty seconds pass before I get onto the platform.

Five seconds too late.

The subway is on the move. Layla's in the second wagon, her back against the window. As the subway nears a bend, she turns to look out onto the platform

But it's not Layla.

The girl stares out of the window, unaware of the agonizing damage her unfamiliar face causes in my system. I grab a handful of hair at the back of my head and tug hard in a half-assed attempt to override the mental pain with a physical one.

"Where are you, baby?" I whisper into thin air.

A heavy hand drops onto my shoulder, and five fingers squeeze me briefly as if only to grab my attention. I spin to find Spades, eyes narrowed, a vein on his neck throbbing. The look he's pinning me down with is sharp enough to puncture a lung as it fluctuates between sincere compassion and the classic *I told you so.*

I had it coming.

Hands in pockets, he takes a wary step back, giving me much-needed space. "You good?" He weighs the words as if he expects me to lose my shit and start shooting any second. He knows me well.

The only reason my gun is still safely tucked in the holster is that we're in New York, not in Chicago.

CHAPTER FIVE

Layla

A white, fluffy blanket covers the left side of my body, my gaze fixed on the wall and ceiling adorned with hundreds of hand-painted, fluorescent stars. Jean has a knack for murals, but she has sure outdone herself with this one.

When night falls over Ivanhoe, the painting looks like a window to a far-away galaxy. Like one of those projectors that you can buy online.

She had no idea when she spent a few days creating this masterpiece three years ago that one day, it'll be the only thing keeping me sane at night. Insomnia might be the most sickening side-effect of a broken heart.

An old-fashioned clock on a dresser by the door ticks loudly, the rhythm of passing seconds a close match for the rhythm of my heart.

A creak in the hallway outside the bedroom breaks the comfortable silence I got myself used to. Aunt Amanda starts work at six in the evening, and Jean hardly spends time at home, always out with her friends. The creak is quickly followed by a light knock on the door. I turn to face the wall, tucking my knees close to my chest, and throw my arm over my face. Not that it'll stop the unwanted guest...

Jean's persistence is tiring.

Another knock. Louder this time. Five more seconds pass before she turns the knob and enters the guest bedroom, uninvited as always. "I know you're not asleep."

What gave me away?

With a sigh, I turn again, away from the wall this time to face the door, knowing she won't leave without a fight. She's relentless in the so-far futile attempts to drag me out of the comfort of the house and over to a nearby bar with her friends Tayler and Rick.

As expected, she stands in the doorway of the small bedroom, an unflattering scowl across her pale, freckled face. She stomps her foot, arms crossed over her chest. Looks like she's resigned to trying a different approach today.

I can't keep up with her mood swings. From cheerful to annoyed in three seconds flat. From supportive at first to pleading the following day. Neither worked, so she worked her way through every emotional sabotage trick known to parents worldwide. Bargaining, bribery, pleading again, and more bargaining...

This is new, though. She looks positively aggravated, so I guess she's ready to shout. Maybe throw around a few unsupported, idle threats. *Clean your room, or I'll take your toys!*

"You've been crying again! And you're not ready! Tayler will be here in half an hour, and you're wearing..." she scrunches her nose, eyeing my top, "this monstrosity!"

"It's pj's, Jean. I'm not going. I told you yesterday, the day before, and all the other days since I came here. I can't go. I don't want to go. I *won't* go. I'm fine here."

She scoffs, sizing me up, one eyebrow raised high enough to hit her hairline. "This is what you call fine? Ha! Don't make me laugh. You're a mess, girl. You're pathetic. And because of a guy... c'mon! You're a Harston, for fuck's sake! Harston girls don't mope over guys. Where's your pride?"

I move my eyes from her enraged face back to the ceiling. "It won't work, Jean. Say whatever you want. Scream, if you must. Throw a tantrum. I. Don't. *Care.*" Neither about the way she sees me nor about anything, really.

Yanking my blanket away, she plops onto the bed, her lips in a slight pout. "I'm sorry. I didn't mean to shout. I'm just running out of ideas on how to cheer you up, you know? You barely eat. You're locked in here all the time. It's not healthy."

"I know. I'm sorry too, but I can't go. Not even if I wanted to. If someone would see me—"

"Of course, someone will see you! It's a bar; people attend, drink, and laugh. Remember? I'm sure you have bars in Chicago, right? You know the drill. And sure, everyone will *stare* at you because you're new here, but they'll get ove—"

"You said it. I can't go."

Jean waves her hand dismissively and rushes to the dresser. She opens the first one, makes a mess, and continues her journey, rummaging through my clothes.

"Here." A pair of jeans lands on my face. A flannel shirt follows thirty seconds later. "Put it on, and don't you dare say no. again. Erase that damn word from your dictionary while you live here. You've been crying for two weeks! Enough!"

"Twelve days."

"Whatever. I tolerated your compulsive, obsessive..." she pulls her eyebrows together, searching for another adjective, "just plain stupid need to spend every evening here by yourself. Not tonight. You're coming whether you like it or not. Either that or you'll tell me *why* you've cried two rivers so far."

A long time ago, Jean knew all my secrets. Her mother's house was my home during the summer months every year until I turned twelve. Back then, we were inseparable. Then Frank killed Dino, and Aunt Amanda found out how her brother made a living. She refused to speak to him or his family ever again, and my friendship with Jean ended... but when I knocked on Amanda's door twelve days ago, she took me in. Reluctantly, under merciless conditions, but she did.

"If anyone shows up here looking for you, I'll lead them straight to your room, Layla."

Neither Jean nor Amanda asked why I asked to stay here. I don't think they had to. They might live in one of the most boring, remote places, but they have TV like everyone else. Frank's death, and the Mafia War getting out of hand, was broadcasted all over the media when thirty bodies were discovered in Chicago. While Amanda doesn't want any inside information as to what exactly happened that night,

Jean asks too many questions trying to force the story out of me in private.

"Damn it, Layla!" she snatches the pillow from under my head. "Get dressed! Tayler won't be pleased if he has to wait for you!" She waves a checkered, red, and black flannel shirt in front of my face. "Do you need an invitation? Should I draw you a map to the bathroom, or will you find your way?"

Enraged Jean resembles an enraged puppy—exasperated, energetic, loud, and utterly ineffective. A lot of yapping followed by a lot of nothing. Of the two of us, she was always fiercer, but it looks like she mellowed a touch since childhood. She used to be a true tomboy, climbing trees, getting dirty, and fighting with boys.

On the other hand, I was a girly girl in pink dresses, weaving flower crowns. I guess Jean's attitude back then left a mark on me. In part, I have *her* to thank for the feisty bones in my body.

"You won't drag me out of here no matter how creative your threats might get. You're wasting your time. Go and enjoy, okay? I'm fine here." I shoo her away.

A string of quiet curses flies past her lips. It sure doesn't suit her to swear like a sailor. With a huff, she whirls on her heel, marching out of the room, each step louder than the last as she takes her frustration out on the old, wooden floorboards. The door slams hard, rattling the frame. Even the windows shake a bit.

Tayler's pick-up truck pulls into the driveway. The engine splutters as the car grinds into a halt. I peek through the curtains, a tiny-bit sad that I won't join them when Jean hops into the car, her signature frown on display.

They stay parked for a minute which doesn't bode well for Tayler. I can only imagine the earful he's getting on my behalf... Jean's very vocal when she's annoyed.

Once they back out of the driveway, disappearing out of view behind a row of maple trees, I make my way downstairs. With a thick blanket in one hand and a steaming cup of hot chocolate in the other, I head outside to the back garden, if the piece of unkempt land here can be deemed a garden. Other than a few trees dotting the perimeter and grass that, although dry and dead now, reaches my knees, there's nothing I'd expect to see in a garden. No flowers, ornaments, grill, or sitting area. Obviously, no pool, either. A beaten-up tractor with half the engine missing is secluded by a wobbly, in-desperate-need-of-TLC picket fence. Jean said it's here to keep wild animals off the property, but the boards are so far and few that even a bear would find his way in.

My big-city, upper-class upbringing or the summers spent on this very farm failed to prepare me for starting fires in the wild. The first time I tried this, I burned my fingers and a hole in my sweater. Now, I'm not as useless. Starting a small bonfire still takes effort, but after a few tries, it blazes in the middle of the small clearing while I sit on a wooden bench, surrounded by the addictive silence.

Back in Chicago, I thought nights were silent, but now that I'm here, in the middle of nowhere, a few miles away from interstates, cities, and at least three hundred yards from the nearest neighbor, I understand what silence is. Or natural silence, at least. No cars, no people, no factories humming in the distance. All I can hear here are the occasional animals howling in the distance, the flap of bird's wings, and the rustling of leaves in the wind.

Flames dance before me, consuming more wood with every soft sigh of freezing wind. Large chunks of pine wood blacken, crack, and fall apart—almost like my heart that's slowly turning to dust. Thousands of sparks take to the biting air, flickering out in a fraction of a second— just like Dante's eyes when he realized I betrayed him.

They say love is a flower in constant need of nurturing, or it dies. They say love is a dream that arrives when we don't need it, but when it comes, we want it to last. They say love is bitter-sweet like a fine wine. And like fine wine, it kicks your butt and makes you dizzy. We do stupid things while drunk, but no matter how much we convince ourselves we won't ever touch wine again, we always do.

In my case, love is a drug that grabbed me by the throat, infested my mind, and spread through my bloodstream. Drug users forever remain addicts, even when they stop using. It's not easy to stop. Not many people volunteer to sever the connection to something that, in their eyes, makes them feel good. Not many have that kind of willpower. I don't. I won't detox. I'll stay in love, forever in limbo, hoping, dreaming, *waiting* for a kiss to wake me up.

Unsolicited tears stain my cheeks. I promised myself I won't cry because tears can't change the past. Nothing can. Tears make me weak, and I need to be strong. I'm on my own, navigating a world in the dark, unequipped to deal with reality now that it's diseased with regret.

Every day I wake up determined to climb out of the ditch. I tell myself that despite how bad things look, the world didn't really collapse. Life isn't over. I should thank God I came out alive, almost unscathed. The finale to Frank's plan could've been much more sinister.

Every day I create a new scenario of what my life will look like going forward. A screenplay where Dante's lead role has been cut. A movie sequel in which he has no part. Regardless of my efforts, I can't change that. Even though he's not around, he's still everywhere. He occupies every cell of my body, every thought, every dream. He's omnipresent but absent, and I fall to my knees like a house of cards every night, pushed to the ground by my sins.

I wipe my cheeks when the sputtering of Tayler's pick-up reaches my ears. There's no mistaking the ear-splitting rattle of a defective engine as it pulls into the driveway. That car is a death trap, waiting to give up on Tayler when he'll need it most. A deep breath helps me bury the pain under a pile of rubble that used to be my heart and mind. Pathetic doesn't begin to cover my current state. I know I should stop wallowing in self-pity, grit my teeth, and push forward, but *this...* this is easier. It requires no effort.

A few pairs of pants rustle in long grass for a moment before Jean plops beside me with two bottles of wine. She hands one over, gazing at the fire, as she unscrews the cap on her bottle and takes a hefty sip. Tayler and his best friend, Rick, plop down on the bench opposite with a handful of beers.

"Is the bar closed?" I ask, guilt like a thorn in my throat because they changed their plans to keep me company.

Jean shakes her head, clanking her bottle to mine. "I won't let you spend another evening crying."

"I wasn't crying."

Tayler snorts, trading a loaded look with Rick. They're two ends of a spectrum. Tayler's twenty-two and the most gullible guy I've ever met in all my nineteen years. A five-foot-eight, one-hundred-and-seventy-pounds of a goofy softie. No one takes him seriously. Not with the ever-present surprise on his young, delicate face, careless attitude, or complete lack of a backbone.

On the other hand, Rick is a tall, over-the-top muscular stiffness. Five years in the army explains the lack of facial expressions and tense stance to an extent, but Rick seems almost robotic, as if he was programmed with not enough emotions. He's gravely intelligent and perceptive, but there's no joking around with him.

"Instead of lying, start talking," Tayler says, opening a bottle of Bud Light. "You can't hide the reason forever. Tell us why you ran from Chicago. You'll feel better when you get it off your chest."

"Exactly." Jean clicks her tongue. "I can't look at you anymore. You're a shadow, Layla. You're getting skinnier by the day. You're absentminded, fucking *frightened*... what happened?" She squeezes my hand. "You can trust us. I promise."

The secret weighs down on my shoulders. I really want to let it out. Vent. Cry. Scream at the top of my lungs, but fear stops me whenever I ponder the idea of opening up to Jean.

Tayler scratches his head, stealing a sideways glance at Rick. "I mean, we know most of it anyway, right? It's all over the news, and Jean told us about your father."

I glare at my Judas of a cousin. "Way to keep a secret."

"A secret? As Tayler said, it's all over the news! You do have the same surname as Frankie, you know? And it's not like I never told them I've got a cousin who used to visit every summer. They would've riddled it out by themselves by now."

Rick? Yes.

Tayler? Not so much.

"What have you told them?"

Jean shrugs, eyes fixed on the fire that's slowly dying down. Rick takes the hint, adding wood to the pile.

"Nothing that isn't readily available online. Only that your father was a mobster, and you dated his enemy, and that Frankie is, *obviously*, dead." Jean huffs. "Oh, go on. Just spill it. Tell us what happened so we can tell you it's not a big deal and take you out for a drink tomorrow night."

I sip from the bottle, weighing my options. God, I want to tell them every last detail and hear an opinion. I want to know if they think there's a chance Dante will ever forgive me. I trust Jean. Tayler's unconditional, one-sided love for her means he'll never breathe a word to a living soul as it'd risk him losing the slim chance he has with her.

Rick is a different story, though. His defense walls are always up. I can't read him, so there's no guessing his reaction. But in the grand scheme of things... what difference does it make if they know?

There isn't much either can do with the truth other than inform Dante of my whereabouts. Deep down, I hope they will, even if all it'll bring upon me is death.

"One thing you should know about my father is that he never should've had children," I say, peeling the wine label off the bottle. "He wasn't fit for the role. Maybe because he was too young when I was born, or maybe because he was a sociopath and a manipulator."

"He was a cold, heartless bastard," Jean cries, imitating her mother's condescending tone as she fakes outrage. "He had no decency! He was a criminal!"

"I see Amanda wasn't too fond of her brother."

"She hated his guts. At some point, she had way too much to say about Frankie."

I can imagine when. Amanda knew nothing about her brother's profession until Frank killed Dino and the media showed his face all over the country as the prime suspect. Nothing came out of the accusations, but Amanda found out what profession Frank chose and broke off all contact.

"He was rotten to his core, but he was my father. The main point of this story is that I never had what most would deem a normal family."

"I don't understand," Tayler mumbles, two vertical creases on his forehead. "You're crying after someone you call a sociopath and a manipulator?"

"Who said my tears have anything to do with Frank?"

He bobs his head twice, gesturing for me to continue. And I do, starting with the poor relationship with my parents, Frankie's hatred toward Dante, my fake boyfriends, and finally onto Frank's master plan.

"He wanted to destroy Dante, but he didn't want to just kill him. He wanted to inflict as much pain as possible and take away more than his life. He wanted to show Dante what it means to lose everything he cared about." I pause, gathering my thoughts. My throat clogs with a new wave of tears that I'm desperately trying to hold in. "The problem was that Dante only cared about work. That's where Frank wanted my help. He wanted me to give Dante something to care about."

"Don't tell me he asked you to seduce the guy!" Jean gasps, positively mortified. "I mean, seriously? What the hell?"

"That was my reaction..." I sigh, my heart aching, racing, and breaking all at once. "To make things even worse, Frankie told me my whole life was a part of his sick plan. He laid the groundwork for years, raising me to grow up into someone Dante couldn't resist."

Tayler exhales a heavy breath. "He wasn't all there, huh?"

No, he wasn't.

Looking back now, I can't believe my own naivety. I volunteered to be led into a trap. I allowed Frank to use me as a means of winning the war over half of Chicago. Just *half*. Frank wasn't normal by any definition. Because of him, neither am I. Emotional instability, an ever-unsatisfied need for closeness, and a complete lack of common sense—not normal. Frankie raised me to follow him blindly. And I did.

Hungry for love and acceptance even though a parent's love should be unconditional.

Frank's wasn't. He was incapable of loving or caring. The one good decision he ever made was to send me on my way to meet the greatest strength in my life... Dante.

"What happened next?" Jean grows impatient, tapping her foot on the grass while Rick adds more wood to the fire. "Did you do it? Did you agree?" She's halfway through the bottle, her cheeks flushed, eyes wide and glossy.

"There wasn't a thing I wouldn't do for Frank. If he'd tell me to jump, I'd ask how high. So yeah, I agreed, and..." I inhale deeply, and a small smile curls my lips. I'm torn between the joy associated with the enticing memories and the regret of hurting the only person who has ever loved me unconditionally. "...and then I met Dante. I wasn't supposed to fall in love with him. That wasn't part of the plan, but I couldn't help it. There aren't many men like him walking the earth. He's confident, ruthless, arrogant—"

"He sounds lovely," Tayler mocks, elbowing Rick under his ribs hard enough to earn a scowl.

"He's intense, protective, and caring, and he loved me with all he had." The bottle of wine in my hand empties faster once I tell them about the night Delta was set on fire.

The look on Dante's face when he understood my part in Frank's plan haunts me every night. Fear writhes inside me, battling with hope. Fear of the man I love and hope that he'll forgive me. With each passing day, both subside.

Amanda's house isn't the safest hiding place; informing Jess that I ran here wasn't the smartest move, but safe or smart is not what I aim for. Dante would have no problem finding me here if he wanted to. It probably wouldn't take more than a few phone calls. One visit to my mother's house...

but he's not showing up. It hurts more than if he arrived with his men and put a gun to my head. At least then, I'd know my betrayal hurt him, that he *felt* something. Now it seems he moved on without an issue.

"Frankie told me to kill Dante." My hands start shaking at the memory of the heavy, cold pistol. "I held the gun. I aimed at his heart. I watched him cross the thin line between love and hate." I wash down the dryness of my throat with more wine. "If Frank hadn't shown his true colors that night, I would've killed him."

"You would've killed Dante?" Jean echoes.

"It's scary how much power Frank held over me all this time. He snapped at me when I hesitated, and it finally hit home that I was never more than a tool in his hands. He didn't love me and would never love me regardless of how many orders I'd fulfill or how much I'd try. He didn't deserve me, my love, or my loyalty."

Jean inhales sharply, eyes wide. "*You* killed him?"

"If I didn't, he would've killed Dante."

One of them had to die that night. I don't regret my decision, regardless of how rushed and emotional it was.

CHAPTER SIX

Dante

A mansion.

There's no simpler way to describe the house of the New York King. Two armed men stand guard on both sides of a tall, brass gate that opens onto a dark-gray, paved driveway. Instead of a water fountain in the middle, like in most gangster movies, a palm tree thrives despite the freezing cold. A three-door garage stands to the right, and the house stretches before us, bathed in an orange hue of LED lights embedded into the driveway. Another bodyguard is guarding the entrance, stiff as a mannequin, eyes focused on something in the distance.

Spades parks out of the way, cuts the engine and spins his head left and right, taking in the over-the-top large mansion. "Nikolaj sure knew how to make an impression."

"He sure did." I agree, stepping out into the cool morning air, though the goosebumps dotting my skin aren't because of the cold. I'm still reeling after that girl in the subway turned out not to be my star.

A thin layer of snow covers the roof, but it long melted on the ground. As we approach, one of Julij's pawns opens the front door, muttering in Russian into a microphone affixed to his jacket. A spacious foyer with marble floors and a high ceiling brings to mind an expensive hotel lobby. A crystal chandelier hangs low on a silver chain, directly over a large bouquet of lilies and roses on a round table. Their aroma hangs in the air, reminding me of Layla's perfume.

The memory of hiding my face in her neck at night, inhaling her intoxicating scent plays on the backs of my eyelids. I push Layla out my head when Julij appears at the top of the grand staircase that snakes on both sides of the room.

A tall, dark-haired man stands right behind him, and although I never met him, his posture, facial expression, and something I can't quite put my finger on seem oddly familiar.

Julij pins me with a hateful stare, his fists clenched. White-hot rage radiates off him as he rushes down the stairs, taking two steps at a time. "What the fuck do you think you're doing?!" He grips me by the collar only to shove me against the nearest wall. "Are you out of your fucking mind?! Call it off!"

Spades reaches for the gun tucked in the holster by his

belt, but Dimitri materializes behind him out of nowhere, pressing the barrel of his gun to Spades' temple. Without much choice, he lets go of his gun and raises his hands to his chest in defeat, but I know that one word from me will have him raining hell on everyone around with his bare knuckles. I'm too stunned by Julij's outburst and the fucking nerve of him getting in my face to say a single word.

A few seconds pass before I process what the fuck just happened. Once it sinks in, a switch responsible for my temper flips in my head.

I catch Julij's arm, twist it back, and watch him bend and arch away, his cheek not far off the floor as he tries to save his bones before they snap. "What is wrong with you?" I ask, my eyebrows furrowed. For now, confusion towers over anger.

"*Me*?!" Julij scoffs, fighting, albeit weakly, to wriggle out of my grip. He's tall and muscular but doesn't stand a chance against me. Not today. Not after the thirteen days of pure fury and slashing agony I've endured. Not after I thought I had Layla at my fingertips half an hour ago.

"Let go of him, Dante." A stoic, low voice with a sharp, Russian accent sounds in the room, the commanding note unmistakable and un-fucking impressive.

I turn my head when the man descends the stairs. "Make me," I hiss, turning back to Julij, "and you," I twist his arm harder, forcing him to his knees, "explain that stunt."

"You want *me to* explain?!" Sweat breaks out on his forehead, but he grinds his teeth, trying and failing to hide just how much his arm hurts right now. "You're the one with explaining to do, but first, call off the hit. Right. Fucking. *Now*."

I let him go at that. His words, like a freight train, crash into my chest.

"A hit? What fucking hit?"

"How many have you commissioned lately?" Julij straightens up, smooths his shirt, and adjusts the jacket before he motions at Dimitri to stand down, cradling his sore arm in the other. "Call it off, or you won't get out of here alive."

I grab him by his throat and pin him to the wall in the same spot he had me moments ago. "Threaten me again, and I'll snap your spine so fast Dimitri won't have time to pull the fucking trigger. Now *explain* what the fuck you're talking about, and you better change your attitude. It's been over two years since I ordered a hit, Julij." I let him go, stepping back. "Who's the target?"

His face falls, eyes widen, and hands tremble as he grabs fistfuls of his hair. "It wasn't you... Blyad'!" he bellows in Russian. "Kak ne ty..." Blood drains from his face, turning his usually pale complexion ashen.

Dimitri steps forward while Spades glares at Julij with one eyebrow raised and one hand back on the holster. Julij tears his gaze away from the wall, pure torment in his eyes. The atmosphere changes from raging to heavy in the blink of an eye. The fine hairs on my neck stand on end. My mind fills in the blanks based on the little information I have.

"Who is the target?" I ask again, my voice almost unrecognizable, muscles tense while I silently beg him not to say what I already know will come out of his mouth.

"It's Layla," he clips, his chest heaving. "She's the target."

An answer I expected and one I'm entirely unprepared for. The words bounce around my head like tiny balls inside a rattle toy. One sentence. One fucking piece of information, and I'm damn near losing my wits. The meaning of Julij's words strips me of my sanity bit by fucking bit. For the second time in my life, I'm powerless. Crushed by the intense protectiveness. By *fear.*

I open my mouth, but words pile up on the tip of my tongue. I grip the nape of my neck, dig my fingers in my skin and squeeze hard to ease the tension. Instead of forcing the chaotic thoughts out of my mind by asking all the supporting questions popping up, I breathe in and out, delivering enough air into my lungs to remain focused, somewhat composed, and in a relatively sane mindset.

Layla in danger is the only thing that can get me from calm to all-out petrified in a matter of seconds. The most excruciating dread sweeps over my entire system, powerful enough to bring me to my knees and leave me weak and defenseless. It robs my mind of its basic functionality: the ability to think straight. It pushes me to act without gathering all the information. I could easily crumble under the weight of my protectiveness that engulfs every nerve in my body. It's crushing. Primal. Uncontainable. My body springs into combat mode. Real, physical pain jabs at my heart because she's out of my reach.

I can't see her.

I can't touch her.

I can't fucking protect her.

"I found out this morning," Julij says, his words distorted as if coming through bulletproof glass. "I don't have much information yet."

"Get the man a drink," the authoritative voice says again.

Spades squeezes my arm for the second time today, pushing me toward the living room. I inhale a sharp breath, grit my teeth, and force my legs to move and my head to snap out of the trance. I collapse on a sofa, my hands shaking, chest tight enough to fucking choke me.

"Drink." The dark-haired man hands me a glass of whiskey.

Instead of drying it in one go to calm my nerves, I set it aside on the side table. No way I'll take that road. It'd numb my chaotic mind, but I can't afford to lose focus.

"And you are...?"

"My name is Anatolij Aristow." He takes a seat on the opposite sofa. "I'm Julij's uncle."

Ah, the infamous Anatolij Aristow. The name doesn't explain the strange familiarity I feel towards him. I've never met the man but can't shake the feeling that I know him from somewhere. He's the complete opposite of Julij and Nikolaj. Broader, coarser, and much more sophisticated. I imagined him to be older, but he looks in his late thirties at the most.

"Who the fuck ordered the hit?" I glare at Julij.

"Obviously, I thought it was you until you made it clear just now that you didn't even know about the job."

I pull a packet of Marlboro out of the inside pocket and pinch the filter between my teeth, lighting it up. Dimitri sets an ashtray on the coffee table while Spades sits beside me, the glass of whiskey I refused to drink now in his hand.

"So, there's a hit, but no principal?" he asks, resting his elbows casually on his knees. It's just a front, though.

I know Spades as I know myself. He's fuming. Delirious with the need to find a kill whoever ordered the hit.

"Oh, there is. At least I think it's him. Or was, actually." Julij shakes his head in disbelief, pinning me with his rude, forceful stare. "Remember when I told you Frank's on the lookout for a hitman last time you were in New York?" He waits for me to nod. "I thought he wanted someone to kill *you*, but it looks like he tried to find someone to kill Layla."

Everything I had for breakfast climbs back up my esophagus, bitter bile pooling at the back of my throat. Jesus, just hearing *kill Layla* has me on the verge of spontaneously combusting.

I can't believe the fucker. He sure deserved the bullet Layla put through his heart. Ordering a hit on his own daughter? How deranged; how bent on revenge was he to revert to murdering his only child? The hit was the one element of Frank's plan that made no sense back then.

Now, it makes too much sense.

"Frank ordered a hit on his own daughter?" Spades asks, his tone filled with disgust and disbelief as he can't comprehend what I already understood. "He was one cruel motherfucker, but he was her father... it makes no sense."

I exhale a cloud of smoke. "It does."

Frank's plan was methodically crafted to perfection. Layla herself was my dream come true. I spent thirteen days and nights analyzing the last few months, and other than the supposed hitman Frank wanted to hire, I found nothing that couldn't be easily explained. But that hitman... what a baffling idea. He wanted Layla to kill me, so why hire a professional?

So he'd kill her if the plan fell apart, as is always the risk in our line of work. So he'd kill the one person I cared about. Everyone knew Layla was my sole weakness. Even Frankie.

Especially Frankie.

Without Layla, even if Chicago fell into my hands, even if I rose to the top of the game, I'd have nothing. My life is fucking worthless without her in it. Unlivable. Because I've not been living the past thirteen days. Merely surviving.

"I'm taking away what you hold dearest."

Those are the words he spoke that night. He was one hundred percent sure Layla would kill me; he meant more to her than me, but he insured himself, nonetheless.

"I doubt he thought Layla would shoot him; otherwise, he wouldn't have given her the gun, but Frankie always had a backup plan in case things turned to hell." Julij sits beside his uncle, mimicking Spades' position with elbows resting on his knees as he leans forward. "He had to consider a margin of error in his plan. It'd take a tiny slip-up to turn the tables. I guess that's why he ordered the hit. "He wanted to make sure that even if he'd be the one to die, you'd still lose her."

There it is again. The jab of fear. The violent hollowness in my stomach at the mere thought of anything happening to her.

I squeeze the bridge of my nose, trying to recall the moment my borderline obsession began. I wasn't like this from the start. But I was already like this before she ran. Somewhere along the way, the rational part of my brain left, and I don't remember what triggered the response.

And I have to. I can't go on for long, acting bat-shit crazy.

"We've got the principal. Who's the hitman?" Spades asks.

He sits beside me, his back straight, muscles tense, a focused, determined look on his face. He can pull the wool over Julij and Anatolij's eyes, acting composed, but I've known him for years. I see past the mask. Fury courses through his veins just as it does through mine. He's ready to leave and not come back until he finds the hitman. He'd take his rage out on him first before dragging him back to me, half-alive, so I could finish the job.

"Anyone who wants to try," Anatolij says with a heavy sigh. "Frank opened the hit to anyone willing."

"An *open* hit?" Spades clips. "He couldn't find a single person dumb enough to take the job?"

I rake my hand through my hair. "Quite the opposite. If he hired one guy, I'd find and kill the fucker. By opening the hit, he took control out of my hands."

It's frustrating how well I know Frank. *Knew* him. Deciphering his intentions is child's play now, but the plan with Layla as bait slipped my attention. Now all I need are seconds to figure out his way of thinking. By opening the job, he turned it into a race. The first one to find and kill Layla wins the money... and anyone can try.

"How much?" I ask while Dimitri refills the glass for Spades.

"Way too much to hope that the professionals will forfeit this time. Not to mention amateurs. Search parties are probably out as we speak."

The difference between a professional and an amateur isn't all that significant. Professionals are those who make a living out of contracted killings. They work for no one but themselves, with no boss to answer to. People like Cai or Jackson who deal with the dirty work daily but report to a boss are amateurs. The way some of those so-called amateurs handle a gun would make a professional blush.

"How much?" I urge, staring Julij down.

"Three million."

Spades chokes on the whiskey, coughing like an asthmatic. He raises his hands, gasping for air as his forehead and cheeks turn purple. "*Three million dollars*?" he pants between ragged breaths, calming down slowly. "Two years ago, Andreas got one and a half for taking out the boss from Florida. You'd think Layla's the president's daughter."

Anatolij rises from his seat, making his way toward a window, each step calculated. An aura of crushing power walks with him. He stops a foot from the glass, staring out to the back garden, hands behind his back. "We seem to be overlooking one issue. We have an open hit and a deceased principal. That means someone must hold the money to pay the winner. Any ideas?"

"You mean a promoter. We call them promoters," Julij clips, clearly unhappy with his uncle. "And no, I've no idea who could be stupid enough to agree to oversee this farce."

"Think, Dante," Spades elbows my ribs. "If we find the promoter, we can close the job."

"Killing him won't retract the job," Anatolij interjects, turning back to face us. "The information is out there. You do not know how many people have been alerted or will be alerted in the coming days. You must force the promoter to close the hit and inform the takers using the same channels."

"I won't chase the promoter and risk anyone finding Layla in the meantime. She takes priority. Once she's back home, I can start looking for the promoter."

I pull out my phone to call Jackson. Apart from his job as my main fighter, he's also the head of the *Lost and Found* department in my entourage. If I require any kind of information, he's my guy. His friends can access an online database with a few keystrokes. Jackson himself isn't a lousy hacker, but I need everyone he can get on the task right now.

I want... fuck, I *need* her back this very second.

"What's up?" he asks, answering on the third tone.

"Find her."

A short pause is his first response, but I doubt he needs an explanation as to who I want him to find. "Why?"

I almost smile at the hesitant note in his voice. He sounds like he dares me to make one false move; say one word wrong that'd warrant him going ballistic on my ass. Despite Layla's betrayal, my people remained in awe of her.

She clawed her way deep under their skin, not just mine. I guess they all knew it was a matter of time before I'd start looking for her. Deep down, I knew it too, but I was too stubborn, riled-up, and hurt to admit it. There's no way in heaven I could let her go. Since the day she stepped into Delta wearing a red dress and a sassy attitude, my whole world revolves around her. Knowing people are out there searching for her, eager to claim three million dollars, flips my stomach. I spent thirteen days in a web of self-woven lies, but in the end, I'm powerless in the face of my feelings.

"Because it's about time I stop lying to myself."

"Took you long enough." Jackson chuckles. "I'll get on it straight away."

"Get everyone on it, Jackson. Right now." I ball my fists, adamant to say what has to be said without losing my fucking shit again. "There's a bounty on her head. Three million dollars, open hit." My voice remains stable even though inside, I'm screaming and sending one bullet after another into the New York sky.

"Shit," he whispers as furious tapping on a keyboard starts in the background. "Who ordered it? And *why*?"

"Frank. I'll explain when we're in Chicago. Get to work."

"On it. We'll find her first, Boss."

He cuts the call, and I turn to look at Spades, lighting another cigarette. "I want to know who the promoter is. Make it happen. Call the V brothers and all our other business partners while you're at it. No one is to even *think* about taking the hit, or I'll cut them off and kill everyone they're related to."

CHAPTER SEVEN

Layla

Jean stands in the doorway again, with a stern look and hands on her hips. "Don't argue. You told us what happened, and nobody cares. You promised to come with us tonight, so you're coming whether you like it or not."

"I didn't promise anything. I'd love to get out of here and stop thinking for a moment, believe me, but—"

"No buts! You've been working with me in the shop for two weeks!"

"Thirteen days." I don't know why I feel the need to correct her, but I do.

She snorts, shaking her head. "More than twenty people see you every day, and yet somehow your lover boy hasn't materialized in Texas, so don't try to tell me that if you go out tonight, he'll suddenly know where you are."

Aunt Amanda owns a small convenience store on her premises and asked me to help Jean despite my weak protests. She refused to take money for letting me stay here, so helping out in the shop is the least I can do to pay her back.

I sit on the edge of the bed, fidgeting with the hem of my flannel shirt. Jean insisted I wear those while at work. It's not a piece of clothing I'd buy given a choice, but there's no denying that flannels are ridiculously comfortable.

"I only work with you because your mother won't take my money to cover my expenses."

"We live in the least interesting town in Texas, Layla. You won't see any new faces at the bar. Only those you already know from the store. We don't have gangsters around here, and no one has any clue who you are!" She brushes out her braid and gathers her hair into a ponytail. "And you know what I think?"

Not really.

I don't care, but stopping Jean from voicing her opinions is as easy as stopping milk from spilling over once it starts boiling.

"I think Dante isn't even looking for you. I mean, why would he? After what you did to him, he sure put a cross on you. I know I would."

His name from her lips forces my heart to pick up the pace. I inhale a deep breath, grinding my teeth, but the walls seem to close in on me. I miss him, and sometimes, I don't understand how it's possible to miss a person so much. How can anyone love *this* much? How can anyone fuck up their life the way I did before it even properly began?

"You hope he's looking for you, Layla. You want him to find you because you think he'll forgive you. I'm sorry for the brutal honesty, dear, but hope is the mother of fools."

It also dies last.

I'm not ready to admit she's probably right. "If he's looking for me, it's not to forgive me."

"If he loved you as much as you say, he definitely doesn't want to kill you. Stop freaking out! You're safe here." She yanks the hair tie out of her hair once more, pulling a few hairs with it, and combs the locks with her long fingers, tucking loose strands behind her ears. "There." She hands me her phone. "Call him. Say goodbye, and let's start a new chapter in your life. I think Rick is into you, you know?"

I hope she doesn't plan on playing matchmaker, or so help me God, I might get uncharacteristically violent.

"You want me to *call* Dante? Are you crazy?! He'll trace the phone. He'll know where I am!"

"Then hide the caller ID." She rolls her eyes, pressing the cell phone back in my hand. "Call him, apologize, and say goodbye. You'll feel better once you close that chapter, Layla. Leaving things hanging isn't healthy."

"Say goodbye?" I stare at the black screen.

How?

How am I supposed to say *goodbye*?

The word won't slip past my lips. Not to him. I don't know the rhythm, the sentence structure, or the individual words and letters required to say goodbye. It would never be just one word; it'd be an entire monologue to make him understand. I'd start begging, for sure. I'd probably bawl my eyes out too. There are no words in my dictionary or in my language that could easily convey all the reasons *why* I betrayed him and why I followed my father's orders. And I don't know a language in which I could say goodbye to him.

I set the phone aside.

Jean sighs, pulling a face that's half pitiful, half annoyed. "Fine. Suit yourself. Get changed and don't even try to protest, or I'll send Tayler here, and he won't be as nice as I am. We're leaving at seven o'clock sharp."

A small smile tugs at my lips. It's six fifty-two. Jean's the only person who can bring a smile to my face these days. She's positively nuts. Since I arrived at the doorstep of this house *thirteen* days ago, she's crawled out of her skin to rebuild our long-lost friendship. She might be two years my senior, but she sure acts five years younger.

Or maybe I'm overly mature for my age.

I grew up in a big city, in a house full of criminals, guns, and drugs. Jean had a happy childhood on a Texan farm in a small town where the nearest neighbor lives three hundred yards away, on the other side of a small river. I could scream bloody murder here, and no one would hear me.

She's innocent, joyful, and behaves adequately for her age.

With a defeated sigh, I fling my feet over the edge of the bed. Maybe getting out of the house will do me some good?

A moment later, Tayler pulls into the driveway in his thirty-year-old Ford Ranger that looks and sounds like it wants to kill you the second you get inside. Rick's in the passenger seat, unmoving, while Tayler hops out onto the gravel to wait outside. He leans against the hood with a cigarette in his mouth, a cell phone in hand. He taps at the screen, seemingly focused on the task, but when Jean stops in front of him, he tucks the phone away immediately and lets his eyes rove the length of her body, dressed in jeans and a flannel shirt. She's borderline cliché in her love for those things.

"Finally," Tayler says, his attention on me long enough to see me standing there. He hardly ever notices anything when Jean is around. "I thought you'd stand us up again."

"She wanted to, but I told her I'll send you up to her room this time." Jean hops in the pickup.

"Am I that scary?"

Not in the slightest. He looks like he's been taken straight out of a cowboy movie: a hat, shin-high leather boots with spurs, and a checkered shirt tucked into his jeans. I have a feeling that's not his style, merely a ploy to weaken Jean's resolve to keep him close, but only as a friend.

"Not so much." I bite my cheek, winking at him in the rearview mirror as I settle into the back seat with Jean.

Tayler slams the door with all his might to force it shut. He does that every morning when he arrives at the store to see Jean before starting work at an old junkyard in town. You'd think he'd find a working set of doors or a locking mechanism of sorts, but no. He's perfectly content with forcing the door shut using the little muscles he has.

"Have you played pool before?" Rick turns in his seat to face me, larger than life and coldblooded with an apathetic expression that sends a fit of unpleasant shivers down my spine. He reminds me of Luca.

Luca reminds me of *that* night.

And *that* night reminds me of Dante.

There's no escaping that man.

"No, I'm quite bad at games. Any games, really. It'll be safer for everyone if I watch and cheer."

He nods, but with that expressionless face, there's no guessing whether he agrees or if he decided to teach me the ins and outs of the pool. After living in Chicago my whole life, I'm used to the street noise: traffic, horns, and crowds of pedestrians on the sidewalks. Flashing billboards, smog, and a sort of liveliness of the place.

There's none of that out here. During a ten-minute drive to the bar, we pass three cars and zero pedestrians. It's odd, almost unnatural, for any place to be this peaceful. Even the interstate, by which our destination looms in the distance, seems forgotten.

A few trucks and bikes are parked outside the tall, wooden building where a scruffy sign hangs over the door with an ever-so-original name: *Joe's Place.* Not a soul loiters in the cold January air. Everyone crowds the spacious bar, sitting at the tables or at the bar on wooden stools. A pool table is tucked out of the way, the place bathed in warm, dimmed lights.

"What's everyone having?" I ask once we shed our jackets by one of the larger tables. It still barely accommodates the four of us.

"Beer, of course," Jean says. Auburn locks dance around her cheerful face as she shakes her head with an amused smile. "Don't count on any fancy drinks around here, Layla. You can have whiskey, vodka, more whiskey, or a beer."

Neither would be my choice of poison back in Chicago. I feel like I went through the looking glass and emerged in a different, unknown reality. I make my way to the bar, resting my hands on the spotless countertop, and wait for a barmaid to approach.

"What can I get you?" she asks, eyes narrowed.

"Four beers, please."

She folds her hands under her impressive breasts. "ID?"

Oh... I did *not* think of that. Again, this is so unfamiliar that I'm instantly taken aback. I'm nineteen, so being asked for ID shouldn't surprise me, but back home, I've never once been asked to prove my age. Being Frank Harston's daughter and then Dante Carrow's girlfriend came with certain perks.

"Relax, Sydney, Layla's with us," Tayler shouts from across the room. A seemingly irrelevant comment, but it's enough for heads to snap my way.

Everyone around drops dead silent, their burning gaze on my head. Sydney cocks a questioning eyebrow, and with a roll of her eyes, she reaches for four beer glasses, then wipes them clean with a crisp white cloth.

"Put it on my tab." I hear behind me.

My heart goes from zero to sixty faster than Dante's Ducati. The voice is different, not as low, not as enticing, but the words evoke a wave of memories.

"Thanks, but I pay for my own drinks." Irritation, sweet and sticky, lace the words shooting out of my mouth, firing like bullets from a nine-millimeter.

The man sits on the stool beside mine, the corners of his lips curled into a coy smile. He's not a drunk idiot. No, he's sober and lethal. A black leather jacket hugs his broad chest and shoulders, hiding a thin, grey t-shirt. It works well with his short, dark hair and sharp features. My cheeks heat when emerald-green eyes meet mine.

I glance at the ceiling, swearing internally.

Of course. The one heterosexual man to ever chat me up out of his own accord has to be the enemy.

Not mine, my father's, but it doesn't change much.

"I wasn't asking for permission," he says, his voice low and rough like that of old rockers.

I crash with reality when Tayler rests his back on the bar beside me.

"I've got money, Tayler. I've got this."

"I know you do. Which is why you'll buy the next round. I'm sure wherever you spent your evenings back in Chicago was a lot fancier than this, but it's not that bad, right?"

Most people around us return to their conversations, but a few still watch me with curious eyes. Mostly older men with large beer bellies and long beards, but there's also a group of young guys in the corner whispering among themselves, their eyes darting to me every few seconds. Jean's still at our table by the pool. Rick stands nearby, engrossed in a conversation with a tall, broad, tattooed man in his early thirties. A deep scar runs from his left eye down his cheek, disappearing under his immaculately trimmed beard.

"That's Archer," Tayler says in a hushed voice, following my line of sight. "He and Rick served together for a couple of years. I don't like the guy."

A note of envy rings in his voice, making me chuckle. Tayler might be the most insecure man I've ever met. Archer's head snaps in our direction as if he can hear me above the hum of the chatting crowd and the upbeat music seeping from a vintage jukebox. His eyes slowly float down my body in a shameless once-over. I feel exposed. Almost vulnerable under his scorching gaze. My pulse would skyrocket if Dante were in his place, but Archer's open staring makes me uncomfortable.

"Oh, great," Tayler huffs, folding his arms over his chest. "Looks like he's into you. He's an ass, Layla, he—"

"*Don't* even start." I spin back around, focusing on the barmaid and the beers she's pouring. "I'm not interested in him or anyone else."

"Good. Well, not good that you're not into anyone, but good that you're not into Archer. He's not worth your time."

He grabs the tray with beers that Sydney pushed his way and crosses the room, his steps small and careful so he won't spill a single drop. Once I'm comfortable in my seat, clutching the cool glass of beer, Jean and Tayler move away to set up the first game. My skin crawls, ears burn, and I'm pretty sure Archer is still watching me, but I don't turn to check.

"Are you sure you don't want to play?" Rick comes back to our table when Jean's almost done humiliating Tayler. She put most of her balls in the pockets while he only managed two.

"No, I'm honestly not very good at games." I laugh to myself, remembering my poor attempt at bowling.

There are more balls here, and even though I wouldn't do much damage with those, the long wooden stick could prove a weapon of mass murder in my hands. We talk until Tayler loses and Rick takes his place. Jean doesn't sit down for the next four games because Tayler lets her win every time. His over-the-top chivalry doesn't appease her, though. The truth is, she's well aware of his feelings but never asked him to stop hoping. It'd save the guy time and effort, but I think Jean enjoys being wooed.

The beer glass in my hand empties slowly. It's not the bitter taste that stops me from upping the tempo. I'm just not in the mood for a bar outing. I'd rather curl into a ball in bed because evenings are the worst. Longing hits hard as if the fact I lived through another day *alone* doesn't mean anything. Still, moping in bed won't do me any better than sitting at the table and watching my cousin win time after time.

An hour goes by before I head to the bar for another round. Archer's piercing gaze catches mine as I rise from my seat. He's in the corner of the room, alone.

Why wouldn't Rick invite him to join us?

He offers me a one-sided smile, but I'm not about to give him the green light in case he gets up to start a conversation. Instead, I nod, aiming for a stern look on my face, and walk away, feeling his eyes follow my every move.

"Four beers," I say, stopping at the bar.

This time, Sydney doesn't bother asking for ID, and no one pays me any attention as I stand there, waiting for her to pour the beers. I can't say it's growing on me, but I could get used to the bitter taste.

I rest my elbows on the countertop, hiding my face in my hands. Jean's words echo in my head, tempting, taunting, and confusing the ever-loving hell out of me.

"You hope he's looking for you, Layla. You want him to find you because you think he'll forgive you."

Naive. That's what I've been called my whole life by my father, mother, and everyone on my path. Even Dante said that once, but it ends now. I'm too trusting for my own good. I might wear my heart on my sleeve, but I refuse to be naive anymore. Frank brainwashed me to the point where I lost all sense of right or wrong. Once he died, the hold he had on me died too. My mind cleared of the clutter.

Dante won't forgive my sins, but he won't hurt me, either. He loved me with everything he had. That kind of love doesn't disappear or fizzle out. It stays with us forever, lingering in the depths of our hearts.

No, Dante won't hurt me.

He won't find me to put a bullet through my head. He won't find me, period. What now seems like a lifetime ago, he made me a promise... although I deserve worse, it hurts more than anything I have experienced so far that he has no intention of keeping his promise.

"I won't control you. I don't have to know where you are at all times, but when you're supposed to meet me, and you don't show up, don't pick up the phone, and no one knows where you are, I will look for you." He moves closer, kissing my lips. "Always." He kisses again. "Until I find you."

"You good?" Rick nudges me gently. "C'mon. I'll help you with this." He grabs two beers from the countertop, waiting until I take the other two. "Stop tormenting yourself, Layla. Dwelling on the past won't help you move forward. You *can't* move forward if you keep staring backward. You need to distance yourself from what you've done and accept that it was unavoidable. You can't turn back time."

"That's the problem," I say when we sit back down. "Even if I could, I wouldn't change a thing."

Tayler peers up from the screen of his cell phone. "You wouldn't change anything? You mean you wouldn't even tell Dante about Frank's plan?"

I shake my head *no*. In a fit of courage and stupidity, I snatch the cell phone from his hand. "I'll borrow this for just a second."

Since Jean gave me her phone two hours ago, I can only think about calling Dante to hear his voice again. Before Tayler can protest, I'm on my feet, rushing out the door. Wind whips at me, tugging on my shirt, but I barely register the cold, too pumped up on adrenaline.

My heart picks up the pace as I change the iPhone's settings to disable caller ID, then check three times that the correct setting is definitely on before I tap ten digits which, in the right order, form Dante's number.

My hands shake so hard it takes me three tries to input the number without mistakes. I stop a hundred yards from the bar and sit cross-legged on the edge of the empty, eerily silent interstate.

The night sky is a sight to behold around here. Back in Chicago, among the skyscrapers and artificial lights, stars are rarely visible. Even when they do peek from between the thick, gray clouds, they don't shine as bright as they do in Texas. Away from Dallas, on a clear winter night, the sky looks even better than the mural in my bedroom at Jean's house. An oily, black canvas stretches high above my head, dotted with millions of bright stars. The moon looks more radiant, too. It's bigger and shines brighter, illuminating the horizon with a soft glow.

One deep breath fails to calm my nerves. Nothing but the touch of Dante's lips on my forehead could elicit any sense of calmness right now. He always had the magical power to rid me of all troubles with one kiss.

I tap the green button, pressing the phone to my ear. Incoherent thoughts screaming over one another in my head come to an abrupt halt...

"Hello?" he answers before the second tone rings out.

My legs turn cotton-candy-soft. Thirteen days have passed since I last heard his voice. Thirteen days filled with more hurt and pain than some experience in a lifetime. I might've killed Frank myself, but I still mourn him even though he doesn't deserve a single tear. Music plays in the background hinting where Dante is right now.

I squeeze his hand, having a hard time believing he's not only real but mine too. Frankie was right six months ago when he said he knows what type of woman Dante's looking for.

He stops to look at me, inching closer not to shout over Britney blasting from the speakers. "Everything good?"

"Yes, all good." I rise on my toes, curious to see whether such a blatant manifestation of feelings will bother him while everyone who can see us watches us with wide eyes.

He doesn't stop me when I press my lips to his and smile, satisfied that he's not planning to hide me like a dirty secret.

I swallow the lump lodged in my throat, unmoving, silent, one hand clasped over my mouth to muffle my ragged breaths. I count to stay focused.

One.

I want to speak, say something, anything that'll prompt an answer so I can hear his voice again; nitpick his tone to guess what's going through his head. Whether he hates me or still loves me even a little bit. My mouth falls open, but my mind draws a blank. No words come out. All I can do is listen to the music pumping around him and his steady, calculated breaths.

Two.

Tears sting my eyes. I imagine he sits in the VIP booth at Delta, a drink in hand—vodka on the rocks or maybe cognac. He's probably surrounded by his men. A focused expression clouds his handsome face, not a hint of softness in his striking green eyes. That softness was reserved for me.

Three.

"You promised," I whisper, twisting the ring he gave me on my finger.

"*Layla*," he says on an exhale, his voice low and coarse as if his throat hurts. "Where are you?!"

The trance I lulled myself into fades when a tendril of panic seizes my chest. An adrenaline rush sharpens my senses as air stalls in my lungs, but my reaction is instantaneous.

I cut the call.

CHAPTER EIGHT

Dante

Delta once again bursts at its seams, overflowing with half-naked women writhing on the dance floor to modern techno remixes of the nineties R'n'B classics. Music blares from the speakers, sifting through the air that smells heavily sweet of coconuts and vanilla.

And *zero* giant dildos are in sight. The club looks more or less as it did before the fire, with a few updated details. A white to red color change of floor-length curtains that hung behind the DJ station happened. It was an unconscious decision. I didn't realize at the time why I craved red...

Now, I crave red even more.

I was heading to my office at the back of the club to meet Spades and Nate when Layla called. She said two words. *Two* fucking words. Enough to briefly put my mind at ease.

She's alive.

Not yet safe, but with the phone to my ear, the solution was simple: ask where the hell she is.

I asked.

She didn't answer.

She hung up the fucking phone. When I tried to redial, a private number sat at the top of the callers' list. It took effort, but I reined the burning need to hurl my phone at the crowd of dancing people. I did, however, squeeze the cell so hard that the screen cracked in three places.

Spades and Nate sit in the office, sprawled on the brand-new *red* leather couches. A bottle of Bourbon, eight crystal glasses, a box of Cuban cigars, and an ashtray sit on the table, ready for unwanted guests.

Too much has happened in the last twenty-four hours... I'm no longer in the right frame of mind to endure a business meeting with the V brothers and Julij. They're due any minute, but my mind is elsewhere. With *her.*

Julij hadn't had the chance to meet the V brothers yet. Which is another reason why this meeting shouldn't be happening tonight. I really can't deal with their cocky attitudes. My fuse is way too short to referee the cock fight, which will, undoubtedly, ensue the second Vinn and Julij step into the same room together. Julij has an invidious ability to piss off a man without saying or doing much of anything. His face is enough. He can't hide his emotions, and Vinn sure is easily offended. He looks for disrespect in everyone he comes across, always ready for a fight. He never takes the *bigger man* route, unable to just fucking drop it. I'm in for one hell of a circus show going forward.

"Caro called," Spades says, but I shush him with one flick of my hand, dialing Jackson's number for the hundredth time since I ordered him to find Layla yesterday morning.

God, it feels right to think about her as mine again.

"I still don't know anything, Dante," he answers, his tone laced with amusement rings in the office loud and clear through the speakerphone. "I told you it'll take time. Longer if you don't stop calling every ten minutes. Get a fucking hobby, alright? Start knitting or go fishing."

Spades and Nate elbow each other like children. They're having a blast watching me lose my shit as I pace the room, growing uncharacteristically impatient.

"Layla called," I say, stopping either of them from offering an alternative hobby or a snarky comment.

My people adapted to my change of heart faster than the light turns on after a switch is flipped. They knew my resolution to leave Layla behind like a figment of my past wouldn't last long, but they stood back and watched from the sidelines while I processed her betrayal at my own slow pace.

So fucking slow.

Now, they organize search parties to locate Layla and contact our allies to thwart whoever plans on participating in the hit. The busy schedule doesn't interfere with their not-so-subtle digs and yanking my chain all day long, though. Spades and Nate took it upon themselves to bug me for waiting so long before chasing after Layla.

I know they're just trying to distract me from the problem

at hand, from the fact that hundreds of killers are out there, salivating at the prospect of earning three million dollars. Keen to kill the one person I care about more than myself.

Surprisingly, I *don't* need a distraction. I'm proud and rather impressed by how I handle the situation. My mind took the wheel, locking my heart in the trunk to focus and work in peace without the unwanted distraction of ache or fear leaping in the way.

"Did she say where she is?" Spades reacts first, his spine straight as an arrow, undivided attention on me. He's waiting for orders, ready to go wherever we'll need to go to get Layla.

"No. And no caller ID. Can you trace it, Jackson?"

"Yeah, sure I can. It'll take a while, but it'll be faster than what I had planned. I need your phone. Send Nate or Spades here, and I'll get on it right away."

Nate's up before Jackson stops talking. He grabs my phone, cuts the call, and leaves the office without a word. It's good to have a crew who knows how to use their brains.

"Here they come." Spades motions at the screens behind my back which show the live feed from cameras inside Delta.

Together with Caro, the V brothers climb the metal staircase leading to the balcony. A moment later, the office door stands open. Vince enters first, a bottle of cognac in hand, a three-piece gray suit on his back. "The club looks good," he says, giving my hand a firm squeeze.

"It looks the same." Vinn clips, sauntering closer to pat my back. "Any news about Layla?"

"Not yet. How are things looking on your side?"

Vince sits on the couch and takes the liberty of standing in as our bartender for the evening. He pours the cognac, glancing around to check if anyone else wants a drink. I'm off alcohol for the time being. I need to stay alert, focused, and sober to jump behind the wheel at a moment's notice.

"None of our clients will touch the job, and all have instructed their people to steer clear."

"That's a start," I say, thinking of the bosses we supply with drugs. "Julij's been calling off Nikolaj's affiliates."

The one in question chooses this moment to make an appearance, stealth as a ninja if I hadn't spotted him on the cameras. Vinn narrows his eyes, scrutinizing Dimitri as if looking for weak spots. Knowing Vinn, that's what he's doing.

I didn't expect Julij to dive into new business ventures one day after the casket with his father was lowered into the ground, but when he learned the V brothers were due in Chicago tonight, he packed a suitcase and left New York by my side.

That's not what struck a nerve, though... Anatolij boarding the plane with us without a word or explanation, did.

There's something peculiar about him. The sophistication of Prince Charming mixed with the wickedness of Scar from "The Lion King." He carries himself with an abundance of respect and an undeniable sense of conviction, and he talks like a Commander strategizing his next move.

He fooled me into believing he's the two-point-oh version of the bosses from the olden days like the infamous Al Capone, whom Julij compared him to a few weeks ago.

But there's more to Anatolij than meets the eye. More layers than most notice. For a reason I can't yet understand, he favors *me* over his nephew. We spent the better part of the flight back to Chicago engrossed in a conversation about the hit on Layla. With no connection to the matter, he offered to help in any way he can.

It got me thinking... connecting the dots.

"How's Jackson doing?" Julij asks, marching across the room to shake my hand.

The king-of-the-world attitude is back in full—a defense mechanism designed to hide his insecurities. He disregards the V brothers and the need for introductions, his eyes fixed on me, awaiting an answer.

I motion behind his back. "That's Vinn and Vince, and that's their right hand, Caro."

"I had an idea," he continues, without as much as a nod in the V brothers' direction. "You're not gonna like it."

Vinn's jaw tightens, eyes sparkling with annoyance that paints his face bright red. Looks like we're off to a *great* start. Under different circumstances, I'd deal with his shitty attitude first, but right now, I don't give a fuck. He's onto something. I can tell. Any idea is worth pursuing if it'll help me find Layla. No way he's referring to anything else. He's on his toes, worried, impatient, and desperate to find her. Under normal circumstances, his feelings would be bothersome, but right now, I don't give a fuck who loves Layla if anyone is ready to turn every rock, check every lead, and kill anyone who stands in my way to her. Julij will. He won't rest until she's back in Chicago. Safe, with *me.*

He'd happily give his arm to make it happen.

I'd happily detach his arm from his body to teach him a lesson. *Don't touch what's mine. Don't dream about it either.*

"Spit it out," Vince seethes.

"I know someone who might know exactly where Layla is."

I narrow my eyes, straining to see the big picture among the white noise of obsessive worry thrashing inside me like a pissed-off snake. The answer leaps in front of me out of nowhere and smacks me across the face.

Fuck.

Why didn't I think of *her* sooner?

"Jess."

Julij's right. I don't fucking like this.

CHAPTER NINE

Layla

My heart beats double-time, ramming against my ribs hard enough to cause pain. The sound of soft footsteps coming from behind me catches me by surprise. I half expect Dante to materialize before me, lethal, ruthless, and unforgiving. I scramble to my feet, my body feeble, fragile. Pulse throbs in my ears when I spin to stand face to face with Jean.

"Are you *insane*?!" she booms, hands akimbo, murder in her eyes. "Why did you call him?!"

"You told me to say goodbye, remember?" My voice mirrors the emotions rolling inside me—fear, helplessness, defeat.

She grabs my arm and tugs hard, manhandling me back toward the bar. "Yeah, but I was just teasing. I didn't think you'd actually do it. Shit, Layla, what the hell were you thinking?! Did you tell him where you are? Is he coming?" An unhealthy dose of panic pushes her voice higher an octave.

"I didn't tell him anything. I cut the call the second he realized that it was me calling."

She stops to turn my way, or else I'd miss her beautifully cocked eyebrow and how she's scrunching her nose at me like I'm certifiably insane. "You *didn't* talk to him? Then why the hell did you call him? Jesus, Layla, you're so fucking confusing! You called him, so you might've as well said goodbye."

I'm confusing? Can she hear herself when she speaks?

"I can't keep up with you. First, you tell me to call him, then you're pissed off I did. What did you expect me to do?"

"Let me think," she mocks, tapping her chin with her long, red nail, a condescending look on her ghastly pale face. "Either call him back and apologize or stop living in the past and get a grip! He's not going to kill you! It's been two weeks, but no show. He doesn't want anything from you anymore."

As cruel as that sounds, as deep as her words cut, Jean's right. Dante's unlike any man I ever crossed paths with. With his connections, money, and several skilled men at his command, he has the means to find me but chooses not to.

It's time to face the music. Accept, that the three months we shared were all fate had planned for us.

Jean tugs my arm again, discreetly jerking her head toward the building. Archer's there, leaning his back against the wooden wall. He lights a zippo and touches the flame to the cigarette's tip, pinched between his lips as he scans the lot with a hunter's look. We're fifty yards apart, but I swear he's staring straight into my eyes. Straight *through* my eyes, into my mind. A disturbing gesture follows the short stare-down.

A signal.

A nonverbal order not to move. He slides his right hand under the jacket, adjusting what I'm sure is a gun tucked in the holster. I can't see it, but it's there. I know it just as I know that one bullet has *Layla* written all over.

Dante's face flickers before my eyes. Hope vanishes, undermining everything I conditioned myself to believe. Pure fear starts in my chest and ripples in all directions. I deserve what's coming, but I hate Dante's cowardice. He should be the one to pull the trigger. Not a hired hitman.

"Get inside," I tell Jean, my gaze fixed on Archer, my voice artificially calm.

There's no reason for her to witness the execution. She doesn't deserve the trauma and doesn't deserve to die if Dante's orders are to leave no witnesses.

Before Jean can ask *why* the door on Archer's left flies open. Rick exits the building, shoulders square, spine straight. Tayler trails close behind, and they split up immediately. Rick marches straight ahead, Tayler veers left toward his pickup, his steps rushed. I think he can barely stop himself from breaking into a sprint. Rick is ruthlessly focused, eyes on me as he crosses the lot, every step calculated to perfection.

"We're leaving." The powerful, commanding note in his voice could rival Dante's tone. "Right now." He looks over his shoulder, taking half a step to the right.

My mouth falls open because I know what he's doing. He's shielding me with his body, purposely stepping into

Archer's line of shot. Fear grips me by the throat. Cold, dead hands squeeze hard enough to cut off my air supply. My face tingles, and goosebumps cover every inch of my skin when I step aside, back into the line of Archer's shot.

"You should go," I tell Rick and Jean, eyes on Archer.

He just stands there, watching, waiting. Lethal. Determined. There's nowhere to run and nowhere to hide.

I'm a sitting duck.

"I'm not leaving you here." Rick grips my arm to hold me in place as he steps in front of me again. I peek over his shoulder, wriggling out of his grasp, but his hold tightens.

Archer grows tired of waiting. He draws the gun aiming it at the back of Rick's head. An earsplitting roar of Tayler's tired pickup truck cuts through the tense silence. He's too far away to reach us before Archer pulls the trigger.

Five bony fingers clamp around my upper arm as Jean inches closer to whimpers in my ear, "he's got a gun. He's got a *gun,* Layla."

Time fails to slow down. This is nothing like in the movies. No slow-motion action sequence. Only me and Archer, eyes locked as he slides his index finger to the trigger. I shove Rick away with all my might but feel him jerk me to the side by the arm he's still holding.

Archer doesn't pause. He doesn't hesitate. There's no loud bang, just a quiet hiss when the bullet leaves the chamber, slicing the air as it heads straight for my heart. It falls short of reaching its destination...

Rick's attempt at moving me out of the way worked to some extent. The bullet goes through and through, half an inch below my collarbone. I'm in no state to stop and register the pain that screams up and down my arm like a lightning bolt, settling into the gunshot wound. Jean yelps, a high-pitched, horror-movie kind of sound. She ducks for cover when Tayler slams the brakes, stopping the pickup behind Rick's back. The rusty piece of metal serves as a barricade, separating the hunter from the hunted... but it isn't bullet-proof. It won't hold Archer off for long.

The passenger side door flies open. "Get in!" Tayler booms, his voice higher than Jean's.

She's inside before the words fully roll off Tayler's tongue. She jumps onto the passenger seat, slides to the floor, and folds her arms and legs to fit in the space under the dashboard. Rick hauls me into the back, arms wrapped around my middle.

"Go, go, go!" Jean yells.

The back door is still open but slams shut when Tayler hits the gas. Chaos erupts all around. Jean cries Tayler swears, the old engine blares louder than a rocket as the car gains speed, and tires squeal when we jump from the gravel of the parking lot onto the asphalt of the interstate. Adrenaline mixes with fear, zapping my nerve endings, and works as a decent ad-hoc anesthetic. I push away the panic, forcing my eyes to stare ahead, not glance at the warm blood wetting my t-shirt, or my mind will cease to work.

"What the fuck did you do!?" Rick tears his shirt off his back, scrunching it into a ball to press against the gunshot wound. He applies enough pressure to balance on the verge of breaking my bones, trying to stop the bleeding. His face shows something other than cold calculation or moderate interest for the first time since I met him. He's worried. His eyes jump between my face and his hands as if he's watching a game of tennis. "You could've died!"

"Better me than you. I'm the one Archer wants. You shouldn't have tried to save me. Tayler, stop the car. Let me out."

"No fucking way!" Rick grips my wrist as if he half expects me to jump out of the moving truck. "Keep driving."

"Oh my God! Oh my God!" Jean chants, tears streaming down her cheeks, tiny rivers of mascara. "What is happening?!" She peeks between the front two seats, scrambling off the floor to look at me, but looks out of the back window instead. "Oh God! He's behind us!"

Rick turns around, checking briefly before his head snaps to Tayler's pale face in the rearview mirror. "Put your foot down. Get us to the city. Somewhere public. He won't shoot with witnesses around."

"How did you know he was going after me?" I ask to redirect my thoughts away from my blood and the sudden onset of blinding pain ripping my arm wide open.

"I didn't like how he acted since he saw you." He glances at me briefly but returns his attention to the back window in a heartbeat. "The way he was looking at you... I've seen that look before, and I don't fucking like what follows. Listen... I know we're both thinking this, so I'll just go ahead and say it. You're not safe in Texas anymore. Dante knows you're here. We need to get you out, hide you better. My sister has a cabin near Montreal. Tayler's pickup won't make the drive, but—"

"You mean Dante hired Archer to *kill* her?" Jean gasps in the front seat, her processing speed slightly delayed.

Was the shooting not enough of a hint?

We're doing about a hundred miles an hour. The car shakes, sputtering from the exhaust pipe, and the engine strains as if on the verge of giving up any second.

And then Archer whizzes past us on a black motorcycle as if we're at a standstill. My heart kicks a riot in my chest, mingling fear with adrenaline, but it all dies down when nothing happens. Archer keeps going, speeding into the darkness of the night until he's out of sight.

Tayler's nervous chuckle fills the confined space. "Shit, that was... God! I feel like I'm in a fucking movie!" He takes his foot off the pedal, slowing the car to a more pickup-friendly speed. The road ahead is empty as far as the eye can see, but a faint glow of city lights looms in the distance.

"This doesn't feel right," Rick says, voicing my thoughts.

And then *fuck!* booms over other sounds. A silhouette of a man standing in the middle of the road comes into view. Archer holds his arm outstretched, aiming his gun at the pickup. Panic curdles the blood in my veins. Clots jam every major artery. I watch in horror as he pulls the trigger.

The front tire of the truck blows up.

The car goes airborne...

This time, it does feel like in the movies. Time slows down; sounds mute. The car flips onto the side, then the roof, and keeps rolling fast. Too fast to comprehend which way is up. Rick holds me in a vice grip of his arms only for a moment before the centrifugal force throws him against the window.

The world unmutes. A deafening clatter of metal bending, glass breaking, and Jean screaming pierces my eardrums like steel splinters. Raw, intense pain resonates all over my body when I bounce off the seats, the roof, and the windows.

The car stops rolling, swinging on the roof several times before it stills completely. Clouds of smoke hiss from under the bonnet.

And then, everything fades to black.

CHAPTER TEN

Dante

Spades attempts to impersonate Rookie, burning across the city toward Jess's house. He emergency brakes at every corner and slams the gas halfway through the turn. My head bows back and forth, hitting the headrest every time. He's fucking hair-raising behind the wheel.

Still, I've been the passenger with much worse drivers behind the wheel. While Spades' skills aren't that bad, he fails miserably in the laid-back attitude department Rookie emanates. Spades clutches the wheel so hard I think he'll rip it out of the steering column. Sweat breaks out on his forehead, eyes glued to the road, Adam's apple bobbing when he swallows hard. I've never seen him this tense.

He's probably never felt so tense either.

Julij's hot on our tail with Dimitri behind the wheel of their rental Camaro. He insisted he accompanies me to meet Jess. He claims she'll be more inclined to talk if she sees that we're both looking for Layla. Maybe he has a point.

He has no reason to hurt her, and that argument might come in handy. With everything that happened, it's safe to assume Jess is not my biggest fan.

I hold my spare phone on my knee and light the screen repeatedly, staring at Layla's picture: a security camera frame from the night we first met. She sits at the bar, her chin high, no smile across her lips. A red dress hugs her body, and an abundance of dark locks frames her doll-like, innocent face.

"You tell me. I'm not a guy. I don't know what's so repulsive about me."

"Frankie." Nothing else is an option. "Men are afraid to touch you because they're afraid of your father."

The fabric of her dress rolls up when she readjusts her position exposing more skin. A beauty mark halfway up her thigh comes into view as if to taunt me as if to say, this marks the spot where you kiss. And, fuck if that's not what I want to do right now. I move in, resting my elbows on my knees, and place my hands on her legs, stroking the small dark spot with my thumb.

Gut-wrenching desire mixes with a cruel, compelling need to taste her lips. The intensity of my lust quadruples because no one has kissed her yet, and no one has had her between the sheets. I feel like Neil Armstrong the day he boarded Apollo 11 with the moon in his sights.

I have Layla, my star, right in front of me. I want to be the first man to do everything to her, and with her, that she should've done by now.

"You're not afraid," she utters, eyes lingering on my hands feeling up her legs.

I dig my fingertips into her flesh, my blood turning into red hot lava. "I'm not afraid of Frank, Star."

Spades pulls into the driveway of what I'd call Frank's house two weeks ago, but what is now Jess's house alone. He kills the engine, slinging the door open. A cold shiver slides down my spine when the cool air seeps through the thin fabric of my shirt. I hadn't stopped to think about the fact that Frank Harston is dead. I know he is. I saw him take his last breath, but while I crumbled under Layla's betrayal and drowned in the pain of losing her, I failed to process Frank's death. Now, standing at the door to his once house, the realization courses through my veins, slow like tar. It feels like fucking *defeat.* The hatred between us grew throughout the years but failed to erase memories.

Frankie helped me when I needed help most. At sixteen, ruled by hormones and rage, I was destined for doom. I rained hell, getting in trouble with Chicago's finest thanks to many idiotic stunts, fighting with anyone who dared to look at me wrong. After a few weeks of wandering Chicago with bruised knuckles, a few weeks of my uncle threatening to ship me off to military school, a few weeks of rage trapped inside of me and begging for an out, destiny placed Frank Harston in my path.

I still remember the first time he invited me over to his house, *this* house I stood in front of, for dinner. He mentioned he had a job for me. He didn't explain the job, but a tailor-made suit on a twenty-something-year-old and the gun

I spotted under his pristine suit jacket clued me into his line of work.

I was in awe of the man back then. He lived the dream. Big house, full wallet, and a beautiful family. A family I became a part of for six years until I went rogue... then, not long ago, one-third of the said family became a part of me.

I raise my hand to knock on the door. The house is dark, the secrets, lies, and betrayals hang in the air like a foul stench. Despite wishing a slow, painful death on Frankie since the moment I learned how he treated his daughter, there's no denying that a small part of me died too when Layla put a bullet through his heart.

He was my mentor.

He shaped me into the man I am now. It fucking hurts that we fell apart along the way. Life would've been different if I had stayed by his side. Perhaps Layla and I would've gotten together sooner. Frankie would probably give us his fucking blessing...

Maybe she'd still be the angel she was all those years ago. She's closer to a devil than an angel now. She has no wings. Frank tore them out. He bruised, taunted, and brainwashed her for years.

A wave of hatred sweeps me from head to toe, bulldozing the regret. It fades quickly when the lights come on in one of the rooms upstairs and then in the hallway downstairs. Angry, hastened footsteps reverberate inside before the door flies open, and I'm staring into the barrel of a gun.

Frank's gun in Jess's shaky hands.

Yeah, I'm definitely not her favorite person.

She shudders all over, her eyes pooling with fresh tears, the slim, pale face bordered by a mess of short hair. "Leave," she chokes, clutching the gun in both hands. I think she's aiming at my forehead, but her hands shake so much it might as well be my throat. "Leave, Dante. *Now*."

"Put it down, Jess," I say, unfazed. She hadn't even flipped the safety. "I'm not here to hurt you. I need your help."

Her grip tightens. Tears roll down her cheeks and her flawless make-up. "Get out of here. Please... get out!"

I grab her wrist, retrieve the gun, and pull her flush against my chest, boxing the petite, scared woman in my arms. She doesn't fight to break free.

Instead, her body gives in and melts against me as she rests her forehead on my torso, fisting my jacket with both hands. A sharp intake of air paves the way for powerful, despairing sobs.

"I need to find Layla." I hold her in a tight embrace, cradling her head to my chest. "I know she was here the night Frank died."

Jess nuzzles closer to me for another three sharp inhales before she steps away, wiping her face with the sleeve of her pink silk robe, half of her make-up stamped on my shirt. Blonde hair sticks to her long neck, and baby-blue eyes look dull, almost dead. She lost her husband two weeks ago, but I have a feeling it's not him she misses the most. It's Layla.

Jess never was a devoted mother; she never had time for Layla, too busy enjoying her youth to appreciate a child, but she's a mother, nonetheless. Losing them both must've been a bucket of ice-cold truth over her head. I'm sure it opened her eyes to everything she fucked up in her life.

"I don't know where she is. Even if I knew—"

"Jess," Julij says behind me, making his presence known. "We need to know where she is. It's important."

Jess glances between us, one eyebrow raised as she awaits explanations. There's no time for a vague chit-chat. I walk around her, inside the house, taking the direction of the kitchen. Not much has changed here over the years. The same light color scheme and expressionist paintings of distorted faces on the walls. The distinct smell of cigar smoke saturated every piece of furniture here over the years.

Spades stays outside with Dimitri while Julij and Jess trail behind me as if I'm the host and this is my fucking house. She sets an ashtray on the glass table, pointing her chin at the opposite chair. Julij settles for a casual lean against the wall, watching Jess with a frown, ready to beat the information out of her if playing nice proves fruitless.

The intensity of his feelings for Layla is staggering. He rivals my protectiveness. Puts to shame my agitation. At least he keeps a careful watch over his possessiveness. Otherwise, his face would resemble one of those in the hideous paintings in the hallway.

"Who killed Frank?" Jess asks.

"Don't ask questions you don't want to know the answer to. Although I'm sure you've already figured it out."

She helps herself to one of my cigarettes. "I guessed that Layla did it. She was terrified when she came home that night and immediately started packing. I didn't want to believe she had it in her to kill him."

"She had a choice. Frank or me." I light a zippo, leaning over the table to light the cigarette for her.

"That explains a lot..." She inhales a deep drag, standing up to fetch a glass of wine. "Ever since she met you, she started seeing Frank for who he was. The longer you were together, the more she surprised me with how she treated him. Until you, she was blind to Frank's flaws. She looked at him and saw the father she so desperately wanted to have, not the one she had. You were good for her."

No objection. We brought out the best in each other. "I need to find her."

Jess bites her lip, and just like that, I'm back in Layla land.

She bites her lip, playing with her fingers. "I think I probably do believe you're here for me and that I'm Switzerland."

"You think? Probably?" I smirk. "You have to know it. And believe me, when you're ready and willing, I won't let you out of bed for a very long time." I fall onto my back, tying my hands under my head.

Layla lays down too, lips swollen from my kisses. "You're not making this easy, are you?" She nuzzles herself into my side. "I shouldn't want to love you."

Love*?*

She wants to love *me.*

One sentence and the arrogant fucker I am, turns into a plush toy. "You're delirious, Star. You must be exhausted." I wrap my arms around her, kissing her head.

I hope she'll love me.

I hope she won't be able to live without me because I sure as hell can't imagine my life without her.

I crash with reality when Jess flips ash off the cigarette, accidentally brushing her hand over mine. Layla and Jess are strikingly similar. Same petite figures, doll-like faces, and full, pouty lips. Frank's the one to thank for Layla's hair and eye color, though. And maybe I should've thanked the fucker. The combination of dark-brown locks and light gray, almost silver irises is striking. In fact, I couldn't peel my eyes off hers most of the time, openly staring as she studied or read.

"Why are you looking for her?" Jess asks slowly, every word quieter than the last. She doesn't trust me. That much is obvious, but I think she *wants* to trust me. "Why did she leave?"

"It's complicated."

She butts the cigarette in the ashtray and leans back, folding her arms over her chest, her chin nonchalantly raised. "I won't tell you where to find her if I don't know why you want her."

Because I can't go on without her.

"She was scared and confused that night. She thinks I want to hurt her."

"Do you?"

My hands ball into tight fists on their own accord. What kind of a stupid fucking question is that? "Do you really have to ask? Frank ordered a hit on her before he died. An *open* hit, Jess. Anyone can try to kill her. And a lot of people will try." I lean over the table again, a vein on my neck throbbing. "I need to know where she is. I need to find her. I can't fucking protect her if she's not with me."

There's no trace of pink blush left on her face. The peachy tone of her skin turns ashen, eyes fill with a new batch of salty tears. She reminds me so much of Layla that my immediate reaction is to get up and lock her in my arms.

"He wanted her dead?" she utters, peering from under her thick, black eyelashes at Julij, then at me, and back as if willing either of us to say it's a sick joke.

I still can't comprehend Frank's sheer insanity. There's no other fitting word to describe the bastard. *Insane* fits perfectly. Treating his daughter like a puppet was beyond absurd. Fucking ludicrous. Requesting that she gives herself to me was even worse. Fucking grotesque. Not to mention the rape or mutilation he ordered—a testament to his deranged mind.

I could easily rip him apart for any one of those sins but ordering a hit on his daughter? Playing God to punish me for insubordination? That's another level of madness.

A level beyond my comprehension.

He should be thankful Layla found the courage in her to kill him, or else I'd skin the fucker alive regardless of her betrayal. I'd bask in his screams, pleas, and apologies. He'd pay for every single time he hurt her. Every threat, every disappointed look, every spiteful word.

"He hated me so much he wanted to sacrifice Layla to leave me with nothing." I weigh every word. Anger rushes over me, bubbling like red, hot soda water in my veins.

Frankie played on Layla's insecurities her whole life. He turned the vulnerable little girl I adored when she was a child into a weapon of mass destruction.

And then... ready, aim, *fire.*

I was hers, whenever and wherever. Prepared and willing to throw the world at her feet, to risk my work and life to protect her. She's a panacea to the diseases infecting my mind, heart, and soul. Life without her just isn't worth the trouble. I've not been living since she left. Barely surviving. I'm stuck in limbo, tumbling deeper into the land of the mad the longer she's out of my reach.

And Frankie knew that and then some. He knew what kind of a man I was. One who'd completely lose his wits if the right girl ever came along.

I wait for Jess to decide what her next move should be, whether she's willing to trust me or not. There's no doubt in my mind she knows where Layla's hiding. I don't harbor the same hatred toward her as I did—and still do despite his *deceased* status—toward Frank. She wasn't a good mother, she hurt Layla too, but hers and Frank's sins are incomparable. Jess deserves a chance to right her wrongs. Frank deserves a few bullets fired from my gold revolver.

Surrendering the information I need will mark the first step on Jess's long road to redemption.

"I've got hundreds of people looking for her, Jess," I say, painfully aware of the ticking clock. "I *will* find her, but it'll be faster if you can tell me where she is. We're working against the clock here."

She peers up, letting out a loud, shaky sigh. "She's at Frank's sister's in Ivanhoe."

"Texas?" Julij cuts in, pushing away from the wall.

I almost forgot he was here. He walks closer as an injection of adrenaline jolts his body.

"Yes. Amanda has a farm there. I'll get you the address." She up and leaves the kitchen without a backward glance.

For a moment, I can't believe this is happening. If we obey traffic regulations, we'll be in Texas inside of fourteen hours. Still, since neither I nor my people give a damn about speeding tickets, the distance is doable in ten hours with breaks for refueling factored into the equation.

Maybe it'd be quicker to fly? A quick search online scraps that idea. The next flight to Dallas leaves at seven in the morning. Flying is not an option. I glance at the watch Layla gave me for Christmas. It's quarter to eleven. I'll have her back by nine in the morning. A shockwave of relief detonates in my chest, spreading to all my organs, soothing my jittery unease.

I'm coming, baby. Hold on a little while longer.

Jess comes back with a small notebook in hand. At the same time, Spades enters the kitchen. A sullen look taints his features, and my relief vanishes instantly. There's no mistaking the torment in his eyes, the expression reserved for relaying the most dreadful news.

He inhales sharply, rubbing his forehead.

"No," I snarl. "Don't you fucking *dare* say it."

"It's not *that*. She's alive, but... she's at a hospital."

"What happened?" Julij asks, his face contorted with worry.

Spades pays him no attention, eyes on me. His tense stance and pained look on his face as if someone kicked him in the stomach make it obvious that he's ready for my outburst. He's leaning closer slightly, prepared to jump in and, I don't know, hold me, maybe? "Jackson accessed her records, but she was only admitted half an hour ago, so the information is limited. Two major wounds to her shoulder and leg, a gunshot wound just below her collarbone, and a mild concussion. She's stable."

My insides tangle into knots at the thought of Layla alone in a hospital bed, scared, defenseless. Unprotected. Vulnerable. "Do we know what happened?"

"It's unclear. The police report places five people at the scene. Out of the five, one's dead. A tire burst. The car flipped over, rolling for thirty yards before it stopped. There's no explanation for the gunshot wound on Layla or the dead guy."

"Who was he?"

"Ex-marine, Archer Hayes. Someone blew his fucking brains out. No witness statements yet, so it's hard to judge what went down there."

Jess slumps into the chair, lips parted in an inaudible shock. She gawks at me with big, scared, tearful eyes.

"*No one* will touch her," I say, catching her hand in mine. "*No one* will hurt her, Jess. They'd have to go through me first, and you know damn well that's not happening." I squeeze her fingers once and rise to my feet, shaking the weakness off my limbs. "I'll have Layla back in Chicago in thirty-six hours."

Spades steps from one foot to another. There's more to be said, but he refrains from speaking until we're out of the house, away from Jess's ears. "She's no longer invisible,." He lights a cigarette while Julij paces on the gravel. "Hospital records aren't protected well. Anyone who's keeping tabs will know where she is."

"It's a twelve-hour drive," Julij adds. He sure doesn't know Rookie as I do. "A lot can happen in twelve hours, Dante. She needs protection."

I nod, a plan of action already fully formed in my head. "Call the guys. I want to be on the road in fifteen minutes," I tell Spades, then turn to Julij. "You're not coming. You're organizing the security detail for when we get back."

CHAPTER ELEVEN

Dante

Blake Davis is one of the few people who remained loyal to Frankie throughout the years. They had been partners since the early days, since before Dino died. He stood by Frankie's side regardless of his sins. The Holy Trinity: Blake, Frank, Nikolaj. Unlikely but powerful affiliates at one point; good friends once Frank's fixation with me and taking over South soared out of control.

And now I need his help.

He's the biggest fish in Texas, a goddamn shark. The boss in Dallas. An old Mafioso who adheres to old rules and frowns upon breaking them. Under different circumstances, securing his help would prove impossible, but the odds are in my favor tonight.

Makes for a nice fucking change, all things considered.

He's one of the old guys, one of those who lived through the eighties when La Cosa Nostra was sacred; when being a mafia man, being a *made* man was a way of life, not just a way to make a bucketload of cash fast. They had different values back then. They *had* values back then.

"Dante Carrow," he drawls, answering his phone. A note of curiosity rings in his voice. "You're the last person I expect a call from." He speaks slowly as if reciting an old poem as if every word is worth its weight in gold. "I imagine this will be interesting. How can I assist the new kingpin of Chicago?"

"You'll have to forgive me, Blake. I have no time for pleasantries tonight. I'm in urgent need of protection." Squeezing the bridge of my nose, I wait, expecting a blatant *no* right off the bat, but Blake keeps silent, waiting for more words on my part. "As you must be well aware by now, there's an open hit on Frankie's daughter, Layla."

"Yes, so I heard," he sighs, pushing a long burst of air down the receiver. "If the whispers are true, I'm not surprised you ordered the hit. Although I must admit, you never struck me as a guy who'd—"

"I did *not* order the hit." Why am I everyone's first guess? Granted, not many people know or could hope to understand how much Layla means to me, but why does every single person consider me the prime suspect? "This isn't the time to divulge the details. You must know two things for now.

One: Frankie ordered the hit. And two—"

"Hold your horses right there." The pace of his voice changes to animosity. Words come out sharp enough to cut if administered correctly. "You're telling me Frankie Harston ordered a hit on his daughter? Don't be ridiculous, Dante. I've known him since day one in this life. He's my kind of guy. He had respect for La Cosa Nostra. He had respect for his family."

"Right up until he didn't," I snap, heat pooling in the base of my stomach. "He used Layla against me and..." I huff the air through my nose. "This really isn't the time for explanations. She's been hiding in Texas, but someone found her. An amateur, a newbie judging by the way he handled the job. She's alive at a hospital in Dallas. News travels fast, Blake. If I know she's there, everyone knows. It's a matter of hours before the place is crowded with hitmen. I need you to take her under your wing until I get there."

Like most old bosses, Blake doesn't make rash decisions. He's scrupulous in his moves. Plans his actions in great detail if his work partnership with Nikolaj and Frank is any proof. They were unlikely allies, but they made it work.

Agreeing to protect Layla is not a decision he can take lightly. It comes with the possibility of stepping on the toes of many bosses and hitmen he might not be willing to cross. With both Nikolaj and Frank dead, Blake isn't well protected. Alone on the battlefield.

Which, come to think of it, could prove to be another ace up *my* sleeve... choose your friends wisely. I might be the best thing that has happened to him in a long time.

"Name your price," I urge, staring out the window at a blur of Chicago's streets.

The bastard sure knows how to build on the anticipation.

Adrenaline burns through my veins like acid, bringing my focus to a very sharp point. Seconds tick away, nothing but heavy breathing in my ear as he weighs his options.

"I'm too old for this," he says after what feels like a goddamn century. Tension in my neck gives way to the defeated undertone detectable in his clipped tone. "My son will soon take my place. I want you to hook him up with the right people. I want him safe up there, at the top of the game alongside you, Dante. That's my price."

My eyes narrow in confusion. "You want him to be my protégé? Where is this coming from?"

Blake laughs softly. "Nikolaj is dead, Mr. Carrow. You have gained a powerful ally in Julij, although you probably don't see it yet. His father's affiliates are now yours, whether they like it. And believe me, the word on the street is, they very much like the prospect of receiving your product. With the business venture you've set up with Detroit and all the other bosses who already bow to you, you're very fucking close to the top of this ladder. I want my son on that ladder too."

Words pile up on my tongue, pushing and shoving at one another to shoot past my lips. I mull over my response just as Blake did his. I wasn't in the right frame of mind for the past two weeks while my world slowly splintered around me. I ignored the consequences and victories brought on by Frank's death. I didn't assess how much power I hold now that he's out of the way, no longer breathing down my neck.

It would've occurred to me sooner if I hadn't been preoccupied with Layla since that fateful night. More than half of the biggest bosses in the country now work with me or rely on my product. I'm where I've wanted to be for years. At the same time, I'd give it all up at the snap of my fingers to keep Layla safe.

"You have my word," I say. The knot in my stomach that tied itself up when Spades said Layla's in the hospital starts to come apart now. "Kill anyone who tries to see Layla. She's your priority for the time being. I don't care if it's a nurse, someone claiming to be related to her, or the president trying to get in her room. No one gets through."

A low satisfied chuckle is his first answer. "I've got just the guys to handle the job. My son will lead the team. Don't worry, she's safe here."

A state of mind where I don't worry about her no longer exists. I don't think it existed since the day she entered Delta.

"I need someone on the inside. Have you got a trusted, reliable doctor at the University Hospital?"

"Yes, of course. I'll send you the details. His name is Mark. A hundred grand will have him dancing to whatever tune you might want to play."

"Thank you. Keep me updated. Anything happens, I want to know first." I cut the call a touch lighter and calmer.

Rookie sits behind the wheel, relaxed and seemingly unaffected by the hundred and thirty miles an hour on the clock. Spades and Nate have a hard time keeping up while Cai and Jackson are no longer visible in the rearview mirror.

It's not that they lack power under the hoods. Last week I swapped the three identical SRT8 Charges we had to Hellcats. We sit on the same horsepower, but neither Spades nor Cai can handle a car the way Rookie can; neither has the balls to watch the speed climb to the max. That's precisely why Rookie's by my side and not Spades. I want to get to Layla as soon as humanly possible. He can make that happen.

"That didn't take much work." With a sideways glance my way, he slams the gas, veering into the other lane to pass a truck that's still miles away. "I expected more resistance."

"So did I."

I check the phone every three seconds, waiting for the doctor's details. Two minutes later, I call Jackson, who's on the passenger seat of the car with Cai at the wheel, ordering him to wire a hundred grand over to a Mark Johnson. Once the transfer is complete, I dial the number Blake sent.

"Hello?" He answers, the Texan accent ringing in my ears.

"Check your bank account."

He doesn't question me, which hints it's not the first call he received with such an opener. Tapping on the keyboard sounds in the background for a few long seconds before he speaks. "I'm listening." An unhealthy dose of excitement spiked with dread chimes in his voice.

Who wouldn't sound excited after becoming one hundred grand richer in seconds?

Money cheers everyone up. It's the bread and butter of our existence in this mundane, shitty world. The main thing people chase. The reason behind the most heinous crimes. Money is power. Whoever says otherwise is either stupid or never had the kind of money that lets you buy everything. Material and immaterial things. A yacht. Obedience. A penthouse in New York. Information.

Money *is* power. Kids are taught from a young age that money is a tool, a means to get by, pay the bills, and buy necessities. Kids are taught that love matters most. That being a decent human should take priority over everything else. One doesn't rule out the other, though.

You don't have to give up love to have money. Believing the blatant lie that you have to choose is an excuse not to get off your ass and earn *more*. It's the mindset of those who don't want to succeed. Those who are perfectly happy with mediocracy.

Thank God average folk exist, willingly living out their average lives, or else rich people wouldn't be as rich.

Don't get me wrong, love *is* the best thing that can happen to a person. The notion is now well and truly cemented in my very being since I got a taste of what true love feels like.

Yeah, love is the best, but try paying your bills with fucking hugs and see how that turns out.

I'd give up all my money if I had to choose between the millions in my bank and Layla.

Layla. Always Layla.

That doesn't mean I'd sit back on my broke ass, basking in the questionable wonders of mediocracy. I'd make the money back fast because I don't settle for average.

"Layla Harston was admitted to your hospital an hour ago," I say, watching the surroundings as they change from city streets to a quiet interstate.

"Yes, she was. I had Blake on the phone just now. You work fast, Dante. I haven't seen Layla yet, but from what I gather, she was involved in a car crash."

"Until I arrive at the hospital in ten hours, you're the only person allowed to touch her. No nurses, no other doctors. Only you. She needs a change of dressing, you do it. She wants a glass of water, you get it. She wants anything at all, no matter how extraordinary her wish, you accommodate. The one thing you can't allow is to let her leave the room. Understood?"

"Yes." He clears his throat. Quiet scribbling in the background tells me he's writing it all down. "Whatever she wants is hers as long as she stays in her room."

"Put her in the most remote room you can think of. Don't note the change in her file. Blake's people are on their way as we speak to stand guard at her door. They have orders to kill anyone who isn't you or me who tries to see her, and they will fucking do it, so you better make sure no hospital staff goes anywhere near the room."

"Of course, I'll ensure no one goes near her."

"Good." I squeeze the nape of my neck, bracing to ask the question to which I'm downright scared to hear the answer. "Now talk to me. How is she doing?"

More tapping on the keyboard follows. "Stable. Strained wrist, cuts, and bruises. A mild concussion. Twenty-six stitches on her thigh, eighteen on her shoulder, four more on the gunshot wound, two at the front and two at the back. The bullet went through and out. Nothing but muscle tissue was damaged. She's conscious, but..." he trails off.

The short pause shouldn't affect me the way it does. My thoughts shouldn't grind to a halt. My heart shouldn't climb up to my throat that pulses and throbs. But it does, and there's shit all I can do about my body's reaction.

"But *what?*"

"She's hooked to diazepam. The attending's note says she had a panic attack on the scene."

I rub my face, eyes closed. The images his words summon, amplify the unease rolling around me like sewage. The car crash alone must've scared her senseless, but I know blood seeping from her wounds had a more sinister effect. "Make sure she doesn't look at blood. She can't stand the sight."

"No blood. Got it."

CHAPTER TWELVE

Layla

My head feels as if someone inflated a balloon inside. The humming and beeping of the machines around my hospital bed aren't making it any better. It's not pain. I'd be astounded if I could feel pain while hooked to IVs with painkillers. No, this is more infuriating. A constant, exhausting pressure as if my head is slowly heating up, tiptoeing closer to boiling point.

My body weighs a tone. Feeble, fragile, and heavy all at once. Stitches pull on my thigh and shoulder, only itchy for now. The itch will morph into pain once I'm out of here, no longer under the numbing influence of whatever glorious pain relief drips into my veins.

I try to remember; to replay the car crash in my head. Everything from when Archer pulled the trigger to shoot the tire is a blur. Straining past the milky fog in my brain is a daunting task. I give up fast, too tired to piece together a coherent, sharp picture.

Greeted by a young doctor shortly after I was brought to the hospital, the initial haze started dispersing. Pumped full of painkillers and with the effects of whatever they used to knock me out at the scene wearing off, the panic eased away. All I remember clearly is that all-consuming, blood-curdling panic, the thick fear wrapped around every muscle, bone, and cell in my body.

And that was before I saw a pool of my own blood around my injured body. By the time the ambulance arrived, I was on the verge of passing out, my breaths sawing in and out, vision blurred by tears, chest so tight it felt like I was breathing around twenty-four broken ribs.

I recall bits. Muffled voices, Rick's distorted face in front of me, the firm touch of his big hands holding my shoulders. His desperate, futile attempts to calm me down.

He couldn't.

The ambulance crew tranquilized me on the spot before they hauled me out of the pick-up truck. I was hysterical. Bat-shit crazy. At least that's the description provided by the attending doctor once I calmed down with however much Diazepam they pumped into my system.

Not my proudest moment, I admit.

When I started to regain consciousness and rational thinking, fear came back, too. The doc hooked me to Diazepam again to suture my wounds in peace. Almost an hour later, the same IV still drips slowly, keeping me calm, weak, and tired. So, so tired. My eyelids want to close so badly, but I fight sleep. I'm waiting for Jean, Tayler, and Rick to visit. Doc promised to send them in once they're checked over.

I want to go home, curl into a ball and pretend that my life isn't a series of unfortunate events. The problem is, I don't have a home. Now that Dante found me in Texas, I'll never be safe again. Running isn't really an option. He found me once, so he'll do it time and time again.

My days are numbered...

I'm thankful for the drugs whooshing through my system. They numb the paralyzing train of thoughts that'd normally drive me insane.

Dante wants me dead.

And dead I'll end up, I'm sure.

The door to the room opens abruptly. Again, if not for the diazepam, I'd be jumping out of my skin. Now, a mild flinch is all my body can muster. My heart, on the other hand, picks up the pace a little when a tall man enters. A hoodie is pulled over his head, and he's not wearing a lab coat, dressed all in black. My pulse hurries again at the sight of a gun shoved into the holster by his belt. He parades around with the metal handle in full view, not trying to disguise it.

The machine that monitors my heart rate beeps faster as he pulls down the hoodie, revealing a wicked, chilling smile. I'm jolted into motion, frantically trying to pull myself up. At least that's what I think is happening. In reality, I'm moving as if through quicksand. My stiff muscles and bones don't want to cooperate while I try to at least sit up.

"Ah, you poor little thing. Let me." The man crosses the room to adjust the pillows behind my back. "You hid well, Layla. I've been looking for you for two weeks."

I silently, stupidly gawk into his dark eyes, taking in the stiff posture, broad shoulders, and exotic looks. His colorful accent and tanned complexion hint at Latin descent.

He sizes me up, snorting softly. "So young... so pretty. How did you fuck up your short life so badly, Imp?"

My eyebrows furrow as a peculiar familiarity washes over me at the nickname. Someone used to call me an Imp... it would probably be easier to access distant memories without three separate drugs in my bloodstream.

"You don't remember me, do you?" he asks, unnaturally pleased, his grin disturbing and taking more real estate across his face by the second. "Oh, come on! Don't hurt my feelings. Think harder, *Imp*."

Again, a strange sense of familiarity envelopes me like a soft blanket. I know him, but I can't recall his name. Even his face doesn't ring any bells. Just the nickname. Knowing that he came here to kill me doesn't help me concentrate. Inside, I'm as jittery as a sinner on judgment day, which, come to think of it, is probably a spot-on definition of me and this day. Outside, I wear a convincing mask of practiced indifference.

Too bad the machines betray what I feel as the rhythm of my heart beeps faster than it should.

I scrutinize his warm complexion, black eyes, and scruffy beard. Broad shoulders, large hands. Tall. Six feet at least. I tilt my head, taking him in as a whole again. Athletic build, probably in his forties... and then I spot it. A clue that untangles the web of memories, pushing the relevant ones to the front. If not for the signet ring on his finger, same as

Frankie's and Dante's, I probably wouldn't have remembered who he is.

Relief comes first. A single, powerful wave. It dies an ugly death after a fraction of a second, morphing back to fear. Our connection doesn't matter. Family or not, there's no room for mercy in the mafia world.

"Morte." I drop my gaze so he can't see fear clouding my vision. Blood drains from my face, and the treacherous hurtled beeping of the heart monitor fills the room.

It's been a long time since I last saw him. Thirteen, maybe fourteen years ago, back when Dino was in control of Chicago and Frankie barely rose in the ranks to his second in command. Morte was a regular guest in our home when I was a child. No wonder.

He's my godfather.

"Hello, Imp. Long time no see." Morte beams wider again, but there's nothing friendly in his smile. He's excited in a peculiar, eerie way. "I'll repeat the question. What did you do to deserve a death sentence at nineteen?"

My fear sets his face alight with sick satisfaction, so I clench my teeth harder, giving up without a fight. My body is too exhausted to hold me up, let alone fight or run for dear life. This is it. Game over.

"Tell him I'm sorry," I look back at my hands, my voice steady, a picture of calmness. I'm still breathing, but I feel dead inside. "And tell him I understand."

And tell him I love him.

Morte chuckles softly. God, it's so fitting. Almost poetic. Out of all the people he could hire, Dante chose *him* as my executioner. He's Portuguese, and so is his name: *Death.* I don't know the story behind the name, but I'm sure there is one. What parent in the right mind calls their child *Death*?

"I assume you mean Dante?" he asks, alive with excitement. "Don't prove Frank right so easily. He always said you were naïve. You're not, though. You just don't trust your gut. Do you think Dante wants you dead? The kill order didn't come from Carrow, Imp. It came from your father."

Pure confusion blurs my vision. Although *shock* is a more appropriate word. Pure, incessant shock. I feel as if someone suddenly pulled the rug out from under my feet as if the sky turned green before my eyes. "Frankie told you to kill me?"

"No, no, no," he hurries closer to take a seat on the bed and leans forward, closer to me, eyes wide, hands raised, ghosting over my cheeks. "I'd never hurt you, Imp." He cradles my face, sweeping his thumbs under my eyes. A disturbing urgency resonates in his moves, gestures, and words. "I'd *never* hurt you. You're my family, remember? This job isn't for me. It's for everyone. Anyone can walk in here and kill you."

"I don't understand..." I'm dizzy with confusion. Frankie wanted me dead. My own father wanted me to die.

Hypocrite. You killed him, remember?

"It's an open job, Layla. Instead of one hitman, you get hundreds." Morte inches closer, lowering his voice the way children do when they want to let you in on a secret. "Frankie wanted Dante to end up with nothing even if things went wrong that night." He throws his head back, cackling like a maniac. The sound sends a fit of shivers down my spine. The hairs on my neck stand on end. I think he's mad. Certifiably insane. His attitude changes every few seconds, dark eyes overflowing with crazy. "Didn't you surprise us all, Imp? *You* turned that night on its head."

This is too much to comprehend so quickly. My life is too fucked up to fight for it or understand the abstract reasons, lies, and secrets. Dante hates me. My father wanted me to die to satisfy his need for vengeance. What's left? Not much. Nothing worth fighting for or looking forward to.

"Dante no longer cares about me, Morte. My death won't change a thing."

"Frankie told me about his plan and your lead role a few weeks before he died. He hired me because he thought Dante might kill him before the finale.... but it was *you!*" he huffs with an ear-to-ear grin, stroking my hair in a monotonous rhythm that could quickly put me to sleep under different circumstances. "You killed your father! You betrayed him despite agreeing to help him take Dante out." Admiration and approval ooze out of every word. Keeping up with his mood swings is impossible. "I didn't expect such a turn of events. This would make a great movie, you know? What a twist! On the other hand, Dante was always good with women. They fell head over heels for him." He clicks his tongue, shaking his head in amusement. "See? You're not as strong as your daddy thought you were."

"You're stalling. Please, just get it over and done with."

He tuts under his nose, lips in a pout. "I told you the hit isn't mine to take. Pay attention, Imp."

"You said Frankie hired you!" I snap, my body rigid as steel, refusing to follow my mind and give up

I don't want to hear any more. I've had enough. My parents let me down at every turn, but I always found a way to justify their lack of love. Now, *this* can't be explained in neither a rational nor irrational way. It's barbaric. Unnatural. Incompatible with every human's basic instinct— to protect your offspring. Frankie was an anomaly.

And I'm an anomaly because of him. Because of the sick genes he passed down to me. I'm no better than him. Nothing in my life makes sense. Everything appears to be one giant illusion. I don't know right from wrong. Truth from lies. How could I have not noticed my own father was a psychopath? How? How the fuck is it possible? There's something fundamentally wrong with my head that no amount of therapy would fix.

"Earth to Imp." Morte playfully wraps a lock of my hair over his index finger, pinching the dark strands with the fascinated look of someone in a coma for two centuries and waking in a new reality. "Did you hear what I said?"

"No, I don't care."

Gritting his teeth, he squeezes the bridge of his nose. "You should. Curiosity is a natural thing, Imp. Frankie hired me for surveillance. Not to carry out the dirty work. I wouldn't agree. Not even for the three million he offered for your pretty head." He stamps a kiss on three of his fingers and taps them at the crown of my *pretty head*. "I'm the promoter. I set the wheels in motion right after Frank's death, but you hid so well it took me two weeks to trace your journey from Chicago all the way here. I only sent the word about your location earlier today."

He pauses for a moment, looks around, and crosses the room to pour himself a glass of water from a plastic jug on the side table.

"The only reason I'm here tonight is that Archer called in your time of death two hours ago. Before I wired the money, I wanted to see with my own eyes that you are, in fact, dead. Imagine my surprise to find he's the dead one." He cackles, coming back to me. "But it's all good fun. I'm glad we got to talk. As I said, I've been looking for you too."

"Why?" I wrap my arms around myself, seeking a bit of comfort.

"Finally!" Morte takes my hand to squeeze lightly. "You're starting to ask the right questions. Frankie wanted me to tell you why he ordered the hit. He wanted you to know you'll die in the name of the greater good." He scratches his beard, seemingly unconvinced. "At least that's how he saw it. He wanted you to understand him. If he knew you'd kill him, there'd be a different reason for the hit, I guess."

"Understand him? How am I supposed to do that? He wanted me dead, Morte. What kind of a parent does that?"

He touches his fingers to both temples, massaging in small, purposeful circles as if our conversation gives him a headache. "Frankie was somewhat crazy all his life, but it got worse after we killed Dino. In a way, you did him a favor when you killed him. It's such a pity you need to die too."

"Frank deserved what he got. You knew him. You know what he was like. When Dino died, nothing mattered more than revenge. He was obsessed. He controlled my life for years before telling me I was supposed to be the bait for Dante. I killed him because Dante gave me all I needed and could've ever wanted. Everything I never had. And he didn't expect a goddamn thing in return. Unlike Frank."

"Dante got a wee bit irritated when he found out you were conspiring with Frank, didn't he?" Morte sits up, straightening his spine. The crinkles around his eyes betray excitement.

I think he wants all the inside information he can get, but I'm not about to relay the worst night of my life for his entertainment. I clench my teeth, refusing to cooperate.

A scowl blooms on his face, but a manic smile covers it up fast. "You said you're nothing to Dante now, right? So, tell me... why did he set a whole army of pawns on their toes to find you? He's nobody without you, Imp, and he knows it."

The damn heart monitor speeds up once more, but this time, my pulse thuds in my ears loud and clear, partially drowning out the background noise. Dante's looking for me.

"He wants to kill me," I whisper, not ready to let my mind wander too far. Not ready to allow hope to break the dam I've built for the last thirteen days.

"He wants to *protect* you, Layla. He's bent over backward, pulled in very expensive favors, and started calling off hitmen yesterday when he found out about the hit."

A tiny flame of hope flickers in my heart, burning shyly as Morte's words sink into the deepest, most vulnerable parts of my psyche, filling the holes in my heart, gluing it back together. The flame morphs into a blazing inferno, burning my fear to the ground. Panic recedes, and real, intense relief rattles every cell in my body. This time, it's here to stay.

He wants to protect me. He *cares*.

Morte inhales a deep breath, eyes full of pity. "I hope whoever kills you does it quickly, painlessly. You don't deserve to suffer, Imp." He leans over to kiss my forehead and winks before leaving the room in a hurry like an unwanted stranger.

I struggle to make sense of my life, staring at the closed door. I'm nineteen, for crying out loud. This isn't the time to die. This is the time to find happiness, have fun, and live the way I'll never live again. This is the time to stay up with friends, drink, and make silly mistakes. The time to fall in love every Friday evening and forget about the guy by Sunday afternoon.

Instead, I wait for death, madly, irresponsibly in love with the one man I want to love until the end of time. Not long ago, I thought the end of my life was somewhere in the distant future, but now my end looms around the corner.

I jump out of bed, adrenaline jarring my limbs, zap after zap, that pushes me to act. I tear the cannulas out of my arms. The sudden injection of raw vitality helps my legs hold me upright when a few drops of blood splatter on the bed.

Dante's looking for me.

He doesn't want to kill me.

I need to get back to Chicago.

The door opens slowly again, stopping me dead in place. This time, it is a doctor who walks in, a white lab coat on his back. He frowns, taking in my state and the warm blood trickling down my arms from the torn cannulas. Maybe it wouldn't be as ghastly if I took more care. My heart beats out of my chest at the thought, but I transform fear into strength.

"Layla, you need to lie down," he says, striding closer, his hands outstretched far to the sides. Either he attempts to block the way out or readies himself to catch me. "You shouldn't be on your feet for a while."

"I need to see my cousin. She was in the car with me."

He takes two steps forward and grabs me gently by the shoulder. "You can't leave this room. Get back to bed."

Does he really think he can keep me here? I just found out there's a bounty on my head, and the one person who can keep me safe *wants* to do so. No one can keep me here. I need to grab Jean, Tayler, and Rick and head for Chicago right now.

In an electrified haze, I scan the room, an abstract plan at the back of my mind. A metal tray sits on the table nearby, beckoning me to use it. I don't stop to consider my predicament, the hospital gown on my back, or that I can barely stand on my own two feet.

Dante is all I can focus on.

I grab the tray, swing at the doctor, and ram him over the head. He goes down, swearing under his breath. By the time he scrambles to his feet, I'm on the run, darting barefoot down a bright, empty corridor. I pass doors left and right, aiming for those at the far end. Again, I failed to take a second and really *think*. I have no idea where I'm going or where Jean might be, but sheer willpower spurs me on.

The double door in front of me swings open. A tall man marches through them, a dozen or so others hot on his tail. His eyes widen when he sees me charging straight at him. I'm no more than ten feet away, too close to apply the brakes. All the man has time to do is open his arms before I ram hard into his chest, almost knocking us both off our feet. Shooting pain jabs my thigh and shoulder, knocking me out of breath.

"Whoa, where do you think you're going, little birdy?" He pushes me away, his hands cupping my shoulders in a tender but firm hold.

"Let go of me!" I claw at his arms to wriggle out of his grip, but despite only holding me by the shoulders, my efforts are pointless.

"I don't think so," He looks over my shoulder with a deep, dissatisfied frown. "What the fuck, Mark? She's not supposed to leave the room."

I turn to see the doctor in the doorway of my room, massaging a sore spot on the side of his head. "I couldn't stop her. She whacked me with a tray."

A murmur of laughter cuts the air. The man in front of me smiles, teeth and all. "Good job, birdy, but I'm afraid you can't leave. Go back to bed. And you better not run again, or I'll have to cuff you until Dante gets here."

My heart thumps faster. If the unexpected news won't stop soon, I might really end up with a coronary. "He's coming?"

"Oh, he's coming, alright." He spins me around to face the way I came. "He's on his way. My job is to keep you safe until he arrives, so do me a favor and cooperate."

I cast him a sideways glance as he falls into step beside me. "Who are you?"

"Me? Call me Johnny." He places his hand on the small of my back, pushing me gently toward the room. "Now, get to bed and let Mark check you over. I think you pulled the stitches on your thigh. You're bleeding."

"Don't look," the doc clips immediately. "I'll take care of it, just don't look, okay? I hear you don't do well with blood."

"I don't," I admit, laying back on the bed, eyes on the ceiling. "How did you know? Oh, and... sorry about your head."

"I had Dante on the phone five minutes ago. Whatever you need, I'll do my best to make it happen as long as you stay in this room."

"Right, I think you've got this, so I'll leave you to it," Johnny says from where he stands in the doorway. "Shout out if you need help."

"Yeah, that won't happen either," Mark huffs, the sound coming out amused. "Dante said no one but me can come in this room, so you better back away."

Johnny chuckles. "I wasn't talking to Layla. I was talking to you. You know, in case birdy here whacks you over the head with something else."

CHAPTER THIRTEEN

Dante

After nine hours in the car, two nights without sleep, and two weeks of functioning mainly on coffee, whiskey, and cigarettes, I'm on my last legs, but I'd run a thousand miles from Chicago to Dallas if Layla waited at the end of the road.

Rookie's still at the wheel, raring to go and refusing to let me drive. My phone rings every so often all through the night. Blake's son, Johnny, called twice, reporting a dead body. Ten hours passed since Layla's admission to the hospital, and already two hitmen had tried their luck in getting to her before me.

I glance at the dashboard, clenching my fists. The fuel gauge slipped into the reserve, and the hospital is still over fifty miles away. I take my cell phone out to call Nate, who sits behind the wheel of the second Charger. "Pull over at the next gas station."

"Yeah, okay. We're almost dry too."

He managed to overtake us a few miles back when Rookie's girl called, distracting his focus off the road for a few seconds. Nate made it a point of honor not to let Rookie back in the lead. It's their way of staying entertained and alert, so Rookie let him have a moment of fun. Ten minutes later, we stop at the station, and Rookie jumps out of the car in sync with me to stretch his legs.

"You want anything?" I motion to the shop.

"Chewing gum and water." He inserts the nozzle into the fuel tank. "Argh, shit, get me a coffee. Large. And sugar. Lots of white sugar."

Jane forced him on a fancy cleansing diet, and he's been torturing himself with homemade salads and lemon-infused water for a whole week now. Cai pulls up behind us and kills the engine when the passenger side door opens.

"I love this car, but next time I'm taking my Range Rover," Jackson groans, stretching out like a cat. "I didn't realize how uncomfortable these are for longer journeys."

Cai rolls his eyes, glancing at me. "He's been whining like this since Arkansas. Can he ride with you now? I can't promise I won't kill him before we get there."

Jackson is ruthless, sometimes even sadistic, but he's comically delicate too. He could break half the bones in a man's body with his fist, then walk around with a cold compress for three days, complaining that his hand hurts.

We're back on the road moments later. As anticipated, the last thirty miles stretch like bubble gum. The closer we get, the more anxious I become, fidgeting in my seat, unsure what the fuck will happen when I see Layla again. I call Johnny ahead of time so he can meet us outside.

He waits by the main entrance to the hospital, a carbon copy of his father, just thinner. "You made a fair amount of time up on the way." He shakes my hand when I approach with Spades and Nate on my sides, two steps behind. "This is Mark. I thought you ought to know how Layla is."

Mark moves the weight of his body from one foot to another, staring me in the eye. He's older than I expected, probably in his fifties. Deep wrinkles surround his eyes as if he smiled too much in his life. "She's good. Awake, alert."

"She's a feisty one," Johnny adds. "She knocked Mark over his head with a tray last night when he tried to stop her from seeing her cousin."

I can't help but smile when my entourage barks out a laugh. "Yeah, nothing new there. She is a handful." Good job I've got two hands. "I assume her cousin was in the car too. Where is she now?"

"Yes. Jean and two guys. They're waiting for you in the cafeteria. Bugged me all night to let them see Layla, but it's your call."

"Maybe later. Layla first, lead the way."

We walk through the sterile corridors, passing hospital staff on the way to Layla's room, my body like a time bomb. I'm heavy, anxious, and overwhelmed at the same time. Something inside me pulls taut like a bowstring until I almost can't breathe around the sudden onset of dread knotting in my stomach when we enter the last corridor. Armed men stand in strategic places by the door, the windows, and the emergency exit.

With every measured, calculated step that brings me closer to Layla, another contradicting emotion resurfaces. Fourteen long, torturous days have passed, each full of attempts to forget, hate, and kickstart my life without her by my side. Who the fuck was I kidding? The day I realized she meant more than anyone else, I crossed a line. A line I've been so perfectly fucking balanced on, it felt like a paradigm shift when I put one foot out. Now, there's no turning back.

The imposing smell of gauze and antiseptic spikes the back of my nose when I grab the door handle and push down, bracing for a harrowing sight. Bruises, cuts, tears.

But the bed is empty, and the heart monitor is flatlining. The sound steals the oxygen out of my lungs. My chest pinches tightly for a split second before adding two and two together. Of course, it's fucking flatlining. It's not connected to Layla. Not reading the rhythm of her heartbeats.

The IV stand is by the bed, the bags empty, and a cannula lays on the sheets stained with a few drops of blood. An open travel bag is tucked under a chair by the wall, and a takeout cup of coffee stands on the nightstand. It must've been the first thing Layla asked Mark to fetch this morning because there's no way this girl can start the day without a dose of caffeine, or she unleashes fire and brimstone.

I'm about to turn around to ask Johnny where the fuck she is when the door on my right, partially hidden behind a room divider, swings open. Layla emerges from what must be an ensuite bathroom, stopping in her tracks. Still, so, so still. Frozen in place like a statue. An unbearable ache swells in my heart. God, she's so fucking beautiful that looking at her feels like a punch to my gut. Wet hair sticks to her neck and shoulders, falling further down her back where it wets the white fabric of the V-neck t-shirt she wears.

A single, silent tear rolls down her cheek. She swats it away, doing her utmost to stop the rest as she squirms under my gaze, trembling like a baby deer. She's thinner than I remember. Cuts and bruises mark every inch of uncovered skin.

Tension leaves my muscles for the first time since Spades told me Delta's on fire. I twitch to cross the room and touch her, but with the first step forward I take, she jerks back, eyes wide, cheeks scarlet.

"*Don't. Move,*" I say, wearing my heart on my fucking sleeve as I pin Layla down with a pointed stare, willing her to stay in place.

There's nowhere to go, nowhere to hide. Even if she locks herself in the bathroom, I'll knock the door down two seconds later. I catch her hand and pull her frail frame close.

Chest to chest.

My heart rate soars, pulse throbs in my throat as I wrap one arm around her back. The world stops fucking spinning. Nothing but her matters when my fingers disappear in her long, damp hair and I cover her lips with mine.

A sort of terrified ecstasy, of being suspended, poised on the edge of a knife, jolts through me, intense and so deliciously sharp it's almost painful. She parts her lips, making a soft whimpering noise that strips me of my inhibitions.

Just like the first time I kissed her, I sink into the silk of her mouth, devouring her sweetness, hungry for the calmness she evokes, for the feeling of being at home.

Her fingers grasp onto a thick tangle of my hair, and everything stills, blurs, fucking implodes. She chokes back tears, trying not to show weakness, but she can't fool me.

Not in the slightest. I feel her emotions as if they're my own when her tongue sweeps and tangles with mine, our lips working in a desperate, breathless sync. She instinctively lets go of fear because she knows I'll take care of it. She knows she's safe with me.

The one thing she clings to is guilt. Every touch of her fingers on my skin, every look, every kiss is designed to prove how much she loves me, so I won't dare to doubt.

I don't.

I *didn't.*

Not for a moment.

"Don't ever leave me again," I whisper, resting my forehead on hers, eyes closed. "Never leave me, baby."

"I promise." She steals another kiss.

Her heart pounds against her ribs, my mind nothing but a slave to the erotic anticipation. The kiss turns greedy, urgent. Forceful. Layla knots her hands on my neck as we fight to say with the kiss what neither of us could explain with words. I don't think there are words in the English language capable of describing the unruliness of my mind.

I grip her waist, standing on the edge, desperate to tear her clothes off and show her who she fucking belongs to. I see it in my head: my hands under her butt, lifting her into my arms, slamming her petite body against the door, so I can impale her on my cock.

I see myself driving into her, burying myself up to the hilt. I can almost feel her vibrating, clawing at my back, nipping at my neck as she comes, moaning, crying out my name.

But we're not alone... we're surrounded by too many people. We're out in the open, not safe from an attack. The hunger burning inside my every cell needs to be tamed.

I break away to cup her face, brushing her tears away. "Never leave me." Her absence is the one thing I can't handle. The hell I refuse to endure ever again.

"I promise... and I'm sorry." She bites her lip. Big, bright eyes stare straight into mine.

"I know."

"No, you don't." She tries to take a step back, but I hold her tight, not ready to let go. Daunting atmosphere brews in the room as her eyes drop to stare at the floor. "I'm not apologizing for following Frank's orders, and I won't." She peers back at me with fresh tears dancing in her eyes. "I don't regret what I did."

"Then what are you apologizing for?" Now I'm the one to step back, my shoulders bunching, tensing, fucking painful again. She's not making much sense, but I'm no closer to hating her than I was a minute ago.

She clings to me. Grabs handfuls of my shirt. Her eyes flicker with panic as if she thinks I'll disappear if she stops touching me.

"I'm sorry I doubted you loved me enough to forgive me." She cups my face with trembling fingers, rising on her toes a little to level with me, which isn't happening at her miniature height. "I love you," she whispers, grazing the bridge of her nose along my jaw line. The alluring, sweet scent of her hits me just right. "I hate what I've done, but I *don't* regret helping Frank. Otherwise, I'd regret meeting you, loving yo—"

I don't let her finish. I catch her lips in mine again, drinking the confession straight from her mouth so she won't take it back. The remnants of contradicting emotions fade away, leaving no trace or proof that I ever wondered if she's worth fighting for. She is.

Christ, the gnawing desire to keep her safe, happy, and at ease, comes back in full force, packing a punch straight in my throat. And she still has the ability to turn the ruthless, filthy, soulless asshole I am into a plush toy.

No wonder I fell for her so hard, so *fast.* Instead of wishing to turn back time, refuse to help Frank, and ensure a death sentence wouldn't hang over her head, she's confident I'm worth all Frank threw at her.

"I'm taking you home, Star." I stamp a kiss on her head. "But first, I want to have a word with your cousin and her friends about what happened last night."

She nods, pushing out a heavy sigh. "Morte was here last night. He told me about the hit. Some family I have."

Fuck. Fuck. *Fuck.*

He's the last person I would've considered as the promotor. The last person who should've agreed to actively participate in this charade. He's Layla's godfather. Frankie's brother by choice. My fucking brother by choice too. I hadn't once considered him to be the promoter. He never had much of a moral compass, but accepting this role should've been out of the question if only because he held Layla five minutes after she was born. He *watched* her being born.

Frankie didn't make it to the hospital on time, even though he had plenty of time. From the stories he told me, Layla was in no rush to get out into the world. Labor took nineteen hours. Morte was there the whole time, Godfather of the year.

"What's the plan?" Layla tucks her head under my chin, cheek plastered to my chest. "You can't possibly think you'll kill everyone who tries their luck."

Watch me.

I tighten my hold around her frame. "I'm here now, baby. This is when you stop worrying. I'll take care of it. No one will touch you." I'll crawl out of my skin to make sure she's safe. I'll sell my soul to the devil himself. The intensity of my feelings is as crushing as the magnitude of power she holds over me.

This isn't fucking normal, surely...

She inches away, a weak smile tugging at the corners of her lips—swollen from my kisses. A glint of unease in her eyes is not what I hoped for. She must think her smile looks believable. It doesn't. It doesn't reach her eyes, so I know it's forced. She doesn't believe I'll close the hit.

Too bad she has no idea what I'm capable of.

Twelve years. Twelve long years, I've been involved with Mafia. The list of my sins is ever-growing. I'm not a good or decent person by any definition of the word.

Since day one, I've had a substantial advantage over Dino's people. They were all clever, crafty, and loyal. They followed orders. They respected the hierarchy. All as it should be, but one thing distinguished me from the rest, which allowed me to rise above my so-called colleagues. Something that made me invincible, unstoppable... I had *nothing* to lose. All Dino's men were vulnerable to blackmail. They had girlfriends, wives, or kids that could've been used against them. They had to err on the side of caution at all times.

I had no one. The only person in my life I cared about to an extent was my mother, but I didn't think highly of her back then. She wasn't any better at being a mother than Jess was to Layla. Once my father died, Isla spiraled into grief and depression. She resented my existence because I reminded her of her late husband.

She nosedived into work to keep sane, spending as much time away from home and me as possible. She left on tours for weeks on end, and whenever she returned to New York, she spent her time composing, shopping, or meeting her friends. I had to grow up fast.

Not an easy task when you're a sixteen-year-old spoiled, entitled brat with an ego the size of Illinois. A stereotypical college douchebag—rich, football team captain, fucking around with the whole cheerleading squad.

That's until I left New York for Chicago to move in with my uncle, Carlton's father. Ruled by hormones, desperate for an outlet for the pent-up rage, I became a lethal weapon in Dino's hands; greedy, untouchable, careless.

Until Layla.

I was in trouble the moment I saw her. I knew then that I'd happily let her wrap me around her finger. Something I mocked for years hit me harder than a freight train the second she opened her mouth. One sassy comment, one look at those big, gray irises, and *feelings* knocked my breath out of my chest. A whole magnitude of feelings.

Three months down the line, Layla is it for me. The one person that anyone with half a working brain can blackmail me with. The one person for whom I'd give up everything. Back in my bachelor days, I pitied the fools who fell in love, making themselves vulnerable... turns out I was the fool.

The kind of vulnerability that comes with love isn't a flaw. Taking caution with my actions is a strength, not a weakness. I'm wiser now that I have something to lose.

A faint knock on the door makes Layla jump. She wriggles out of my arms, keeping close enough to hold onto the hem of my jacket as if she's afraid that severing the connection between us means I'll apparate out of here like a Death Eater.

"Come in." She drapes her damp hair over one shoulder as a pink glow heats her otherwise pale cheeks.

The door swings open inward slowly. Spades enters, stiff

as a board when he stops two steps inside, eyes on Layla. He sizes her up with an unreadable, emotionless expression that has Layla squirming beside me.

"Hey, girl." His scowl morphs into a crooked smile. "Glad to see you're okay."

Two wrinkles sprout on her forehead as if she can't understand why Spades isn't mad. Where the hell is her confidence? Where is the biting tongue and her godawful attitude? I want it back. Right now.

"Remember what I told you when you ditched classes and I found you in the cafe?" he asks, giving her a second to recall the afternoon.

Shit... *that's* my answer. The one I've been looking for lately. That very afternoon is when my protectiveness over Layla spiraled out of control. I waited for her outside the college building, leaning against the side of my car as I flicked through my phone to check recent emails.

The crowd of students thinned within five minutes. Soon enough, the courtyard was empty. No Layla in sight. I called her once, twice, and a disgraceful number of times after that. No answer. Not a single idea where she could be or what could've happened.

Cue the dark scenarios: kidnapped, raped, dead.

My anxiety hit a crowning point, spiking my mind with rage, dread, and fear too intense to express. The tiny possibility of Layla being hurt set a match to my composure, and *poof,* it went up in fucking flames.

I remember dialing Spades' number. The tension in my voice, back, and throat. A rope tightened itself around my chest. What a sad state of affairs. The inner turmoil was irrational. I never felt or acted so out of character before. I'd also never felt anything remotely close to what I feel for Layla.

The sudden onset of jitters was both justified and infuriating. Absolutely *crazy*.

"It stands," Spades continues, watching Layla with a small smirk. "Dante still has hay instead of brains when you're not around, so be a doll and don't leave his sorry ass again. Deal?"

As hard as it is to admit to my weaknesses, he's right. I really can't deal with reality when Layla isn't mine. Fourteen days without her were a blur of pain, regret, and self-loathing.

This can't be normal.

No way people experience this kind of emotional instability. I'm sure it's just my twisted mind working this way, or else people would fall off the tallest buildings more often than they do now, driven mad by the intensity of their feelings.

Layla bobs her head once, relief flashing across her exhausted, beautiful face. "Deal."

"Now." Spades moves his attention to me. I think he'll ask me to step outside for a second, but he changes his mind. "I sent Nate to find Layla's cousin. She threatened to claw his eyes out if he won't let her come over here and refused to talk to anyone who isn't you."

"Stay with Layla until I'm back. Get Mark to check her over again. *Thoroughly*." I start in the direction of the door but don't make it far. Layla holds onto my jacket, keeping me in place. I turn back to kiss her head. "Give me fifteen minutes, Star."

Reluctantly, she opens her fingers, letting me leave. I'll have to work on her insecurities, whatever they might be, because this version of Layla doesn't fucking suit her.

Before I follow Nate to the cafeteria where Jean waits, I take the emergency exit, stepping out onto the staircase. Slim chance this will work, but it's worth a shot. I pull out my phone, scrolling through the contact list to *M* so I can call the son of a bitch I considered a friend long ago.

For four years, Morte, Frank, and I were Dino's main entourage. Morte was like Luca—a skilled, merciless killer. We took care of the dirty work together, although the list of my sins is substantially shorter than his. I witnessed him murder at least a hundred people. He was there the night Dino died, too, then went his own way. I had no idea he stayed in touch with Frank all those years.

"Dante Carrow," he answers so fast I bet he was waiting for my call. "Took you a while to figure it out. Although I guess you didn't really, did you? You arrived at the hospital half an hour ago, so I bet Layla told you I paid her a visit."

Son-of-a-bitch.

He's around here somewhere, hidden in the shadows, watching me from a perfect vantage point. He's probably on his stomach with a sniper rifle to keep him company. Even if I were to send my men out there, they wouldn't find him. They'd end up dead before they could get near him.

The tone of his voice alone, cheerful and superior, is enough of a clue that this conversation won't do me any fucking good. It's pointless. He will not retract the hit.

I'm not surprised. I was perfectly aware of this before I dialed, but... "Ten million. Ten million wired straight to your offshore account inside of an hour if you end this farce."

"Tempting," he muses, purring down the line like an obese, lazy cat. "Ten million is a lot of money for one woman. You only met her because Frank wanted your head, heart, and that black soul of yours. What's so extraordinary about the girl, Dante?" He pauses for a moment, though I doubt he expects me to actually answer the question. I'm not here for his entertainment. "You know you can't bribe me, my friend. You know that a job is sacred. No one but the principal can retract a hit, but a drowning man clutches a straw, doesn't he?"

"Frank is gone." I tighten the hold around my cell. "Layla shouldn't pay for his obsession."

"Wrong. She's not the one who has to pay. You are. She'll just die while you'll live knowing she died because of you." He speaks slowly, no emotion or humanity to his voice or his fucked-up world ruled by a deranged moral hierarchy. "By the way, how could you be so stupid? You're weak. You're helpless because of Layla. You can be threatened, *blackmailed* because you're in love. I thought I taught you better than this."

My jaw locks painfully, but a cunning smile is there too, begging to be unleashed. Years ago, days after the love of his life, Sandra, left him without a word, Morte and I talked about sentiments, scruples, and love.

None of those belong in our world.

A woman always complicates business and brings confusion and chaos into a well-organized world.

I never realized the accuracy of that statement until Layla became my priority. Until she took the shine off what I once considered key: power, respect, and money. All became less relevant when she—without my consent—entered my heart to keep it under lock and key.

"You were an easy target for Frank because you fell for his daughter. You did exactly what he wanted. Exactly what he *knew* you'd do. You walked right into that one, my friend. Learn from your mistakes because it's clear that you didn't learn from mine."

"Frank commissioned the kill order to get back at me. Why did you agree? What happened to *never threaten a man's family*? She's your goddaughter. You were there when she was born."

"And now I'll watch her die," he clips with maniacal satisfaction. "It's quite poetic, don't you think? I watched her take her first breath, and I sure fucking hope I'll watch her take the last. Don't take my involvement in this personally. No hard feelings. This is business, Dante."

He no longer sounds robotic. I could even risk and say he feels sorry for me. Back in the day, we were close-knit, brothers by choice, but in the face of the hit, the past doesn't matter. He wouldn't help me even if I were his biological brother. Even if I gave him all I have. There's no turning back. There's only a race.

Who'll die first?

Morte or Layla?

I draw in a harsh breath. "I'll see you very soon."

"My death won't change a thing."

True, but I'll kill him anyway, even if just for the sick satisfaction of making him pay for the one mistake he made in his life—threatening my girl. I cut the call, light a cigarette, and lean against the wall, staring at the opposite wall with a menacing scowl.

I need a minute to gather my thoughts, clear my head, and refocus because all I want to do now is run out of the building to find the fucker lurking close by, untraceable. The moment doesn't last long, ending when Nate shoves his head out the door.

"Jean, Tayler, Rick," he says, pushing the door open further. "She's a world-class bitch, Rick's ex-marine, and Tayler's afraid of his own shadow."

I drop the cigarette on the tiled floor, butting it with the heel of my leather shoe. "Lead the way."

Once in the cafeteria, I have no trouble spotting Jean. Long, messy hair, arms crossed over her chest, and an annoyed expression makes her stand out. She sits out of the way with two guys and three disposable cups on the table in front of them. Over the years, I came to realize my presence alone can straighten people's backs. Literally. It works on Jean and Tayler, who pull themselves up in their seats, sitting taller, but Rick remains unaffected. Nate doesn't need to tell me which one he is. I can spot a soldier in any room. They carry themselves with respect and a sense of higher purpose, a superiority of sorts. He must've seen his share of gruesome reality by now, so he's not easily intimidated.

"Well, well, well. If it isn't the infamous Dante. Am I right?" Jean waits for confirmation before unleashing her anger. "How thoughtful of you to finally join us. I've gone gray waiting. I want to see Layla, and don't even try to bullshit me about safety measures. We had her back last night. You can't forbid me from seeing her!" She blows an unruly lock of red hair from her face, chest heaving.

"Wasn't my intention." I sit on the last empty chair, sending Nate away to order coffee. "You can say goodbye in a minute, but first, I want to know what happened last night."

"Goodbye?" Rick asks, hands crossed over his chest. He scrutinizes me, waiting for one false move the way he was taught in the army. I'm not sure what's going on in his head, though. Does he really think he can take me down? Doubtful. "What do you mean by *goodbye*?"

"I'm taking her home." I keep my tone casual not to enrage either of them any further. They have the information I need. Playing nice is in my best interest. "So? Fill me in."

CHAPTER FOURTEEN

Layla

"Are you sure you want to leave?" Jean asks in a hushed voice, cross-legged on the hospital bed, playing with my fingers.

Doctor Mark signed my release papers and checked every one of my bruises, cuts, and stitches, leaving Dante with detailed instructions on how to take care of my dressings. Not that he needs the information. He was on the phone with Carlton earlier. He'll pay us a home visit every forty-eight hours to check me over. Dante's overreacting, but I won't disagree with him just two hours after I got him back. I still can't believe he's here. That he had it in him to forgive me, to act as if there's no one he wants or needs more than me.

The unease that settled in the pit of my stomach when Morte left the hospital disappeared when Dante arrived. I might not understand why he wants me, but I know he'll bend over backward to keep me safe.

"You can stay with us forever, you know. It's nice having you around even if you weren't the most outgoing person lately," Jean continues, almost pleading. Her gaze burns through my retinas. I think she's waiting for a sign. A slight nod, a flicker of my eyes, *anything* that'd warrant her going full-on Hades on Dante and his men.

He agreed to let Jean, Rick, and Tayler in here so I could say goodbye. The get-together couldn't go ahead without supervision, though. *His* supervision. He watches me from his casual lean by the window, outwardly relaxed. I treat myself to cursory glances his way every few seconds, unconsciously checking if he's still there. It'd be nice if I could calm the panicked little girl inside my head; reassure her that Dante won't go anywhere, but I can't. We are one. I just hide my anxiety better than she does.

"I know." I offer Jean a tight-lipped smile and a tight squeeze of her fingers, "But I don't belong here."

She narrows her eyes, still searching for a sign, her face stern, a no-bullshit attitude on display when she huffs and looks over her shoulder at Dante. It's a ploy. She's teasing him, and it would work a treat if not for the blooming smile that threatens to split her mouth from ear to ear.

Whatever Dante told them must've made an impression. Jean seems in awe of him, and so does Tayler. He watches

Dante with respect sprinkled with a handful of fear. Only Rick's eyes stay trained on me, making me uncomfortable. He's the one who got out of the car crash unscratched, and, from what Dante told me after he spoke to them, he's the one who killed Archer.

Jean points a finger at Dante. "I won't wait another seven years to see her."

"Once I get the situation under control, you're welcome to visit anytime you want." He glances at me, the look loaded with a silent *time to go*. His eyes darken a notch, triggering a pleasant spasm that seizes the muscles in my abdomen.

Anticipation blooms between my thighs like a blood-red rose. We're supposed to stay at a hotel until late evening before we get on the road to Chicago so the guys can recharge their batteries ahead of another ten-hour drive. Dante and I will be in bed too, but we sure won't be sleeping.

Ten minutes later, I'm in the back seat of a matt black charger with Rookie in the driver's seat. He seems happy to see me. Along with the rest of Dante's men, they act as if the night I killed Frank never happened. I should be relieved. I should be glad, thankful, and *happy*, but all I am is scared. Scared that none of them processed my betrayal. That *Dante* hadn't processed it, and at some point, it'll detonate in his head like a delayed bomb.

Clearing the air is on the agenda. We need to talk through the subject, scream a little, and put it behind us but tonight is not the night.

I'm not ready to hold that conversation. Bringing up the fateful night is a risk I'm not willing to take yet. I need to be with him like this—peaceful, for at least a little while before we re-open hell's gates.

"What time are we setting off tonight?" Rookie asks as he reverses into a parking spot outside of the hotel.

Dante looks into the rearview mirror. "Ten o'clock."

It's only one o'clock in the afternoon, so the guys have plenty of time for a good day's sleep. We enter the monster of a building in the heart of Dallas: all glass, luxury, and LED lights. In the lobby, Spades waits at the reception desk with a handful of keycards in hand, hungry eyes on a young receptionist hidden behind a tall, oblong desk.

He holds one card out for Dante when we approach. A suggestive smirk on his lips. "You're on the top floor in the Executive suite... far away from all of us."

Dante leaves the remark without comment as he drags me toward the elevator, his touch urgent, impatient. The door slides shut, separating us from dull reality. Lust erupts below my skin, elevating desire to an almost unbearable level. I want him more than I've ever wanted him before.

We spent half an hour in the back seat of the Charger fidgeting, willing the journey away so we could be alone. Now, the elevator ride feels like a never-ending story. My breaths come in shallow, shaky bursts, my pulse accelerates, and the backs of my thighs tingle eagerly. Neither of us dares to speak; to belittle the tension.

Dante pumps his fingers around mine, pulling me behind him down a narrow corridor toward the room at the far end. He inserts the card into the slot and pushes the door open.

The bag in his hand lands on the floor two steps in.

The door slams shut.

Desire takes over.

He cups my face, pushes his fingers in my hair, and presses me against the wall with his big body. A lustful, demanding kiss bruises my lips.

We rush, grabbing handfuls of the moment, drunk on desire. He grips the sleeves of my cardigan, tugging until the soft fabric slides down my arms, sighing to the floor in a puddle of gray. With both hands, he grabs the white t-shirt I'm wearing and rips it open in the middle, his mouth on my neck, trailing a line of open-mouth kisses. It's chaotic and demanding, but in the midst of mind-jarring urgency to get inside me, he remembers how bruised my body is when he lays me on the bed. He takes care of sliding my jeans off and kisses me around the dressing.

"No foreplay." He strips off his clothes. Dark, ravenous eyes devour my naked breasts. "Not this time, Star."

No foreplay is necessary. I'm wet, ready, and aching. I need him close, as close as I can get him as fast as possible. He kicks his boxers off, and his long, buzzing erection stands proudly, twitching with every move as he climbs back onto the bed to cover my body with his.

He rests the weight of his body on both elbows, spreading my legs with his knee, nestling himself between my thighs. The swollen head of his cock rubs against my clit a few times before he catches my lips with his and drives into me hard. Muscles in my abdomen contract. My stomach wrenches with an almost painful sting as a bolt of intense pleasure zaps my nerve endings. The familiarity, fullness, and warmth of him force a satisfied moan past my lips.

"I missed you so fucking much, Layla... never leave me." He jerks his hips back and slams into me again, introducing a hasty, frenzied rhythm as he holds my head in place. "Say it. Say you won't fucking leave me. Say you love me."

"I love you." I draw long lines down his shoulder blades every time he thrusts deep, up to the hilt. Each thrust pushes me further up the bed. "I won't ever leave you."

"Good girl." He dips his head to kiss my neck. "Mine. All mine. You belong with me." He nips my ear, sucking the delicate earlobe as he buries himself in me time and time again, hitting the perfect spot. "No one will touch you. No one will hurt you. No one will get to you."

Every word spilling from his lips is a quiet growl, sounding like a prayer, a vow, an unbreakable promise.

I push him onto his back, flinging one leg over his to sit on him, my hands on his chest as I lower myself on top of him. I love when he's in charge, but dominating fills me with a certain kind of courage I don't usually feel. Endorphins spike my pleasure, numbing the pain screaming up my thigh, but it grows every time I fall on top of Dante, taking him in deep while upholding the hasty pace he introduced.

The hunger glistening in his eyes, the insistence of his hands grasping my hips to rush my moves, sends me toward the edge inside of three minutes. I grit my teeth and ignore the sting of stitches pulling my skin. I push through the pain, desperate to come and make him come too. Dante's not easily fooled, though. Not even two minutes later, he grips my waist, halting my moves.

"Your leg hurts." A note of annoyance weaved with accusation stains his hoarse voice.

"It's okay. I have painkillers."

He lifts me up, sliding his cock out in the process. "It's *not* okay. Get on your knees and turn around." He cuffs my wrists to clasp my hands on the headrest. "Hold on tight, baby."

Kneeling in front of the wall, I feel Dante get into position behind me. He drapes my hair over one shoulder, exposing the nape of my neck, one hand between my breasts and pressing hard to hold my back flush against his chest. With the other, he holds onto the headrest for support, his forehead against the back of my head when he thrusts his hips forward, filling me in one move. I arch back, tilting my head to reach his lips.

"You're so wet for me," he mutters in my hair. "So soft."

We're no longer rushing, no longer greedy, to take everything in the shortest time possible. Dante changes the pace; slows down his frantic thrusts enough that I'm not jolted half-upright every time he buries himself up to the hilt. The moment evolves into passion and love that swells within us, and my moans are no longer a breathless staccato.

"I won't let anyone hurt you." He ghosts his fingers down my stomach, stopping at the bundle of nerves on the apex of my thighs. "You're mine, Star. Always mine." He circles my clit to bring me closer, and my long, erotic moans fill the room. "Don't hold back. I miss feeling you come."

He circles faster, sliding in and out, and hits the right spot every time. The release comes suddenly. Violent. Glorious. My body vibrates uncontrollably as dark spots twinkle before my eyes. Dante turns my head to the side with a satisfied smile before he drinks my moans straight from my lips. He holds me flush against his chest as my knees buckle.

"I'm not done with you, Star... I never will be."

CHAPTER FIFTEEN

Layla

I'm a princess locked in the highest tower, waiting for prince charming to conquer the archenemy. Just... instead of a tower, there's a bulletproof house. And the archenemy is already dead, taunting me from the underworld. In this tale, the prince may well be the archenemy himself. He carries a gun, talks dirty, fucks angry, and loves fiercely. He's also the one who locked me in the bulletproof house.

Not that I mind.

We've been back in Chicago for twenty-four hours now. Julij organized the security detail before we arrived. Six armed men secure the perimeter of Dante's house, two more stand their ground at the gate, and three Rottweilers growl, bark, and bolt toward the slightest movement.

In a see-through, lacey nightdress, which covers... well, not much, I stand under the noisy smoke alarm in the kitchen, waving a cloth. The idea was to prepare breakfast for Dante, but it backfired fast. He was sound asleep while I tossed and turned in bed for an hour before I decided to surprise him with scrambled eggs. Unfortunately, my culinary skills are sound asleep, just like Dante. With the grace of a proverbial bull in a China shop, I turned the kitchen into *Hell's Kitchen.*

Gordon wouldn't approve.

Not only have I made a mess, but I also forgot to whisk the eggs. They burned, and black smoke triggered the alarm—an awfully sensitive, far too loud thingamajig.

The front door bangs against the wall, stopping me dead in my tracks. A second passes, and the sound of footsteps suddenly comes from not one but two directions: the corridor and the stairs. I tug the lacey fabric, covering my butt as much as the short nightdress allows. Unfortunately, despite the effort, I still show much more skin than Dante's men should see. Too bad I didn't think about modesty before entering the kitchen, ready to cook breakfast dressed like Victoria's Secret model.

Jackson stops in the doorway, eyes sweeping the room. Once his gaze falls on me, he stumbles back, face bright red, eyes flying to the floor, the ceiling, and back to me in a frantic, uncoordinated way. I think this must be the very first time I've had the doubtful pleasure of seeing a man blush.

He turns to the front door, holding his hand out to halt whoever else is approaching. "It's fine. She just burned the eggs. Turn off the alarm."

Taking advantage of a moment of his inattention, I scout the kitchen in search of an apron or a large cutting board, but short of hiding in one of the cupboards, there's not much I can cover myself with. For the lack of better options, I unfold the cloth, holding it to my chest. The shrill beeping of the alarm dies away, leaving an unpleasant ringing in my ears.

Dante joins Jackson in the doorway, stormy, green eyes on me, hands clenched into tight fists at his sides. "Get out," he snaps at Jackson, staring at the back of his skull until the front door closes with a click.

With the cloth firmly against my chest, I feel both the warmth of my cheeks and Dante's burning gaze.

"What are you doing?" His voice drips with unrestrained annoyance, jaw locked tight to stop an outburst.

I pull at the corner of the cloth, squirming. "I'm sorry, I tried to make you breakfast but burned the eggs."

"And you're burning the toast too."

I ditch the idea of modesty, slapping the cloth on the island as I rush to save the toast. It's beyond saving, though. I turn the toaster off, throwing away the charred bread.

Dante crosses the room, his bare feet tapping on the tiles. He grips my waist and hauls me off the floor and onto the kitchen island, the marble counter cold under my butt.

"Both mine and Julij's people are part of the security detail, Layla. All know the access code. Any one of them can walk in here at any time. Don't parade around the house in your underwear."

"I'm sorry. I didn't think."

He hangs his head low for a moment to suck in a deep breath. When he glances back into my eyes, there's no sign of nerves. He looks better than yesterday after we arrived back from Texas. Despite Rookie taking the wheel, Dante didn't sleep. He spent the ride in the back, cuddling me to his chest like a little girl, kissing my head as he encouraged me to sleep. The warmth of his body, the familiarity of his scent, and the calm rhythm of his heart I felt under my fingertips helped me doze off.

Not for long... whenever I fell asleep, the car crash replayed in my dreams, waking me up drenched in sweat.

Dante leans closer, tracing his lips along my neck. Pajama pants hang low on his hips, and he smells of *me,* thanks to sleeping with my limbs wrapped around him as if he were a tree and I were poison ivy. "Don't do it again."

"You mean, *don't cook*?"

Amusement dances on his handsome, rested face when he straightens up. "That too. Also, don't leave the bed without permission and don't show this body to anyone who isn't me. Understood?" Satisfied with my energetic nodding, he returns to the previous task, nipping the skin in the crook of my neck. "Good girl."

We've spent most of our time in bed since we arrived back home, but I'm still thirsty for him. I can't get enough of his closeness, warmth, and smell. The roughness of his calloused hands worshiping my body. The barked orders, filthy, mesmerizing words, and the bombs detonating in my body every time an orgasm hits. I love feeling his lips on my collarbones, shoulders, and the nape of my neck.

He pauses to check the time on his wristwatch.

"Are you expecting someone?"

"Carlton will be here in an hour to check you over and the maid is due any minute." He slides my nightdress off my non-injured shoulder. "Come on, baby, we'll take a shower."

"Subtle." I wrap my legs around his middle, urging him to carry me upstairs. A minute of jumping under the smoke detector didn't do my stitches any favors.

"Too subtle for you? Fine." He bites my earlobe. "I want to be inside you right now. In your mouth first, so you better be on your knees for me in the next thirty seconds. Then, I want to watch the water drip down your naked body, and I want you to scream this fucking house down when you come."

Check, check, and check... twice.

Forty minutes later, I stand in front of the closet, my legs weak. The intense orgasm from ten minutes ago lingers in the base of my spine. I wore nothing other than the nightdress or lingerie for the last twenty-four hours. I dug out both from my suitcase that Jean kindly packed and delivered to the hotel before we set off from Dallas.

Now, I stand in the walk-in closet, scrunching my nose because I don't recognize the clothes hanging neatly alongside Dante's shirts. They're new, and none of my old clothes are here. The question about the whereabouts of my old clothes lingers on the tip of my tongue, but I decide not to ask. The answer is obvious. I'm not sure if I can stomach hearing Dante tell me he threw them away because he wanted nothing to do with me.

"When did you have time to go shopping?" I ask instead, reaching for a plain, straight-neck white dress so Carlton can easily access my dressings. I grab a long olive-green cardigan to keep warm too.

Dante sits on the bed, strapping on the wristwatch I gifted him for Christmas. Droplets of water fall from his hair to the white, long-sleeve jersey he wears. Strong, woodsy cologne hangs in the air, indulging my obsession with the masterpiece of a man before me.

In Dante's world, wearing anything other than a suit is a rarity. Sometimes he wears sweats and a t-shirt when we're alone, but ninety percent of the time, he favors his suits. Now that he's in a white jersey and a pair of black jeans, I can't peel my eyes off how perfectly the jersey hugs his hard, chiseled pecks and broad arms.

The dress-down look doesn't belittle the authority and power he emanates; it fails to decimate the aura of ruthlessness. It's visible in his eyes and how he carries himself with undeniable confidence.

"I sent Grace shopping when we were in Dallas."

"Grace?" I twirl around. "Who's *Grace*?"

A satisfied smirk is his first response. "Hide your claws, Star. She's our new maid. Marie quit."

"Where was this *Grace* yesterday?" My eyes narrow into slits as he strides across the room to help me slip into my cardigan. "And why did Marie quit?"

Dante shrugs, ever so casual, spins me around, and brushes my hair away to kiss the nape of my neck. He snakes his hands around my chest, rests his forehead on the back of my head, and exhales slowly, making the hair on the back of my neck stand. "Why are you afraid of me, Layla?" His hold on me tightens. "Have I scared you? What did I do?"

I swallow the lump in my throat that lodged in there, like swallowing too big of a bite. "I'm not afraid of you. Where did you get that idea?"

"*Don't* lie." He spins me back around. Annoyance tugs at the corners of his eyes. "You were afraid at the hospital. You were afraid at the hotel, and you fucking *flinched* earlier when I found you in the kitchen."

I wriggle out of his embrace and sit on the bed, my heart pounding against my sore ribs. The time has come to talk, explain, and leave the past where it belongs. I'm entirely unprepared for this conversation but aware it has to happen.

"You no longer disagree with everything I say, baby. You don't talk back. You haven't even rolled your eyes at me yet. You didn't complain when I told you to sleep in that see-through nightdress." He sits beside me and pulls me into his lap as if sitting side-by-side isn't close enough. "You're afraid of me, but I don't understand why. It's driving me crazy, Layla."

My eyes dart to the cream carpet and stay there while I search for the right words, untangling the web of thoughts to explain my reactions the best I can. "I'm not afraid of you," I say quietly. Dante curls his fingers under my chin, so I'll look him in the eyes. "I'm just scared to be without you. I'm afraid I'll do something that will push you away, even by accident."

"I won't put you out the door because you burned the toast. Not because of that and not because of anything else. Not now and not *ever*."

I knot my fingers behind his neck, plastering my cheek against his shoulder. "Don't be mad, just... give me some time so I can learn to live with what I've done."

His muscles harden under my touch on cue. Neither of us wants to revisit what happened in the warehouse, but we can't pretend that night never happened. This conversation is inevitable. We have to work through the mess if we want to come out on the other side. With the weight of my betrayal hanging over our heads, we won't ever move forward unless we confront the subject.

He slides me off his lap and stands, taking a few hard

steps toward the French doors that open onto the balcony overlooking Lake Michigan. He's tense. His muscles bunch under the thin fabric of his jersey with every breath he takes. My hands grow cold, stomach ties itself into a double knot.

Maybe he has a point. I am afraid of him a little. Of his reaction, words, and rejection.

"I won't tell you that nothing changed. Or that it didn't hurt when I realized you used me," he says, looking out the window, his back to me. "I tried hard to leave you behind and pretend that you didn't fucking exist. That you were never here with me. I tried to convince myself that you belong in the past and I should leave you there because you don't deserve me or my forgiveness."

His words hit like sharp pins stuck in a Voodoo doll resembling me in scary detail. I don't blame him for feeling that way or speaking the truth, even if his words hurt more than I could admit aloud. He doesn't hate me, and that shows me how pure are his feelings, but... why is there always a but?

Because life isn't a bed of roses. It's not made out of only good moments. Life is hard, uncompromising, and amazing at the same time. And love? Love isn't perfect. If anything, it's a far cry from perfect, but no matter how bad things get, how dark and turbulent, the sun always rises again.

This conversation needs to happen if we are to ever move on. Still, every sentence slipping out of his mouth is a hard slap across my face. A well-deserved slap.

"I couldn't do it." He turns to face me. "I physically can't hate you, Star. You demolished my moral framework, turned my world on its head, and highjacked every one of my thoughts when you walked into Delta. You knocked me out of my comfort zone. You tore apart everything I thought I knew about myself, and you built me back up, changing my outlook on life and changing my focus point. Since then, *everything* revolves around you, baby." He speaks slowly as if such a blatant manifestation of feelings doesn't come naturally to him. I'm sure it doesn't. Dante's thrifty with words. He's a man of action, better at showing than telling. Now, not only do I hear how much he loves me, but I also get to see it in his eyes. "I don't want you to be afraid of me or that I'll tell you to leave."

I'm ashamed that the need to earn Frank's acceptance remained my priority for so long. Until the very end, I was ready to kill the only person who loved me selflessly. "Turn the tables. Wouldn't you worry? I lied for months."

"It doesn't matter."

"Of course it does!" I hide my face in my hands, suddenly powerless. All-out furious. His forgiveness is what I'd hoped for, but the way he's brushing off what happened is not. Not in the slightest. I don't think he really understands my reasons. I don't think he's dealt with my deceit. It's not just Frank's plan that turned Dante's world on its head. Everything that happened since is an extension, a line of consequences to a decision I made almost a year ago.

Like an avalanche, that decision packs more problems to this day. The bounty on my head, Dante's issues with the FBI, CIA, DEA, and whoever else is involved, the fire at Delta, millions he spent and will spend to keep *me* safe: it all adds to my sin, blowing a small *yes, Daddy, I'll help you* to apocalyptic proportions.

We can't go on like this. Dante can't keep brushing the issue under the carpet, pretending it never happened. I'll forever worry that it'll resurface and we'll fall apart.

"Don't ignore it. Don't pretend it wasn't that big of a deal."

"I didn't say it wasn't. You stabbed me in the back, Layla. It was a big deal. It fucking *is* a big deal, but that doesn't mean you're right in what you're thinking and believe me, I know exactly what's going on in your head. You're wrong. I don't need to hem and haw the subject over again to accept, forgive, and forget. Everyone makes mistakes. I know why you made yours. I've accepted what happened, and you should stop beating yourself up. It's in the past."

I shake my head firmly, earning a frown from Dante, who seems to be growing aggravated in sync with me. "I have to explain. You need to know why I agreed to help Frank and why I didn't tell you when I realized I love you."

"I *know* why you agreed." He rests his back against a brand-new dressing table, arms folded tightly over his chest. "You told me you were never loved or cared for. You told me how much you wanted Frank's attention. I pieced the rest together. I also know that if you weren't afraid of my reaction, you would've told me about it very early on." His green eyes bore into mine, looking right through me, peeling the layers protecting my mind to sift through the darkest recesses of my being. "And we're back at the drawing board again. You're afraid of me. You were afraid for a long time... I guess you just hid it better before."

A bitter scoff leaves my lips, forcing Dante into defense mode. His hands ball into fists at his sides, his patience hanging by a thread. I can tell. I know him well enough now to decipher his body language. The way his jaw ticks on both sides under his ears is a clear sign he's moments away from snapping.

At least we're getting *somewhere*.

The hint of accusation prickling his voice is exactly what I'm after. We both need to shout a little, place the blame, let go of animosities, and draw a clear line between the past and the present, or the repressed emotions will backfire like Tayler's faulty engine at the least convenient moment.

"I'm not a good actress. You saw what you wanted to see," I say, blame dripping from the tone of my voice like blood drips from a wound. "A pretty face, a damaged mind, a scared, scarred, innocent girl in need of attention. A *virgin...*"

Dante's jaw works in furious circles. He grips the dressing table with both hands, his knuckles white with the effort as if he's ready to rip the top off. I'm hitting all the right spots, but as always, when dealing with me, he's calm and in control.

"Don't do this, Layla. Don't fucking push me."

It's too late. The atmosphere's already shifted. An argument hangs in the air, brewing overhead like the foulest of storms, threatening to unleash its full power. And it will be glorious. We're both basic elements, forces of nature. Fire and water. Air and earth. Opposites attract, but they clash equally well.

Right now, Dante's a grenade without the safety pin. The clock is ticking. Every one of my words brings the countdown closer to a spectacular explosion. I'm afraid to be on the receiving side of his fury, but I'd rather have the blast now than wait for it for years.

"A tool to get back at my father," I continue, steadfast in my attempt to force him to show me what he's made of. "You liked showing me off any chance you got. Rubbing me in Frankie's face like a trophy, feeling like you were winning."

Dante pushes away from the dressing table, halting my rant. He's pulse-pounding as he towers above me, a bottomless pit of cataclysmic consequences, a spectacular supernova of anger on the brink of eruption.

But nothing happens. The next thing I know, he flies out of the room and doesn't even slam the door.

"Don't ignore me!" I rush out of the bedroom, following in his footsteps. "Stop acting like you're okay with this because I can see you're not. "Say what needs to be said so we can move on!" I grab his arm, halting him at the bottom of the stairs. "Don't pretend it didn't happen!" I claw at his arm when he turns to face me. "Tell me I hurt you. Tell me you don't trust me. Tell me I don't deserve you. Tell me something. *Anything.* Don't act like you don't care! Scream, for fuck's sake! Do—"

"Shut the fuck up!" He booms, the bass of his voice reverberating in the house like a clap of thunder. He cuffs my wrist in one hand, tugging hard to force me down a step into his arms. "First of all, don't ever curse again. It doesn't fucking suit you. You're too sweet. Too delicate for *fucks.*" He's not shouting. There's no need. The low, threatening undertone to his husky voice conveys his emotions clearly. "Do you think your betrayal means anything in the face of what's happened since? It doesn't fucking matter. You chose *me.*"

He catches my lips in a forceful, brutal kiss, fighting his way inside. His tongue skims along with mine, distracting the nest of cobras hissing in my head for a few seconds.

"Listen to me now," he clips, inching away. "I'll say it once, and as it befits your beautiful mind, I expect you to accept it. For two weeks, you weren't mine. The very awareness you weren't, drove me halfway to the fucking grave. I can't and won't let you leave me again. Never. You're mine. You belong to me. You belong *with* me. Now and always. Understood?"

There's something about the way he speaks that has me swell inside. He makes the confession sound like the most natural and obvious thing in the world. I am his, and I'm always supposed to be his.

"You killed your father because *you* love *me*. Now I'll kill anyone who'll try to hurt you because *I* love *you*."

My mouth turns dry, and my lips fall apart. Three simple words, powerful enough to squeeze the breath out of my lungs. I can count on one hand how many times I've heard those words in my life.

I'm sure Dante is the first one who means what he says. I knew he loved me. I've felt it for a long time but knowing, and hearing are two different things.

"Again," I breathe, my mouth twisted into a smile. "Please."

"Don't pretend you didn't know. You accused me of loving you some time ago."

"Of course, I knew. You did a half-ass job of hiding it."

"I wasn't trying to hide it."

An innocent smile covers my face, the anger I felt three minutes ago no longer there. "Say you love me, please."

"I love you, baby. I love you so fucking much. I want my feisty, sassy, annoying star back. I've got something for her." He drags me back upstairs and sits me on the bed, walking away toward the nightstand behind my back.

The familiar sound of a gun being tucked into a holster reaches my ear, prompting a frown on my forehead. A gun? He wants me to carry a gun.

He comes to stand in front of me, runs his fingers through the artistic muddle of his dark hair, and crouches down, placing one hand to cup my knee. He holds the other one open.

A small, black box sits on top of his palm, and the lid is up, revealing a ring with a diamond the size of a pea.

"You already have one, but *this* is the engagement one."

Dante presses his cheek against my temple. "It's not what you think," he says, amused. "I mean, yes, it's a ring, but not an engagement ring."

And I'm not sure if I'm relieved or if my heart finally broke.

I'm full of joy, pride, excitement, and love this time. More than I can handle. More than Dante could hope to accept. I look from the ring to his handsome, content face. No hint of uncertainty in his eyes. He's confident in that sexy, arrogant manner of his. He didn't ask the question, but he didn't have to. I'm his... now and always.

And I'm about to throw myself into his arms when one potential explanation for the sudden, extraordinary proposal springs to mind.

"Clever." I take the ring out of the box. Regardless of the reason, it's mine. It'll look pretty on my finger, shimmering as it catches the daylight pouring inside the room through the windows. "You don't touch the boss's wife, correct? You hope at least those who respect the unwritten rule will refrain from hunting me down if I marry you?"

"If?" He smirks and stamps a kiss on my forehead. "You don't have a choice. You know you're too smart for your own good? The idea didn't cross my mind, but it sure isn't stupid. Few bosses respect the rule, especially when big money is concerned, but I know some who do." He stands, pulling me up with him. "The ring is yours because you're supposed to be Mrs. Carrow, not Miss Harston. I hate your surname."

"I will be Mrs. Carrow, but only after the hit is closed."

CHAPTER SIXTEEN

Layla

Carlton waits for us downstairs, and just like all of Dante's men, he acts as if I never left. He's giving Dante a hard time, making fun of his protectiveness while checking my stitches to make sure the wounds heal at an expected rate.

"She needs the pill, too," Dante says when Carlton finishes the thorough examination.

I cock an eyebrow in question.

"You're not wearing the patch, and we've not used other protection the past two days, so you need the *after* pill. This isn't the best time to get you pregnant."

My cheeks turn hot when I understand what pill he has in mind. And because he so blatantly spoke about our sex life with Carlton and Grace in the room. She's dusting the wine in the wine rack, avoiding eye contact with me since Dante introduced us. I guess she can sense I don't like her. She's young, pretty, and Dante adores her. What's there to like?

Dante and I were so hungry for each other at the hotel, and all day yesterday, I paid no attention to protection or lack thereof. We only used a condom the first few times we had sex before Carlton put me on birth control. The *have you got protection* catchphrase never rooted in my brain.

Dante considers me from where he stands by the kitchen sink, sipping his coffee. A frown makes an appearance out of the blue. "Forget it." His clips, his tone sharp. "Don't even ask."

"What?" I frown, confused by his sudden annoyance.

"No." He takes a step forward, pointing a finger at me. "And that's the end of this conversation."

Grace chances a glance in our direction. Her ears perk up, and her cheeks flush pink as she skims over Dante. She averts her gaze hastily when she catches me watching her every move.

I focus back on him. "Don't boss me around, or I swear to God—"

"No," he snaps again, boiling the blood in my veins. "This one thing is out of the fucking question, Layla. We won't even talk about kids for a few more years."

"Stop interrupting me!" I throw my hands in the air and smack them on my thighs. Not the best idea, considering the stitches that sting like crazy. I wince, breathing through the pain. "You're not my father; you're not my boss. You're my fiancé, so start acting like one."

I didn't have to point out Dante's new status, but I can't help the green-eyed monster rearing its ugly head because of Grace. The enormity of my betrayal blew my insecurities out of proportion.

Dante exhales, squeezing the bridge of his nose. He closes his eyes briefly as if fighting an internal battle. "You're too young..." he mutters before his eyes fly open. "Fuck it." He crosses the room to crouch before me, hands on my legs. "Fine. You want a baby; you're getting a baby."

I exchange a confused look with Carlton, who watches Dante with one eyebrow raised that does little to hide his mild amusement. He shakes his head at me, shrugging his shoulders. I guess I'm not the only one who has no idea about what's going on.

The look on Dante's face is soothing and disturbing all at once. He's willing to scrap whatever plan he has for us in the near future based on my whim. Non-existent future, but he doesn't seem to acknowledge this dreaded fact. Selfishly, I cheer inside that he holds my happiness on a pedestal.

"If you'd stop interrupting, I'd tell you I don't want a baby."

His shoulders sag, relief painting his face. "Good." He takes my hand, kissing the inside of my wrist. "You're too young, Star."

"My imminent death poses a bigger problem than my age."

"You're *safe*. I told you no one will touch you. I told you to stop worrying."

Easier said than done.

Grace walks into the house with an enthusiastic *good morning!* that bounces off the walls. Her smile slips when she realizes I'm the only one home. She only smiles when Dante's around, infuriating me beyond reason. As long as she keeps her hands to herself, I don't attack. I wouldn't mind her presence half as much if he didn't like her, but he does. A lot. Too freaking much.

"Good morning." I cross my legs where I'm sitting on the couch. "Start upstairs today."

If she wants to say something along the lines of *you're not my boss*, she doesn't let it show. Good for her because I *am* her boss, and she better not piss me off while I'm already jumpy. With a curt nod, she climbs the stairs, leaving me alone.

Unable to sit still, I get up to pace the living room, treading a path in the plush carpet I asked Dante to buy to keep my feet warm while we watch a movie in the evening. My eyes dart to the clock on the wall every few seconds while I'm waiting. Waiting way too long.

Dante left half an hour ago to meet a high-profile hacker Jackson found. He's known for tracing those who can't be traced. The prospect of this guy finding Morte lifted Dante's foul mood ten times more than the best blowjob I gave him earlier could.

He's on edge, worrying about my safety so much that he'll end up gray-haired by the end of the month. I try to relax him whenever he's home, but even sex isn't enough to ease the tension of his muscles for longer than a few minutes.

I'm not sure why he's so worried. So far, we're in luck. I've been back in Chicago for five days, but no one has tried to kill me yet. It'd prove troublesome considering the armed army of Dante's and Julij's men outside the front door, the vicious dogs on the premises, and bulletproof windows throughout the house, which I'm not allowed to leave. Not even to inhale a mouthful of fresh air on the terrace.

I sigh, set my phone on the table, and glare at the door as if I can summon Julij if I stare at it long enough. What is taking him so long, anyway? He was at the hotel, not far from Dante's house, when I called. He should be here by now.

For three days, I begged Dante to let me visit Jess. Be that as it may, she *is* my mother. Since my future has a big question mark painted all over it, I want an opportunity for a healthy, peaceful conversation, a few answers, and burying the hatchet. Maybe even a chance to build our relationship from scratch without Frank's meddling.

As expected, Dante refused to let me visit or bring Jess over here. He claims he can't trust anyone right now, not even the woman who told him where to find me.

No matter how many times I tried to convince him, his answer was always the same.

"No, Star. It's not safe."

He might've forgotten I'm not the type to be ordered around. He wants his sassy star back. He wants me to stop being afraid of him...

Here you go, baby.

I pace the living room back and forth for fifteen more minutes before Julij arrives in a whirlwind of blond hair and a steel-gray suit. He wraps his arms around my middle and lifts me a foot off the floor to peck my cheek in greeting: something he refrains from doing when Dante's around.

"What do you need, sugar?" he asks, throwing himself against the couch, a sly smile on his face.

"How do you know I need something?"

"You told me to come as soon as possible. You sounded upset. Dante isn't here. Your hands are shaking," he counts, bending one finger at every point. "What happened?"

"Nothing." I glance toward the door leading to the garage, motioning for Julij to follow me downstairs. I'm not allowed out of the house, so I have to settle for the company of Dante's many cars if I want to avoid prying ears.

Julij cocks an eyebrow, watching me for a moment as he rests his back against the Charger. I wonder if asking him for help is a good idea. Their business partnership has evolved into something close to a friendship. I'm not sure if I can trust Julij. Too bad I'm desperate and have no one else to turn to. Five days in lockdown and under constant surveillance is starting to take its toll on my agitated mind.

Dante's unusually tense mood doesn't help.

"I want to see Jess, and Dante won't let me."

Julij's lips curl into an exaggerated horseshoe. "You poor thing! Would you like me to scold him?" he dramatizes with a chuckle. "Dante's right, sugar. You shouldn't leave the house no matter the reason; that's one and two: are you one hundred percent sure you can trust Jess?"

"Are you saying I shouldn't?"

"I'm not saying anything. I'm asking."

With visible satisfaction, he lights a cigarette, inhaling a cloud of smoke. He closes his eyes briefly, letting it all out, surrounding himself with the gray cloud. The smell of tobacco hits my face, tempting me for the first time ever. I shake my head, dismissing the urge to snatch his cigarette.

For a moment, I watch the delight on his face, the longish blond hair, and blue eyes that seem lighter because of the steel jacket and snow-white shirt he wears. He's a younger version of his father, their kinship unmistakable, but unlike Mr. Capone, Julij has a sense of style. Modern elegance. No hats or lengthy coats.

"I don't know if I can trust her, but I want to see her. Who knows how long I have left? Dante won't take care of everyone, even if he bends over backward—"

"He will," Julij says, rubbing his temple in small circles. "He'll walk on fucking water to make sure you're safe. So, will I. We'll bring this to an end, sugar. Don't doubt us."

I force a smile. He firmly believes that, but approaching the matter realistically, a happy end is out of the question. "Will you help me? I'd like to leave before Dante comes back."

Julij stares at something behind me with a frown. Or maybe he's staring into space, chasing his own thoughts. I'm not sure if he's wondering how to sneak me out of the house or how to let me down easily.

If he says *no*, I'll have to steal one of the cars and drive it myself. That might be an even worse idea than going with Julij. At least he has a gun and knows how to use it properly. I might've shot targets with Luca, but I'd be useless in the face of danger.

Julij inhales again, puffs up his cheeks, and parts his full lips, blowing out the smoke slowly, making a tasty-looking show of it. "Dante will lose his shit when he finds out. And he will. Fast. Probably within fifteen seconds of the garage door opening." He pushes away from the car. "No way I can get you past security unnoticed, so we'll do it Toretto-style."

"Toretto?"

He rolls his eyes. "And you call yourself an American? "The Fast and the Furious" ring a bell? It's a movie with impressive, high-speed car chases." He looks around the cars in the garage until his gaze stops on Dante's custom-tuned, neon green Challenger.

"That's not very clandestine." I frown when he snatches the key from the hanger by the stairs.

"True, but there's nothing faster here. They'll realize you want to run when we open the garage door, so we need a good kick to start with, and this," he trails his fingers over the hood, "this definitely has a kick, sugar. Do you need to grab anything from upstairs?"

"No," I say as I slide into the passenger seat.

My hands start to sweat as adrenaline rushes through my veins. The engagement ring weighs on my finger as if to remind me that I'm breaking all the rules and promises. Behind the wheel, Julij talks on the phone in Russian. He disconnects the call, glancing at me with undeniable glee glowing in his blue irises. I think he enjoys the idea of infuriating Dante.

"Fasten your seat belt."

He doesn't start the engine right away. Instead, he opens the garage door with a remote. It glides up slowly. With every inch of clearance, my pulse accelerates, whooshing in my ears, and pulsing in my neck. Several pairs of legs appear on the other side, but the engine is still dead.

"What are you doing?" I whisper, holding onto the seat.

"Waiting."

I look at him with wide eyes, but before I say anything else, Julij turns the key, and the roar of the V8 cuts through the silence. Spades and the rest of the security appear in the half-opened door. Julij revs the engine, winks at me, then slams the pedal to the floor, forcing everyone to flee out of the way as we jump out of the garage.

The sudden change of ground from concrete to gravel throws the back of the car sideways. Julij steers the Challenger out of a most likely intentional oversteer. We gain speed, driving straight at the gate where Dimitri stands with a grave expression. He nods at his boss as we burn past, fitting into the hole between a concrete pillar and the still-opening gate. In the side mirror, I spot Jackson, his gun raised, aimed at our car. Spades jumps in front of him, knocks the pistol out of his hand, then shoves him toward the garage, gesturing and yelling.

"They're about to chase us," I say.

My throat constricts with the nerves, accompanied by a hollow feeling in my chest. I've always been a rebel, but this time, my rebellion doesn't result from the desire to give Dante a hard time. I simply don't believe I'll live happily ever after. I want a chance to see my mother before I'm dead.

"Of course, they will. Hold on."

I don't have time to grab anything. The car turns sideways again when we make a sharp right at a far too high speed. I'm thrown at the door and knock my head against the window.

"Ouch," I hiss, massaging the sore spot.

"I told you to hold on!"

"Yeah, well, I'm not exactly prone to taking orders, am I? Apparently not even when they're supposed to keep me from harm's way." I wince, eyes glued to the side mirror.

A moment later, a cacophony of horns filters through the closed windows, ringing in my ears. Traffic ahead veers off to the sides, splitting like the sea.

I brace my legs against the floor, my hands clasped around the door handle. Julij turns a blind eye to every red traffic light on our path, burning through the intersections and ninety-degree corners as if he really is the lead character in a high-budget action movie, escaping imminent death.

His blatant disregard for traffic regulations will have us six feet under before the villain can catch up.

"Watch out!" I cry, pressing my back as far into the leather seat as humanly possible, when a truck moves from the right to cross the busy intersection ahead.

Julij slams on the brakes. Tires squeal, filling the car with a stench of rubber and burned brakes. Not even my tight hold on the handle keeps me in place when centrifugal force shoves me forward. My seatbelt locks, and the sudden *stop* knocks the breath out of me.

"Shit, hold on! Grab the fucking doorhandle and don't let go." he booms, then mutters something in Russian. He shifts into gear, stomping on the gas. The back tires lock, spinning fast before we shoot forward, crossing the intersection in a cloud of smoke. "And the fun begins." He points to the rearview mirror.

Two Chargers, a Mustang, and Camaro emerge from the gray cloud, hot on our tail. Not even the police can organize a chase as fast as Spades.

"Turn right at the next traffic lights. We'll go through the estate and lose them in the maze of short streets."

Julij nods, his blue eyes firmly on the road. His unwavering focus is reassuring. The obstacle course ahead calls for undivided attention. Rush-hour traffic barely slows down Julij or the cars behind.

"You need to guide me, sugar. I don't know Chicago well. Tell me when I should turn."

My fingers ache from clutching the handle. My whole body is so taut it'll take days to relax the muscles in my shoulders and back. Next to me, Julij's the exact opposite. Annoyingly laid-back as he bites back a smile. Utterly unaffected by the heart-stopping close calls we just, somehow, lived through. He's having a blast.

I straighten up, pumping my fingers to rid the stiffness, inhale two deep breaths, and attempt to control my trembling hands before I play the role of sat nav. Neither the

Chargers, Mustang, nor the Camaro is visible in the side mirror. Either Dante's people chose a different route or fell behind. They probably figured out the purpose of this trip. Spades was around when I asked Dante about meeting Jess. He's a bright guy; he must've guessed where we're heading. Even if he didn't, he's surely called Dante by now.

"I think we lost them," I say five minutes later, directing Julij toward the house I used to call my own.

"Call Jess. Tell her to open the garage. Just because I took you doesn't mean I'll take any risks."

"Do you think a sniper hunkers by the gate, and I'll drop dead the second I exit the car? Don't be ridiculous. It's really enough that Dante's overreacting for all of us." The seatbelt saves me from a broken nose for the second time when Julij slams the brakes, stopping the car at the curb.

"Don't underestimate what's happening, Layla." He turns his body my way. "It's been five days, and there are already more bodies to account for than my father disposed of during his career. You have no idea how many amateurs and professionals found out about the hit and the price for your beautiful head or how many will try to kill you."

A nasty chill starts at the top of my head, radiating to the tips of my fingers. "Dante said no one tried to get to me yet," I swallow around, the pulse throbbing in my throat.

"What did you expect?! You thought he'd inform you every time we kill another hitman?" Julij huffs out a sharp breath, shaking his head. "Some people would skin their kids for three million dollars. You're the target of dozens, if not hundreds of people. They'll kill you the first chance they get." He curls his finger under my chin. "I won't risk your safety any more than I already have." Poorly disguised fear buzzing in his voice coupled with worry crinkling his forehead forces my heart into a higher gear. "I'll take you to Jess, but you're under *my* protection right now. I won't let a hair fall off your head."

More words seem to linger, unspoken. The air between us hums, teeming with tension sharp enough to bite my skin. I don't understand why his sharp, assessing eyes bore into mine in such a steadfast way until he glances at my lips.

That's not good. Looks like the infatuation that started in Dubai never went away. Instead, it evolved into deeper feelings. How have I not noticed this sooner?

He cares more than he should, and now, by stealing me from Dante's house, he's risked his alliance, business partnership, and friendship with Dante. A friendship that bloomed despite past animosities and will now most likely die an untimely death thanks to me.

Blood roars in my head the longer his eyes linger on my lips. He looks like he wants to eat me. Like he's seconds away from gripping my face to catch my lips with his. The creases on his forehead deepen, and the determined look turns into a pained scowl. His Adam's apple bobs up and down as he lifts his hand, ghosting his thumb along my lower lip.

I watch, paralyzed, too stunned to say a single word.

"Call Jess," he rasps quietly, moving his hand back to grip the steering wheel. "Right now, sugar."

"But—"

"No buts! Either call her, or I'll turn us around and take you straight to Dante."

Irritation heats my insides, helping me out of my confusing haze fast. If I were standing, I'd oh-so maturely stomp my foot. "But I don't have my phone!" I snap. "I left it at home."

He pushes air through his nose—a long, amused exhalation, and hands me his cell phone, setting the car in motion.

"Turn right here," I say.

And that's a mistake...

A black Charger jumps out from the side street and stops in the middle of the road. Neither Spades, Jackson, nor any one of Dante's men fly out of the car. Dante does.

His look of quiet contempt has my heart relocating, climbing up my throat. Rage radiates off him, flooding the air and my senses. It feels overwhelmingly like a hand on the back of my neck, forcing me to my knees.

Julij glances between me and Dante, who's closing in on us, every step determined, shoulders tense. Anger surrounds him like an invisible force, stripping me of my courage. He's a few steps from the bonnet when Julij's hand smacks the steering wheel again. And then *fuck!* He throws the car into reverse pressing the pedal all the way down.

"That'll take some fucking explaining, sugar."

My eyes are on Dante, but the subtle change in how Julij said *sugar* doesn't slip my attention. Something changed. A few seconds of his fingers on my lips turned our relationship upside down. Friendship flew out the window.

Dante's back behind the wheel before we reverse onto the main street. Bitter bile churns in my stomach, and a cold sweat breaks out on my back. God, this was a stupid, *stupid* idea. "I'm in so much trouble," I mutter, staring at my hands.

I redial Jess's number and, without an explanation, tell her to open the damn garage. Ten more minutes pass before we arrive at our destination. I expected Dante's men to get here faster, but we're in luck. The driveway's empty. Julij parks in the garage, kills the engine, and holds my hand, so I'll stay inside until the door slides shut.

"Layla," Jess chokes from where she stands in the doorway leading inside the house. An elegant black dress hugs her skinny frame, her hair is immaculate as always, but her ashen skin and eyes rimmed with pink, hint she's still mourning her husband.

I shush the voices in my head telling me to stay away from my mother. They've been whispering at the back of my mind for years, but an invisible barrier that used to stop us from interacting is no longer there. That barrier was Frank, influencing all aspects of our lives.

"What are you doing here?" she asks when I wrap my arms around her in a tight, rigid embrace. "I thought Dante would hide you somewhere."

"I'm staying in Chicago."

She pushes me away, cupping my shoulders with both hands. She stares into my eyes for a moment as if willing me to understand everything she doesn't know how to put into words. It seems to be a rule of thumb around here. We're all so much better at loaded looks than an audible, *I'm sorry*.

Words aren't necessary, though. Not this time. I'm sure we're thinking the same thoughts. I'm certain we're equally unsure how to proceed and if we'll ever build a lasting, healthy relationship, but at the same time, we're both willing to try.

We go inside to the living room, but neither of us sits before the front door bursts open, hitting the wall with a bang. A clatter of elegant shoes resounds in the house.

Dante enters first, followed by Spades and Jackson. They stop three steps in, Dante's body rigid, eyes pinning Julij with a menacing stare. "What the fuck were you thinking? Who said you can take her?"

"She did." Julij motions to me. "She's not your prisoner."

"No," he admits, his tone far from calm. "But she *is* mine. You don't get to decide what's good for her."

"Neither do you," I clip.

I should probably learn when to bite my tongue. Dante's not a dominating, alpha male. He's usually the one to cave, apologize, or drop the argument whenever we disagree. He's careful, protective, and always puts me first. My comment is unjustified, but I can't, for the life of me, keep my mouth shut.

He shifts his gaze to me, perfectly composed on the outside—a clear sign his anger oscillates around at a cold-fury level. A cold sweat rushes down my back—an unjustified reaction once again, but the grim possibility of losing him is stronger than reason.

As if my thoughts are piped straight into his head, his attitude changes instantly, reducing anger to dust. His fists open, jaw relaxes, and shoulders drop an inch when he takes the first step toward me. I stumble back, the mechanical reaction something I have no control over.

A barely perceptible grimace pulls his face, but he doesn't stop. He takes my hand, drawing me closer. "What did I say? You shouldn't be afraid."

"Then stop giving me reasons. I didn't do anything wrong."

"You tricked Julij into bringing you here even though I said no. It's not safe, Star."

"You *said*? Get. A. *Dog*."

He lets go of me, pinching the bridge of his nose. "This won't work if you don't trust my judgment."

"Trust?! Funny you should mention trust. How am I supposed to trust you when you keep things from me?"

Julij casts a warning glare my way, shaking his head softly behind Dante's back. Too little too late...

Dante cocks an eyebrow, eyes roving my face as if he's trying to find more information in my expression. I'm sure he can. There's no need to spell it out. A pink glow of anger heats his skin like a flame running in dry grass, swiftly wiping off his carefully maintained composure. His eyes close briefly, and nostrils flare. The way he chews on his teeth and cracks his neck tells me he's fighting to stay calm.

Just when I think he's past the outburst stage, he turns on his heel and eliminates the distance separating him from Julij in two long strides. He throws his elbow back. Then forth, fast. His fist connects with Julij's face. A loud *crack* sounds in the silent room—Julij's nose or Dante's knuckles. I can't tell.

"You told her?! Was my *don't tell Layla* too fucking subtle?"

"She's not a helpless little girl!" he seethes, holding onto his bleeding nose. Drops of crimson find their way between his fingers, seeping down to stain his shirt. "She's stronger than you think. You can't shield her from everything."

I feel myself drifting into the dreaded panic. Elastic, wobbly legs won't hold me upright much longer. I suck in ragged breaths, peeling my eyes from Julij.

"Maybe," Dante says. "But nothing will stop me from trying." He steals a glance my way, his eyes full of something much more profound and feral than love. If not for the high-pitched ringing in my ears, I'd easily melt under the savage gaze of his green eyes, under the weight of his protectiveness pressing in on me from all angles. "Fuck." He strides back to where I stand, silently, pathetically panicking. Warm hands cup my face. "Eyes on me, Layla. You're okay."

My head moves up and down like a bobblehead. "I'm okay, I... I shouldn't have looked."

His mouth twitches as he tries to don a smirk. "Yeah, you shouldn't. You shouldn't be here, either. I go where you go."

Goosebumps break out along my spine because I know he means more than following me here. "Good thing you'll make sure I don't go."

CHAPTER SEVENTEEN

Dante

Twenty-eight years of searching. Learning. Finding out who I am, eliminating flaws, and perfecting my character. It didn't come easy. Change never comes easy. A few months ago, I was confident that my priorities were in order and my life was on the right trajectory. And then Layla arrived, introducing a new era of significant changes.

Six months ago, nothing mattered more than power. Respect and money took the rest of the podium.

Now, neither make up the top five.

Layla is *it.*

Nothing matters more. First, her safety, then health, happiness, love, and trust. She brought a different side of my character to life; she peeled my layers to uncover a man capable of feeling more than synonyms of angry or powerful. She changed the way I see and treat women. There's no taking my star for granted, no bossing her around. Words like *please* and *sorry* were long extinct in my vocabulary until she came along.

Consciously, I accepted the changes as they came. I volunteered to grow as a man for her. She hadn't asked me to change, but I'm consumed by a gnawing desire to better myself, grow as a human being, and make her proud.

Among the multitude of positive, intentional changes, there are also those that happened without my knowledge. Changes I wasn't aware of until the situation betrayed me, that my brain no longer occupies the throne. The fucking muscle in my chest seized control.

I understand why my world has been reappraised. I can rationally explain why I feel or act the way I do. Nothing surprised me much. Not the newly acquired reflex of reaching for a gun whenever Layla's in the slightest danger. Not the desire to protect her regardless of the consequences. Not even that I hold her on a pedestal, superior to every other aspect of my life.

I thought nothing could ever blindside me, but I proved myself wrong. My rational thinking was defeated by emotions for years. I'm not a man who calmly assesses a problem. I act first and think later, too late for a change of heart. A turmoil of feelings buzzing in my system thanks to Layla's escape pushed me to make Julij bleed, just as it would in pre-Layla, but today I took a moment to *think*.

Not only does Julij deserve a few punches. So do Spades, Jackson, and Cai. Layla's desertion would come back to bite them all if not for one small detail—she would be the only one affected by my outbursts. My people would brush off the punches. They'd forget my temper a few days down the line.

Not Layla.

She'd torture herself if anyone suffered because of her stunt. And since her happiness is one of my top priorities, I couldn't nail Julij. Well, at least I tried very fucking hard. If he hadn't told her about the bodies piling up since the moment we arrived back in Chicago, I would've succeeded.

"I left her under your protection, Spades." I aim my finger at him while we stand outside Jess's house, giving Layla a few minutes alone with her mother. "You were supposed to watch her. How the fuck did she get by security?!"

He glares at me from the casual lean against the hood of his car, hands in pockets, two vertical wrinkles in the middle of his forehead. "I'm not a babysitter, Dante." Annoyance shudders his stance. "I'm supposed to keep Layla safe, but I sure as fuck won't do it against her will. Do you want someone to blame? Blame him." he motions behind me at Julij. "How would you have me stop them? Shoot?"

Jackson scratches his head, pulling a sour face as he pushes away from the car to stand beside Spades. "Should I point out I tried to shoot the tires, but you didn't let me?"

"You *what*?" A vein pulses on my neck. "You aimed a fucking *gun* at the car she was in? What if you'd hit the tank?"

"Or Layla's head," Julij mumbles, kicking the gravel.

"You better shut the fuck up, and you," I point at Spades, "Go back to my house. Get your shit together. Get *everyone's* shit together. No one has access to the house except security, Layla, and me. Is that fucking clear?"

The mild reprimand pisses him off, but he's not prone to holding a grudge. He should be happy I'm holding onto my self-control. Barely, but points for trying.

He jumps behind the wheel with a tight nod, prompting Jackson to follow suit. Fifteen seconds and I'm alone with Julij. He shuffles his feet, spinning the keys around his finger to the car he stole from my garage, an artificial mask of poise in place. The aura of pomposity, a defense mechanism of some sort, returns, pissing me off big-time. Instead of admitting his mistake and owning up to the fact that he fucked up, he pretends not to give a shit about what I think.

"It was your idea, Julij. It was your fucking idea to meet at the club so we can get a plan of action together. And what did you do instead of heading there? You drove to my house and took *my* girl from the only safe place in this country."

"Safe?" he scoffs, arms crossed, eyes on me now. I'm having a déjà vu moment. Julij from six months ago appears with a zero-fucks-given attitude. "Twenty-six bodies in five days. Two of your men are dead. Three more guys Carlton barely managed to keep alive. That's *safe*? Don't be absurd. Quit being stubborn, Dante. Send Layla to Moscow. Stop fooling yourself. I know you want her close, but don't tell me she's safe here."

"She's safe. No one got anywhere near the house. Security's good." At least at keeping people out. Not so good at keeping them in. "Once Morte dies, the bounty will become insolvent, thus closed." I shove my hand in the pocket to retrieve a pack of smokes and pinch a Marlboro between my teeth.

When I brought Layla back home, both Julij and Anatolij were adamant that she shouldn't stay, that she'd be better off hidden off the grid, somewhere foreign. Somewhere out of reach. Anatolij offered his house, or rather a *castle,* in Moscow as the destination. Nobody would dream of making a move in Russia without his consent. The country is enormous, but all mafia bosses report back to Anatolij. They need his approval for business deals, new ventures, allies... the lot. He's a God over there. Which makes his offer to protect and hide Layla rather suspicious.

Julij keeps quiet, aware I'm not done talking. He waits until I organize the mess of my thoughts and get a hold of myself. However difficult that may be without Layla by my side. A few punches to Julij's nose wouldn't calm me as fast as her touch.

"I tolerate it that you love her, Julij."

He stands taller to showcase his confidence and uphold the Don Corleone persona he has going on. "I don't love her."

I inhale the smoke, resisting the urge to all-out laugh in his face. "Who the fuck are you trying to fool? I don't like that you do, but I can't do much about it short of killing you." I'm still contemplating that option. "Keep your feelings in check, and we'll be good. I trust you."

As fucked up as the logic might seem, because of his feelings, I trust him where Layla's safety is concerned. He doesn't love her as I do; no one can, but his feelings run deep. Deep enough that he'll go to extreme lengths to protect her.

"She asked me to come." He stares at his brown leather shoes, a cigarette in hand, searching the jacket pocket for a lighter. "She sounded upset. I didn't think the crown would slip off your head if I made you wait a bit."

I scoff, hurling my Zippo at him. Between us, Julij's the one with an imaginary crown on his Russian, aristocratic, big head. "You should've said no."

A sad smile curls his lips. "I can't."

He stares me dead in the eye, non-verbally admitting his feelings. No need for admission. Verbal or not. His feelings are as obvious as a day in the sun. His shitty attitude disappears faster than it appeared, and the Julij I respect resurfaces. We both know his interest in Layla is undesirable, but we also know not much can be done to change the way he feels.

"I wouldn't let a hair fall off her head, and you know it."

That's the problem. I do fucking know it.

A black Mercedes with tinted windows lazily enters the driveway. My gun is out of the holster and raised before the wheels come to a full stop beside my Charger.

"Relax." Julij taps my shoulder, urging me to lower the gun. "It's just Anatolij."

"What's he doing here?"

"Good question."

The chauffer rounds the car to open the back door. Anatolij steps out onto the gravel, maintaining an exterior of practiced indifference. He zeroes in on me and lifts his chin in greeting, blatantly disregarding the gun aimed at his head. I tuck the Beretta away when he gets closer.

"Given the circumstances, I'm pleased you don't take any chances. I'd consider you wiser if you'd admit that and allow Layla to go to Moscow for the time being, where she's safer."

"What are you doing here?" I change the subject, refusing to get drawn into the same discussion again.

They both have a point. I'm playing with fire, keeping Layla in Chicago; amid the new war. Moving her off the grid could, in theory, reduce the risk, but it'd also induce my paranoia. She should be here where I can check in on her whenever I want, where I can personally protect her and see with my own eyes how she's doing.

Anatolij glances at the house, his expression unreadable. "I'm visiting an old friend."

"Nikolaj never mentioned that you know Jess." Julij descends the concrete steps to shake his uncle's hand.

"There are many things you don't know about me, Julij."

A train of thoughts pulls away from the station inside my head. I don't have much information, but Anatolij paying Jess a visit leaves me all kinds of wary.

"Jess and I met when she worked as a waitress at Nikolaj's restaurant," he supplies, his pointed stare probably designed to speak volumes. Too bad I don't know him enough to decipher the hidden meaning.

Questions multiply as abstract answers swirl in the depths of my mind, begging me to connect the dots. I've had a bad feeling about this guy from the start... looks like my suspicions were correct. His words don't strike a chord, but I finally put my finger on where the strange, unwarranted familiarity has its roots—his eyes.

Anatolij offers a tight-lipped smile, reading me like an open book. "I think we should talk."

"What's going on?" Julij glances between us, clearly unappeased not to be included in this weird non-verbal conversation we're somehow sharing.

"This doesn't concern you," Anatolij clips, his steel, almost silver gaze trained on me. "Come see me at the hotel at eight."

"Why do you have to be so stubborn?" I ask Layla once we're on our way back home.

Anatolij's cryptic, between-the-lines, half-assed fucking message and all the newly discovered yet unconfirmed information has me poised on edge. Possible explanations play in my head on repeat, summoning crazier scripts that were undoubtedly written by a drunk. What I'm making of this doesn't make much sense...

The animalistic roar of the V8 floods the streets every time I accelerate, eager to get home fast. The clock is ticking. Layla's desertion threw me back almost two hours—time I don't have tonight.

"You like that about me," she says, faking a cheeky smile.

She can't fool me with that. Something bothers her, but I really don't have the time to inquire.

"I do, but I like knowing you're safe even more. Considering the situation, I also like to know where you are. And above all, I like when my people *don't* call to tell me you ran."

Jackson was the one tasked with relaying the news. I'm sure he pulled the short straw. He had to repeat one sentence three times before I caught the words among a litany of fucks, assholes, and a whole lot more stuttering.

"So that's the problem," Layla huffs a forced laugh. "Were you worried that your future bride ran away? No need. You can't get rid of me."

"If we're mixing feelings into this, then all I worried about was whether Julij confessed that he's in love with you and decided that kidnapping you is a good idea."

"In love? That's silly. We're friends."

If I hadn't already parked and turned toward her, I would've missed how she's nervously tugging on the hem of her sweater.

How the hell did she lead me on while under Frank's orders? She can't lie. Even now, she can't hide her emotions. She knows about Julij's feelings. One question remains: did he tell her or show her?

Neither is acceptable, but the latter earns him a one-on-one with me, then with Jackson, and then an abrupt end of our business partnership. I may tolerate—barely— that he loves her, but if he tries to adore her, he'll end up preparing Happy Meals for the rest of his fucking life.

My jealousy is in no way linked to trust. If there's one thing, I trust Layla one hundred percent with, her feelings for me are it. This is about rules. You don't touch a man's girl. Ever. Look all you want, but don't fucking touch. Lack of respect for the rules is the worst flaw of a good accomplice.

"What did he do?"

"Hmm?" She turns to me. "Oh, um, nothing. He said and did nothing. He didn't have to."

She steps out of the car, signaling the end of the conversation. Maybe she needs time to process her newfound admirer, or maybe she knew all along but didn't realize that so did I.

The passenger side window slides down before she takes three steps. "Can you please stay home now? Spades will be here with Nate, Cai, and five others until I get back. I'll be late, so don't wait up. You'll be safe if you stay at home."

She spins around, throwing me off my game with a pointed stare of those big, steel-gray eyes of hers, lips in a defiant pout. "How late is late?"

"Don't expect me before eleven, but—"

"I know, I know. The gun is in the nightstand, the walk-in wardrobe is a bunker, and all the windows are bulletproof."

She wasn't pleased when I told her about the new security feature added to the house: armored doors Julij kindly installed in the walk-in wardrobe while we were in Texas.

"Just in case she needs to hide," he said. And I approved.

Layla rounds the car, climbs onto my lap, and clasps her fingers on the nape of my neck. She leans in to steal an innocent peck, grazing her nose over mine with an ever-so-soft sigh. Cheeky little bug. She knows damn well how hard those needy whimpers make me. I can't get enough of her body now that she's back and mine again.

My head hits the headrest. A low, strained growl rumbles at the base of my throat as my fingers climb under the hem of her skirt to graze the soft skin of her thighs. "Go, Star. I have a lot to do, and it's getting late."

She sighs again, moving her small hands to cup my face as she leans in for another kiss. Deeper this time. The rhythm of her lips is slow and gentle, but her breathing turns shallow. "I'm sorry I left. I had to see Jess."

"I know, baby." I pat her hip. "Get going."

Hot, plump lips draw a line across my jaw to stop at my ear. I dig my fingers into her hips as a rush of desire floods my system when she nips at my earlobe. "Don't keep me waiting too long. I'm so, so wet..." With one last soft sigh, she steps out of the car to climb the stairs.

Now she's fucking done it. I'm sporting a bad case of wood, aching to find release in her wet pussy. I rake my hand through my hair, mesmerized by the seductive sway of her hips. She stops at the top step, looks over her shoulder, and winks with a cute smile. God, she's fucking perfect.

With an exasperated huff, I exit the car. This evening is far from over, but I know I'll be distracted for the rest of the night if I don't get my fill of her now. Layla's in the living room, kicking her shoes off when I catch up with her.

"I thought you needed to leave." She bites her lip when I grip her by her waist and sit her on the bar. "Don't you have *so* many things to do tonight?"

"Yeah. One of them is you." I take her sweater off and fling it over my shoulder, only now spotting Grace on all fours, polishing the skirting boards. "You better leave."

She scrambles to her feet, red in the face as she whirls out of the room into the kitchen. Not the best choice. The only way out of there is through the living room, but I honestly couldn't care less now that my fingers are under Layla's skirt, touching the wet fabric of her panties. I rip them off, destroying the tenth pair since she came back to me.

I yank her closer to the edge of the counter, ready for a feast. "Legs on my shoulders." I bunch her skirt around her waist. "Knees apart. Show me how wet you are." I dip my head, high on her smell, the silky-smooth texture of her skin, and the perfect pink paleness of her pussy. I lick her bottom to top, groaning in pure delight. "So sweet."

A soft moan slips out of her mouth. She inhales, her ribs showing, and when she exhales, I push two fingers inside her, earning a strained gasp. No way I'll ever get enough of hearing and seeing her come. We had sex this morning, but I'm starved for her already.

"That's it," she breathes, grasping my hair when I curl my fingers to stroke her G spot. "Don't stop, please, I..."

Words fail her—the most arousing thing of all when she can't articulate her thoughts. I work faster the more her legs shake on my shoulders, and she grinds her hips over my face searching for her high.

"Not so fast." I stop when she's close and rob her of my fingers and lips, taking her by her arm. "On your toes, baby, legs apart, hands and cheek on the wall." She's such a good girl when she obeys without hesitation. "You think you'll get rewarded for leaving the house without permission?" I slide my zipper, free my cock, and yank Layla's skirt up again. "Naughty girls don't get rewarded. They get punished."

"This is supposed to be punishment?" she half says, half moans when I drive into her, burying myself as deep as I can in one smooth thrust. "Feels like a reward."

"You'll change your mind."

I clasp my hand around her throat, forcing the back of her head to rest on my shoulder. She's on her tippy-toes, spine arched to expose the brain-melting curve of her hip. I thrust harder, making her more audible each time I hit a sensitive spot. I know she loves it when I fuck her against the wall, and I sure love the easy access to her clit this position offers.

She's soaking wet. The slickness coats my cock; her erotic gasps and moans spur me on, filling the house and my head. I'm pretty sure the whole fucking neighborhood can hear her right now. She's not one to keep quiet.

"Oh God!" she cries out when I circle the swollen bud with two fingers. Ten seconds and I stop when she's right there, on edge. "No... don't, please, I—"

"I told you this is not a reward. You want to come, baby?" I graze my fingers down her thighs.

"Yes! Yes, please." She wriggles her sweet butt, pressing herself to me as she tries to cheat the system, looking for a bit of friction that'll set her off.

I grip her hips, holding her still. "Promise to behave."

"What?!" Her knees buckle when I circle her clit again just a few times, enough to drive her mad, enough to tear another loaded moan out of her lips.

"Promise not to be so fucking reckless, Layla. Promise to do as I say until the hit is closed." I tease her again. She's always sensitive, but right now, she's a few shallow thrusts away from coming undone in my arms. So I stop.

"I promise!" she cries. "Don't stop. I promise I'll behave."

I pull back to drive into her again, resuming the hastened pace. "I'll fucking die if anything happens to you." I close my teeth on her shoulder, pumping harder when her walls tighten around my cock. Five thrusts, and she's coming. My name on her lips among a melody of erotic moans. Snaking my arm around her middle to keep her upright while her legs shake, I hold her flush to me as her body vibrates. "That's it. That's my good girl. I love seeing you like this." I follow her into the pleasant, inviting abyss, holding my petite star in my arms for dear life until the blurriness clears from my eyes.

She pants, whimpering when I slide out of her wet warmth, readjusting her skirt in the process. "I should get on your nerves more often if this is how you want to punish me." She spins around, resting her back on the wall, eyes glossy, cheeks flushed.

Maybe she should. Make-up sex, even though we didn't fight, is something else. Then again... "You get on my nerves enough as it is." I clasp my hand on her throat, closing her lips with mine. "Go and take a long bath. Read a book or watch a movie. I'll be home as soon as I can."

"I'll be good."

"That'd be a first."

She chuckles, whacking me over the head playfully. "Go, you're late." She grabs her good-for-nothing panties off the floor, stuffing the lacy, ripped scrap in the back pocket of my trousers. "Something to remind you of what's waiting for you, right here."

With a peck on my cheek and a wink, she walks away. Once she disappears upstairs, I enter the kitchen where Grace sits at the breakfast bar, cheeks scarlet, eyes wide.

"Next time I tell you to leave, you *leave*. Understood?"

She bobs her head vigorously. "I'm sorry, I-I... it's just that I didn't think you'd—"

"That I'll have sex with my fiancée while you're in the next room? Lesson learned; I trust. Next time, don't assume. This is my house. If I want her, I'll have her wherever I feel like it."

"Yes, lesson learned. I'm sorry."

CHAPTER EIGHTEEN

Layla

Piles of papers litter the coffee table: lecture notes that Rookie kindly brought for me courtesy of Jane. I haven't missed much yet, but there's no telling when I'll attend classes again, so I'd rather stay on top of the material while I have time.

Despite the ambitious plan to study, I only managed an hour before I was forced to call it a day, pushing the papers aside. Now, I'm at the breakfast bar with my laptop. Three pretty faces watch me from the screen. When he stopped by earlier, Rookie explained that neither he, Nate, nor Cai want to risk their girls' safety by letting them pay me a visit.

The comforting news is, they *want* to visit.

Since we can't make a girl's night happen in reality, we settled for a virtual chat with a very real glass of wine. The three of them met at Bianca's house, dressed as if we're hitting the club later.

"Jeez, I'm glad you're back, girl. We need a night out! The last time I danced was with you in Delta." Bianca adjusts her pink, strapless dress, which barely contains her large boobs.

"That sure won't happen anytime soon." Luna pulls a face. "Layla's not allowed outside the front door. No way Dante will let her out of the house until the hit is closed."

"True. I don't know how you keep so calm! I'd be freaking out if there was a bounty on my head."

Jane elbows Bianca under the ribs, offering me a tight-lipped smile. "Don't listen to her. She's already drunk. You'll be okay. Dante will skin the fucker who's overseeing the hit, and we will all go dancing soon."

Surprise, surprise. I'm not the only naïve one out there.

"Don't hold your breath."

They stare into the camera on their laptop and consequently right at me.

"Oh, hell no. What was that supposed to mean?" Jane frowns. "Where's the negativity coming from?"

"Can we please change the subject?" I grab a bottle to refill my glass. "Anything but the hit. It's bad enough. I think about it twenty-four seven. I don't want to talk about it."

"Sure, and I know just the topic!" Luna bounces in her seat, spilling a bit of red wine down her cleavage. "Bitch, you're *engaged* to Dante fucking Carrow! We want to know everything!"

"Yeah, but first, show us that big ass rock!"

I raise my hand, showing off the diamond, still not quite accustomed to the thought that Dante wants me forever.

They bombard me with wedding ideas, shouting one after the other as they devise the most insane settings. Monaco, Hawaii, Seychelles. The last one does have a ring to it, and once I check the pictures online, I'm officially in love with the idea of a beach wedding.

It'll remain just that: an idea. There's no way in hell Dante will share my enthusiasm.

Ten o'clock comes and goes; the bottle of wine beside me is almost dry. My mood lifts while alcohol silences my screaming mind and pushes the problems to the background.

"Oh. *My*. God!" Jane giggles, polishing the last of the fourth glass of red. "Get this! A *themed* wedding!"

"Yes!" Luna claps, spilling more wine down her cleavage. Those stains might not come out. Pity, her dress is stunning. "How about Disney? You could be Belle!"

I burst out laughing. "That makes Dante the Beast."

"Well, he kind of is, isn't he?" Bianca wiggles her eyebrows. She's been asking inappropriate questions about our sex life for the last half an hour. "Oh, come on! You're such a prude! Give me something! Is he rough? I bet he likes it hard. I bet he eats pussy like a pro!"

I bite the inside of my cheek, toying with the glass. Is this what girl talk is usually like? I've never had a group of girlfriends. The learning curve is real.

Our childish giggles are cut short at the sound of tires squealing and metal bending outside. Despite the closed, bulletproof windows, the commotion that just erupted out front floods the house as if the chaos is happening two rooms away. A blend of different voices screams orders for a few seconds before a round of gunshots rumbles above all else.

My legs turn weak. Dread fills my lungs like cold mud.

"Are those gunshots?!" Luna cries, eyes wide and tearful.

Cai's still here, securing the house, while Dante's at Delta with the V brothers and Julij. Nate went home an hour ago, and I guess he's the one Bianca tries to reach, pressing a cell phone to her ear.

"Get back to Dante's!" she yells a second later, catching me off-guard. I didn't expect her to send Nate back here where he might get hurt. "Something's wrong. Go back there, someone's shooting outside!"

"If anything happens, hide, Star. Understood?"

Dante's words bounce in my head, but Luna's tearful gaze has me running to the nearest window overlooking the driveway. Dante's men back away toward the house, shooting at a black van that battered down the gate. Its back door stands open. A man dressed in black fires a series of shots from a machine gun bolted to the van's floor.

I scan the driveway, searching for Cai and Spades to check if they're okay, but before I spot them, a movement behind a row of bushes on the left side of the house catches my eye. In the mayhem of bullets flying in all directions and a disorderly rumble of screams, no one noticed a group of men running toward the back of the house.

The van is just a diversion.

I spin on my heel, rooted to the spot. My mind is going as fast as my heart slamming against my ribs like the kickback of a gun. The sounds become muffled, distant, an unclear obbligato of blood whooshing in my ears.

I stare at the glass wall on the other side of the living room. My reflection stares back at me, and the clock ticks slower and louder.

Two hands slam on the glass. I nearly jump right out of my heels. The gunshots become louder, and my breaths shorter, faster. Bianca's panicked voice hits my ears, but I can't make out words. Whoever's outside takes a step closer. A hooded silhouette like a modern-day reaper. The only thing standing between us is a sheet of bulletproof glass.

"Layla!" The high-pitched shrill of Luna's voice cuts through the haze. "What's happening?!"

I don't answer. Blood in my veins turns to cherry slurpy as I watch the hooded reaper raise a saw—the kind firemen use— and press it against the glass. I hope it won't work, but the blade penetrates the glass without a hitch. The man tramps down, cutting a vertical line to create a doorway.

My heart leaps to my throat. All my instincts rebel against such an effortless acceptance of death. I run back inside the kitchen. "Cai's okay. Someone's trying to get inside."

"Hide!" Jane screams. "Now, Layla!"

I take two steps at a time, slamming all doors shut behind me until I burst into the bedroom and halt in front of the armored door to the walk-in-wardrobe. My fingers hover over the keypad on the right, but I fall short of tapping the digits.

I can't lock myself in there defenseless. If whoever's coming brought tools to break through bulletproof glass, it's wise to assume they have tools that'll penetrate the steel door.

From the nightstand on Dante's side of the bed, I retrieve his spare gun and flip the safety with trembling fingers. Memories of the last time I held a gun threaten to weigh me down. For a second, my mind just blanks.

The code to the door plays hide and seek inside my mind. I can't focus among the chaos of bullets flying outside, and my concentration is put to the test when the sounds become louder. Whoever was trying to barge inside did.

"Here-kitty-kitty-kitty. Come out, come out wherever you are!" Resonates throughout the house.

Fear tries to choke me. My mind ceases to work, to stay in the moment, to focus on the task. Heavy footsteps on the stairs elevate my panic to the nth degree. A click of the alarm being disarmed sounds above the anarchy happening all around. The front door slams against the wall: the only *bang* that fills me with a sense of relief.

Four digits pop into my head, and I burst inside the walk-in-wardrobe, slamming the door behind me, and backing into the corner. I slide down the wall, aiming at the closed door as I force even, deep breaths into my lungs. The one thing keeping me sane right now is that Dante's on his way. I can feel it in my bones.

He's coming.

He's close.

He'll be here soon, and I'll live to fight another day. The thought calms me down right until more shots ring close by. The unruly riot of my pulse starts again when three bullets smash against the metal door, forcing my back to press further into the wall as if I can fuse myself with the concrete.

Just as fast as it all started, everything comes to a sudden stand-still. A deafening silence falls all around, spoiled by the violent tempo of my heartbeats throbbing in my neck.

"Layla!" Spades yells, and furious tapping on the keyboard follows. One, two, three tries. "Fuck!" He bangs something—his fist, I think—on the door. "Open up! Are you okay?"

"I'm fine," I rasp, my throat rough as if I suffer from a nasty infection.

And then Dante arrives.

His booming *Layla*! shakes the foundations of the house. His rushed footsteps clap on the stairs. Two more pairs of shoes follow suit. I put the gun down, trying to hoist myself up, but more tapping on the keyboard halts my efforts. Dante enters, a gun in his hand, worry on his face, *blood* on his shirt.

In a flash, I go back in time. I'm no longer in the closet, no longer an adult. I'm seven, in Frank's house on the day my paralyzing fear of blood started.

I stand in the doorway to the kitchen, watching Dante. He sits on the table, his white t-shirt red, face white, twisted with pain.

"Get her out of here, Jess!" Daddy screams, yanking every cabinet door open. "Fuck! Where's the first aid kit in this shithole?!"

My chin trembles when tears spill from my eyes. I want to run and hug Dante, but my legs won't budge.

He turns to look at me too. He's no longer frowning. Now, a small smile crosses his lips. "It's okay, little bug." He tugs his leather jacket closer to cover the bloody t-shirt. "Don't cry. I'm fine."

I sniffle, wiping my runny nose with the back of my hand, nodding vigorously. Tears still stream down my cheeks, but I know I have to be strong, or Daddy will scream and call me a wuss again.

That evening, I cried into my pillow for hours hoping Dante would be okay. I must've pushed those memories out of my system; buried them somewhere deep because thinking about him in pain was too hard. He was the only person in my life to show me any form of affection back then.

And he still is now.

He crosses the room, helps me up, and pulls me into his warm arms. "I'm here." He takes my face in his hands. "You're okay. You're fine, Star. It's over."

I cling to the safety he offers. He acts calm, but the urgency of his touch and the way his eyes scan every inch of my body betray just how worried he is.

With a kiss on my head, he huddles me to his side and turns to Spades. "Everyone okay?"

My gaze travels further into the bedroom, and my barely regained poise snaps like a dry twig. I stand there, motionless, eyes trained on the hole in the forehead of a man lying on the floor. Blood seeps from the wound, marking the cream carpet with crimson stains. My stomach somersaults back. I can't move; I can't say a single word, despite channeling effort into remaining in control of my emotions while my mind traps me in a dark corner.

"Two dead," Spades says in a rueful tone. "Cai and Rookie both got hit, but nothing major. They'll be okay."

"Get Carlton over here," Dante orders, moving his attention back to me. "Hey, don't look."

But that's just it... the first thing anyone does when told not to look is *look*. I can't avert my gaze until Dante curls his finger under my chin, forcing my eyes on him. Simultaneously, he steps into my line of sight, blocking the gruesome view.

"Layla. Eyes on me. I'll get you out of here. We'll stay at a hotel until the house is back in order."

He's focused on walking me out of the house and down to the garage. My eyes fall shut to make things easier but fly open once the image of that man's lifeless body bleeding onto the cream carpet flashes before my eyes.

Dante squeezes my hand tighter. "That's exactly why I didn't ask you to close your eyes."

I take one cautious step at a time. Dante walks backward, steering me so I won't trip over dead bodies. We're downstairs when the door opens, and my head snaps in that direction. Wrong choice. Blood is everywhere. It looks as if someone tipped a bucketful over the floor and walls. My head starts swimming, and I hold my breath, transfixed.

Dante grabs my face to turn my head away from the horror-movie scene. “Breathe, baby. You’re fine. Just breathe.”

I nod vigorously, gritting my teeth

“Good girl.” His lips on my forehead work like Novocain.

CHAPTER NINETEEN

Layla

I gasp, closing my teeth on Dante's shoulder. He leans over me, one hand entangled in my hair, the other on my hip, lips on my neck as he thrusts his hips back and forth in a slow, passionate beat. His fingers dig into my flesh, and hooded eyes watch me in-between kisses. The quiet rustling of bed sheets, Dante's low, throaty growls, and my almost inaudible moans create a stimulating atmosphere that fuels our desire.

Cold drops of water, remnants of a recent shower, trickle down his neck and drip onto my hot skin, introducing more goosebumps, more shivers, more squirming. Dante rests on his elbows, holding his arms along mine to trap me as if he never wants to lose sight of me again.

A greedy, lustful kiss burns a new dose of desire through my bloodstream. Like a boost of energy, it changes the calm, passionate moment into a heated battle. I free myself from the makeshift cage of his arms, drawing long lines on his back as the muscles in my abdomen tighten in anticipation.

We've been in bed for a while, but Dante's not ready to let me come. He brings me sky-high, to the brink of an orgasm, and then stops at the crucial moment. Pleasant pain spreads in a wave of vibrations through my body when he stills, buried deep inside, denying me the release.

He sucks in a deep breath, combing my long, damp hair behind my ears. "You're trembling, Star. And I didn't even let you come yet." Satisfaction paints his handsome face, but a cheeky smirk means he wants to torture me for a long time.

"I'll be sore for days." I press the back of my hand to my forehead. "Enough, please." I brace against his chest to push him back and dictate the pace so I can take what I need.

"Don't even think about it." He straightens his elbows, hovering higher. "I love when you're on top, but today I prefer the look on your face every time you're so close."

I trail my hand down my stomach, desperate to come. I expect Dante to stop my efforts, but he arches back further, dark eyes on me when I circle my clit with two fingers, mimicking his moves when he touches me like this. Gathering a handful of the sheets, I throw my head back, holding my moans on a tight leash.

Dante dives between my legs, guiding his hot tongue along my entrance. "You're so fucking sexy, baby, don't stop."

Like a balloon filled with helium, I rise higher and higher, closer to the all-encompassing release. Dante slips two fingers inside, stroking my G spot. That does it. Stimulation overload. My moans bounce off the walls as I clench my thighs together, holding his head in place until the waves retreat.

I'm still shaking when Dante pushes my legs aside, climbing back to kiss me. The orgasm hasn't completely faded yet, and I bite my lip instead of his, hands on his shoulders, when he slips his hard cock back inside, making me cry out.

"Eyes, Layla. Show me those gorgeous eyes."

I look at him, smiling down at me. "This is too much..." Pleasure mixes with a sting of pain that has me writhing beneath him as another orgasm looms nearby.

"Too much? We've barely scratched the surface."

He thrusts harder, igniting every nerve ending in my sensitive, exhausted body. I wrap my legs around his hips, disappearing into the depths of my own consciousness as my mind explodes with fireworks. Dante pins me to the mattress, pumping in and out to prolong and magnify the sensation. A brutal kiss bruises my lips before he stills, holding me in place as he sinks his fingers into my flesh.

His green eyes flutter shut, muscles shift beautifully under his skin, and lips part when he comes.

I have no strength left to embrace him. Dark spots in front of my eyes disturb the image of his handsome face inches from mine until he collapses beside me, wrapping one arm around my middle to haul me closer. I'm limp, a rag doll in his hands. I can't move. All I can do is attempt to calm my heartbeat and catch enough air to remain conscious.

Dante comes to his senses first, as always.

A wrinkle marks his forehead when he rises on his elbow to look at me. His jaw clenches, and *puff*, the satisfaction is gone, replaced by worry.

I lift my head from the pillow. "What's wrong?"

"You bit your lip."

I move my hand to touch it, but Dante stops me before my fingers come across the blood. The metallic, disgusting taste fills my mouth, and my stomach ties itself into a knot. I hate that. I hate that I can't control this reaction or lessen the heavy feeling in my chest. A pang of anxiety replaces the last of my pleasure.

"Give me a sec." He pulls on a pair of boxers, heading to the bathroom only to emerge back a minute later with a wet towel in hand. He sits on the edge of the bed, parting my lips with his thumb to wipe the cut clean.

"You should be happy," I say. "I didn't register the pain. Too much pleasure."

"I'd rather you didn't panic minutes after sex."

"I think I might deal with blood better now that I know what triggered the phobia in the first place."

He considers my words for a moment as if trying to find the answer for himself. Looks like he found the wrong one because anger taints his features. "Did Frank hurt—"

"No! No, he has nothing to do with it. I promise."

"Okay, what is it then?"

"You... I was seven, and you got hit. Frankie was looking for a first-aid kit in the kitchen when I walked in."

"I remember that. You were the cutest little thing. I hated seeing you cry." He pulls me in and falls back, cuddling me to his chest. "I still hate it now."

With my head on his torso, I contour his biceps with my finger, enjoying the soft kisses he presses to my hair. "I forgot about it, but when I saw blood on your shirt last week, it all came back. Looks like I loved you back then too."

"You'll have to be careful for a few days, Star. I won't be around to take care of you if you open up this cut on your lip."

"Don't remind me. I have eight more hours of acting like I don't have to go anywhere. Let me pretend I can stay here with you and that no one is trying to kill me."

After the shooting, Dante made the difficult decision for us both, to evacuate me from Chicago. If I'm being honest, the idea is the safest bet right now, but the destination leaves a lot to be desired. I had no say in the matter. Even if we could vote, I'd lose because Dante's not alone in his conviction. He and Julij think there's no safer place than Julij's uncle's house in Moscow.

Dante gets out of bed again, pulls one of his white shirts off the hanger, and throws it at me, announcing a break from all the sex. I sincerely hope it's time for food.

"Dinner? I want a big burger with grilled chicken and a rainbow of vegetables."

He takes his cell from the nightstand, eyes on me, while I button down his shirt. "Go to Bellissimo. I want the usual. Layla wants a burger with grilled chicken and vegetables." He looks away when I cover my boobs, wriggling my butt into a pair of sweatpants. What a fashionable composition: sweatpants and a smart shirt that falls down to my mid-thighs. "Then pay him enough to do it."

I gather my hair into something that's supposed to resemble a bun and tangle a bobble around the masterpiece, ready in under three minutes to go downstairs and wait for food.

"Stella Meridionali?" I wrinkle my nose, glaring at my new passport.

Dante handed it over after I went through the passport control. The airport representative, probably bribed, led us through *Employees Only* corridors into a small room reserved for passengers departing on board private aircraft.

"Meridionali..." I test the word. "Sounds Italian. Change of plans?" My voice fills with excitement. Italy is warm in February compared to Russia. "Rome? Milan?"

Dante wraps his arm around me, and with his other hand, he pulls out a small manilla envelope from the inside pocket of his jacket. "It's not Italian, Star. It's Latin. Unfortunately, no change in plans. You're still going to Moscow. New York first, though. Julij will join you there."

"Latin? Why Latin?" I rest my forehead against his torso.

"That's a secret. Stop asking questions."

"We're scheduled to take off in fifteen minutes," a stewardess says from the other side of the room. "We should board the plane now."

"They won't leave without me," I mutter.

Dante pushes me away enough to get a look at my childish pout. "No, but they'll have to wait for the next takeoff window, and you only have forty minutes in New York to get through security and on board the next plane."

I cling to him once more. "I'll fly tomorrow."

"Do not do this, baby." He presses his cheek to my temple. "You think I want you to go? I don't, but more than that, I don't want you to get hurt."

I hate it when he's right. Leaving Chicago to hide in Moscow is the smartest choice. Without me around, Dante will focus his whole energy on closing the hit.

I clench my teeth, taking a rickety step back, and the cloud of anxiety that's accompanied me since Morte's visit to the hospital in Dallas grows in strength, moving with me. An unwavering, irritating companion. My eyes pool with tears as I sniffle pathetically, staring into Dante's eyes—as sad as when I aimed the gun at his heart.

He cups my face, bending down to catch my lips in his, the kiss full of contradicting emotions we both can't shake. "I don't want to see your tears. You need to be strong for me, and you need to miss me like crazy. Understood?"

I nod but don't dare speak, too worried that my vocal cords will break the dam, giving my tears a free pass.

"Good girl. Call me when you land." He pecks my forehead. "I love you, Star."

With that, he turns on his heel and leaves, not daring to look over his shoulder. A single tear trails down my cheek, but I wipe it off with my sleeve, annoyed that it had the nerve to escape its confinement.

I fling my purse over my shoulder, drape my coat over my arm, and follow the flight attendant out of the building, leaving Chicago, Dante, and everything familiar behind.

All I hope is that I'll live long enough to come back.

CHAPTER TWENTY

Dante

I swear under my breath, glance at my watch for the hundredth time, and redial Layla's number.

It's Layla. Try again soon, but don't leave a message. I won't listen.

The flight schedule on Moscow's airport website claims that the plane with Julij, Anatolij, and Layla on board landed twenty-five minutes ago, but none of them have switched their phones on yet. Considering Anatolij's position in Russia, the passport control should've taken all but ten minutes.

It's Layla. Try again soon, but don't leave a message. I won't listen.

"Stop it. She'll call when she can," Spades snaps from where he leans against the bar in my living room, a glass of water in hand. "Your hands are shaking as if you've been drinking for a week."

"She landed half an hour ago."

He shakes his head, treating the ceiling with a surly glance as if begging God for patience, then pushes away from the bar to cross the room. "She'll call. Don't fucking panic. We have a lot to discuss. Nate will be here with Cai and Jackson in a minute. Sending Layla away was supposed to help you focus on closing the hit, but you still got hay here." He taps the back of my head with his finger.

"Once I know she's there, and okay, I'll focus."

"Yeah, right. I'm not saying sending her to Moscow was a bad idea, but there's no way you'll focus when she gets there. You won't fucking focus until Julij flies back." He crosses his arms over his chest, a vein throbbing at his temple. "He *won't* touch her."

"I know he won't."

If he did, he'd die a slow, painful death, and he's well aware of that fact.

It's Layla. Try again soon, but don't leave a message. I won't listen.

Layla's absence is a challenge to my overworked psyche. The excess of problems I pushed into the background while she was by my side knocked me off my feet when she boarded the plane. Everything I tried to keep in check resurfaced to keep my head occupied. The hit, Anatolij, Julij's feelings, Chief Jeremy Smith, screaming his head off over the phone every time I report another dead hitman, Morte, Johnny, the business that still operates despite the undeniable disorder. It's tiring. That's without adding worrying about Layla to the mix.

While she's within my reach, I control the anxiety residing in me since I learned about the bounty on her head, but now that she's gone, I'm a ticking bomb. There's a lot to do, but in the disarray of my own thoughts, I can't find a direction; I'm blind to a way out of the mayhem. I have a hard time prioritizing the tasks. What do I do first? Where do I go? Who do I kill, and who do I bribe?

I try to outsmart Morte, not worry about Layla, trust Anatolij that he knows what he's doing hiding her in Moscow, and at the same time, I try to believe that she's safer away from me.

I shake my head to refocus on the matter, taking a cigarette packet from my pocket. Spades is right. My hands shake as if AA meetings are in my weekly schedule.

"So? What are we doing? Looking for Morte? Paying the big players a visit? Countering the bounty? What's the plan?"

Countering the bounty by ordering a hit on Morte did cross my mind. Five million could tempt many people, but few would take the risk. A bird in the hand is worth two in the bushes. Layla's an easy target. The probability of killing her versus Morte is fifty to one. Ninety percent of killers will prefer to look for my girl than chase the ghost that Morte is—always one step ahead.

Under normal circumstances, i.e., if I were a random guy trying to find and kill the fucker, it'd be mission impossible. Good thing I'm not a random guy. Morte and I fell from the same apple tree. We both worked under Dino. We were both mentored by Frank. We spent six years side by side. If anyone can kill the son-of-a-bitch, it's me.

"We come at it from all sides," I say. "Cover all the bases. Jackson's looking for Morte. Until he finds him, we'll be paying off everyone willing to be paid off and disposing of those who aren't. Security stays in place. I didn't make Layla's relocation such a fucking secret for no reason. The longer the information stays buried, the better."

"You want to kill Morte? That's a shitty plan. It'll work, sure. No money equals no takers, but it'll take weeks, if not months, before the news reaches all the daredevils. I'm sure you don't plan to keep Layla away that long."

True. Good thing killing the bastard is only a plan B in case plan A: forcing him to call off the hit fails.

"What if Morte has a second-in-command?"

"You're overthinking this." I butt the cigarette in the sink and turn to grab a bottle of water from the fridge.

I haven't poured anything alcoholic down my throat for over three weeks. From the moment I found out about the hit, I refused to numb my mind with booze. Layla's safety depends on my ability to think straight.

"Frank hired Morte because he's the best., but he also has a major flaw. He's arrogant. He thinks he's invincible."

The alarm clicks once, announcing the arrival of someone who knows the code to disarm it. A clatter of a few pairs of elegant shoes resonates in the corridor, and a moment later, Nate, Cai, and Jackson appear in the doorway.

"Where's Rookie?"

"He'll be here in fifteen minutes. He's running late coming back from Milwaukee. He doesn't want Jane here when it gets too hot, so he took her to stay with his parents."

"It's not her they're after, am I right?" Jackson smirks, elbowing Nate.

It earns him a whack to the back of the head.

"Better safe than sorry, jackass. I packed Bianca and shipped her off to my mother's house last night. Luna flew out to see her brother. We've got a shitload to do. It'll be better if the girls aren't here for it. They won't get in the way, and we won't worry."

I press the phone to my ear again, ignoring Spades, who nudges Cai, pointing his chin at me.

"You won't, but he's nowhere near done overreacting."

"Hey," Layla answers softly

"Finally." I exhale, no longer brimming with tension, when I step out of the kitchen onto the terrace, sliding the door shut behind me. "You landed forty-five minutes ago, Star. What took so long? How was the flight?"

"It was okay," she sniffs. "I slept through most of it."

My palms ball into fists on their own accord. It's a fucking reflex by now. A tic. My tell of sorts. I hang my head low because thousands of miles away, on the back seat of some Russian car, Layla's plastering her tear-stained cheek to the window. The image of her sad face flashing in my head feels like a punch to the gut. "You promised not to cry."

"I know, I'm sorry. Somehow, it just sunk in that I'm alone, and you're so far away."

I still can't believe I dared to entrust the safety of everything I hold dear to a man I know so fucking little about.

Well, I know he'll put his life on the line to protect her, and that's all I can ask for in the grand scheme of things.

"It won't take long, Star."

A cloud of smoke surrounds me when I light another cigarette, giving her a moment to pull herself together. As always, she doesn't fail me, rising above her anxiety.

"The security guy was an ass. He didn't speak English, so I'm not sure what the problem was, but Anatolij took care of it. It took a while, though. Do you know how cold it is here? It's *eight* degrees outside! *Eight*! My breath freezes as it comes out of my lips."

I chuckle at her irritated tone. She's okay. She's got this, and she's going to be just fine. Not that I have any reason to think otherwise, but I can't help the protectiveness squeezing my heart as if it's a sponge. God, I'm so fucking whipped.

"You'll find another manilla envelope in your bag. A bank card is in there, the pin number saved in your phone under your new name. I opened a Swiss account for you. There's more than enough to pay for a few furs so you can stay nice and warm."

"You said I won't be here too long. I think I'll manage for now without wearing dead animals."

"You won't stay there any longer than necessary. Tell Julij to call me when he has a moment."

"I love you," she says, and the line goes dead.

I shove the phone into my pocket, throwing the cigarette butt over the railing.

Time to face the fucking music...

I have no sense of right and wrong left in me.

CHAPTER TWENTY-ONE

Layla

Five days.

It feels like I've been in Moscow for five weeks, but no. Just five long days. Other than being thousands of miles away from Dante and missing him like crazy, I have no reason to complain. Anatolij is a true gentleman. The kind most women consider extinct. Impeccable, aristocratic manners,

IQ north of one-fifty for sure, and one of the most pleasant-to-talk-to people I've ever encountered.

We only spend time together in the evenings because, during the day, Anatolij is either away or locked in his office on the third floor, nearby my bedroom. Still, even those few hours every evening are enough for me to like him.

He's nothing like his brother, Nikolaj. No, Anatolij is polite, well-organized, and infernally intelligent. There isn't a topic he can't hold a conversation on. His intelligence doesn't impress me half as much as his impeccable manners.

When we arrived in Moscow, he took the time to show me around the castle and personally accommodated me in a large bedroom overlooking the rose garden. He said it looks beautiful when the flowers are in full bloom, but I enjoy how it looks covered in snow too.

The first evening when we sat down to dinner, he gathered his men, ordering them to speak English in front of me or remain silent if they couldn't. My protests were dismissed. Anatolij wants me to feel comfortable in his home. And I do. All it took were a few hours spent alone with him after Julij called it a day, heading off to bed early on the first night. Now, I feel almost right at home.

Nikolaj and Anatolij are like two ends of a spectrum. One was ostentatious, obnoxious, and loud, while the other is an oasis of calmness. It's all the more surprising because Anatolij is only thirty-eight. I would've considered a man his age to be more like Dante—eager, impatient, always rushing, but Anatolij has all the time in the world.

A soft knock on the bedroom door halts my attempt to zip-up a white halter dress. There was no reason to pack a dress for freezing-cold Moscow, but I did, just in case.

What a great choice that was...

I've been gifted a free-access pass to my dream come true. The last thing I expected to find in the basement of Anatolij's fourteen-century castle is a ballroom, but it's there. Modernized like the rest of the imposing structure, and mine to use when I please. I plan on spending a couple of hours down there every morning to help the time pass quicker.

"Come in." I stand in front of a long mirror, twisting my arm back to reach the zipper.

Julij enters the room in a white shirt, with two buttons popped at the top. It goes well with his baby-blue jacket and beige trousers. "I need to go. My flight leaves in two hours."

I've dreaded this moment since we landed. Despite feeling welcome here, unease jabs my mind at the prospect of being left here alone, without Julij. He wants to go back to Chicago, adamant that Dante needs his help, but I'm not dumb. I know the unsaid truth. Dante doesn't want Julij here alone with me.

He crosses the room and grips my arm to twirl me around. "I'm not thrilled about leaving you here alone with Anatolij." His fingertips brush against the skin on my lower back when he reaches for the zipper. "Don't be naïve, Layla. You're a guest here, and you're safe but don't get too close to anyone."

He sounds like Frank and Dante.

They both accused me of naivety on more than one occasion. Now, Julij joins the pack. His condescending tone drives me mad. If only he knew how hard I try to draw a line that separates Layla, who thought of herself as nothing more than Frank Harston's daughter, from Layla, who realized there *is* more.

"Don't beat around the bush, Julij. If you want to say something, say it. What have I done wrong this time?"

He slides his calloused hands down my arms, slowly, gently, before he cuffs me half an inch above my elbows and tugs, pulling me in, my back to his chest, our eyes locked in the mirror. "Nothing, sugar. You did nothing wrong, but I am worried about you being here alone."

He wraps one arm over my chest, eyes scrutinizing our reflection as if memorizing how we look together. It's a pretty picture, a striking contrast of complexion, height, and hair color. Julij can't deny his heritage. There's not one particularly noticeable feature that betrays his heritage, but high cheekbones, a heavy brow ridge, and a pointy chin clue you into his Slavic descent. Especially when coupled with his height and slim but broad build.

"You're beautiful, you know that sugar?" he whispers. His warm breath fans my neck, introducing a wave of goosebumps. "I remember the first time I saw you in Dubai. You wore a see-through beach dress over a yellow bikini."

The memory brings a smile to my face despite Julij's awful attitude at first. I remember the first day in Dubai as if it was yesterday. Maybe because I was in pain throughout the evening. We arrived early in the morning, and once the sun came out, I resigned myself to a lounger by the pool. Five hours later, I woke up from an unintentional nap... my back burned bright red by then. I considered my sunbathing time to be over at that point.

Nikolaj arrived with his family later in the afternoon, and Julij's mother healed my sunburn with two tubs of natural yogurt. The idea seemed abstract at the time, but it worked. Two days later, I was sunbathing again, covered in SPF30.

"I've liked you since the moment you introduced yourself. I didn't like feeling that way. I thought I was too young to want more than sex from a girl, but I couldn't shake those feelings, and—"

"And you acted like an ass for two weeks," I cut in, uncomfortable with where this conversation is heading.

The fondness in Julij's voice and how he holds me tightly in his arms is too intimate. Too close. There's too much awe in his eyes and in the tone of his voice. I hope the forced smile masks my embarrassment well when I wriggle out of Julij's embrace.

His shoulders sag, but he shifts his weight from one foot to another, standing tall again. "You spend a lot of time with Anatolij, Layla. Don't get me wrong, there's nothing wrong with that. I'm glad you two get along. Just don't let him pull the wool over your eyes. I'm pretty sure he wants to sleep with you."

"Excuse me?"

I've spent every evening with Anatolij, engrossed in a polite conversation. He never once paid me a compliment or looked at me suggestively. He's hospitable and well-behaved. Nothing more. Anatolij or the fact we get along isn't the problem. Julij's vivid imagination and jealousy are.

What I pegged for an innocent crush evolved into unwanted feelings. I pray he'll stop acting so infatuated in front of Dante, or else our friendship, if I can still call it that, won't last another week.

"How could you think I'd cheat on Dante?" I fume, the unspoken accusation like a slap across my face. "You're ridiculous. Where is this even coming from? I know I'm not ugly, and you could say I'm nice sometimes, although that'd be slander, but not every guy is out to sleep with me!"

Julij squeezes the bridge of his nose, inhaling deeply. "I didn't say you'd do it. I said he'd do you if he got the chance."

"No! No, he wouldn't. You would. That's why you see a rival in everyone. News flash," I point to the ring on my finger,

"I'm engaged! Neither you nor anyone other than Dante will ever touch me."

Julij grinds his teeth, pinning me down with his freezing-blue stare. "He's all you know. He's the first man in your life, Layla, but he doesn't have to be the last. You've no idea if he's the one because—"

"You're playing with fire, Julij, and you will get burned."

"Too little too late for that." He turns on his heel but turns back halfway to the door, reaching for my hand. His hot lips touch my forehead, and a tight embrace follows. "Stay safe, sugar. It'll all be over soon."

Then, he leaves, and my anger leaves too. I can't stay mad at him for long. The heart doesn't choose… it feels. Julij's heart feels what it never should. Not for me.

My heart feels for Dante more than it can handle. A long list of all the reasons why I shouldn't have let myself fall in love with him didn't mean a thing almost from the very start. My heart knew better.

Who am I to hold Julij's feelings against him? There's not much he can do about them.

I finish getting ready, pull my hair up in a ponytail and leave the room. Julij's voice echoes through the long, empty corridors as I descend the stairs. My name on his lips stops me dead in my tracks. I shouldn't, but I hide around the corner. They stand in the hallway outside the dining room, Julij with a travel bag in hand, Anatolij with the morning paper by his side, an impassive look on his face.

"You promised to keep Layla safe, Anatolij. While I'm grateful, I'm not blind. Keeping her safe is all I want you to do. I'd rather you didn't spend time with her."

God, I want to punch him right in the gut. He's crossing a line he'll regret crossing once Dante finds out about this.

Anatolij's expression morphs from unreadable to irritated. "Are you suggesting what I think you are, Julij? I sincerely hope not."

They fall silent, staring each other down. I glance around, checking for Anatolij's men wandering the castle. I should've retreated upstairs instead of eavesdropping, but my legs are glued to the spot they occupy.

"You're my nephew," Anatolij says slowly. "But not even that gives you the right to voice absurd accusations. I know you love her, but—"

"This isn't about me," Julij growls, gripping the handle of his suitcase harder. "Dante trusted my judgment when he agreed to send Layla here. It wasn't a decision he took lightly, so if anything happens to her while she's under your protection, it will be on my head."

"Don't flatter yourself. You suggesting my home as a safe place for Layla was *not* why he agreed. He's not one to trust anyone's judgment but his. I assure you there's a very good reason why Layla is here of all places."

Julij has no chance of retaliating. The front door opens before them, and Lew enters. Great timing. His arrival gives me the perfect opportunity to emerge from my hiding spot.

The following day, I'm downstairs for breakfast an hour earlier than usual. Anatolij's already there, dressed as if he's due to make an appearance at the Oscars. Just like Dante, he favors his suits. While Dante alternated between cobalt blue, black and gray, Anatolij is always in black.

"Good morning." He peers up from above the morning newspaper. "I'm glad you're here. I want to talk to you." He falls silent, one eyebrow slightly raised as he watches me take a seat on the opposite side of the long table, able to fit twelve people. "Are you feeling okay?"

As okay as one can be given my situation, I guess. "Yes, I'm fine." I point to my face and red, puffy eyes. "Lack of sleep. I woke up a few times hearing someone outside my door. I struggle to fall back asleep once I wake up."

I swear, at one point during the night, someone stood in the doorway when I opened my eyes and rolled over. The creepy silhouette disappeared when I blinked, though.

"That's my fault. The door on the other side of the corridor hides a library. I couldn't sleep, so I went over there to read."

"A library?" That knowledge would've come in handy while I've been bored out of my mind for six days. There's only so much TV a girl can watch. "You didn't mention it when you showed me around the first day."

"I didn't peg you for a bookworm. All the bookcases on the left wall house English books. Feel free to read whatever and whenever you want."

"Thank you. There's not much to do around here. Especially in this weather. Any distraction is worth its weight in gold."

He nods absentmindedly. His eyes bore into mine, but he looks lost in thought while the maid fills his cup with fresh coffee. "I'm hosting a charity event on Saturday," he continues once she leaves the room, presumably to fetch a cup for me. "It's an annual occurrence. I invite influential people and squeeze as much money out of them as possible."

"I'll stay out of the way." I spread honey on a piece of toast. Neither Anatolij nor the cooks asked me what my favorite dishes are, but I'm served something I love every day. It's a silly thing, but I'm warm knowing that Dante took care of the smallest details trying to make sure I'd feel good around here. "I'll take a book and lock myself in the bedroom for the day."

"You misunderstand, Layla. I'm not telling you about the ball, so you'll stay out of the way. I'm telling you because I'd like you to join me. Lew will take you shopping this afternoon. I reserved the best boutique in Moscow for private shopping. No one will disturb you."

A ball sounds much better than a day alone in my bedroom. After a short stroll in the garden with Anatolij last night, I realized that I truly am a princess once he pointed high up to where my bedroom is in the western tower. The castle stands on a hill, surrounded by miles of woodland as if conjured from a children's storybook.

Despite the imposing, intimidating structure, it's perfect, with no sign of wear on the stone walls. I couldn't help but imagine unicorns galloping along the tree lines in the distance because, why not? If castles with high towers, kill orders, and men like Dante are real, unicorns might as well be too.

As enticing as the idea of dancing the night away in a shimmery ballgown might be, I'm in Russia for an entirely different reason than entertainment.

"You do remember that thanks to my Dad, there's a bounty on my head, right? With all the safety measures already in place, I don't think attending a ball is a good idea.

"No one can lift their finger around here without my consent. You're safe, Layla. You have my word."

"I appreciate the offer, really, but I'm sure Dante won't agree. Safety first."

A shadow of a smile crosses Anatolij's handsome face. "I wouldn't extend an invitation if I hadn't cleared it with your fiancé first. Dante's aware of the ball. He approved all the security measures I put in place. The choice is yours alone."

Oh. Isn't this an unexpected turn of events? Dante must trust Anatolij more than I anticipated if he agreed. The ball sounds great, and shopping, or rather the possibility of leaving the castle tempts me like the snake tempted Eve.

"Will there be dancing?"

Crinkles surround Anatolij's eyes when he smiles, rising to his feet. "The theme is The Great Gatsby. Choose something, as you Americans say, *bling-bling*."

I tilt my head to the side to look him over. "You do have something in common, you know?"

"Me and Gatsby?"

"No. You and Leonardo. Your hair is just too dark."

With another dazzling smile, he bows slightly and leaves me alone to finish breakfast.

CHAPTER TWENTY-TWO

Dante

"Weapons?" A bald bodyguard stands in front of a red curtain on the top floor of *Grande*—a members-only strip club in the heart of Las Vegas.

Spades reaches into the holster, placing his gun on a black, high table in the corner. Julij does the same, and I put my gold revolver over there too. I don't leave the house without it, just in case, by a miraculous coincidence, I'll bump into Morte.

This isn't the first time we've been asked to leave our guns behind. For the past two weeks, since Layla left Chicago, I've visited major bosses all over the states, paying them off in return for protection. Most don't care about money. Some already ordered their people not to touch the order. Others want a few million before calling off their hunters.

We landed in Vegas a few hours ago. With time to kill, Spades thought it wise to hit the casinos. Precisely one hour later, he left the Bellagio twenty grand lighter but smiling, nonetheless. The meeting with Mauricio DelVannie is scheduled for ten p.m. He's one of the oldest bosses in the States, one of the last native Italians.

In theory, he should respect the old rules, but in practice, he has dealt with Frank and Nikolaj for the past five years. There's no telling how deep their alliance reached.

Our paths never crossed until tonight. I have no idea what to expect. Rumor has it that Mauricio is a no-bullshit, no-mercy kind of guy, which doesn't bode well for me. I have a gut feeling I'm wasting time here because he won't help. What's more, I'm ready for a bloody finale to the evening.

The storm raging inside every cell in my body won't help me convince Mauricio to cooperate. The longer Layla's away, the shakier my self-control. I'm supposed to focus on the job, but instead, I think about her more. There's no winning here. I can't stop worrying, no matter where she is.

When she was in Chicago, I worried someone would kill her. Now when she's away, in safe hands, I can't find peace because she's not with me. As if that's not enough to drive me nuts, I'm jittery like a sinner on judgment day because *tonight* is the Charity Ball Anatolij hosts every year.

I've been climbing the fucking walls thinking about her out in the open, mingling with people I don't know, but...back in Moscow, no one can hurt a fly without Anatolij's permission. I trust his judgment. Still, I'd rather she'd sit this out, locked in her room, invisible.

The one comforting piece of information came from Julij—no one knows Layla in Russia. No one knows me either. I only work with the Dutch and the Hungarians, but three million dollars is a hefty sum for a target as easy as my star. Knowing that she'll be there, dressed to impress, dancing with other men doesn't help the situation one fucking bit. She's been gone for two weeks. I've not kissed, held, or felt her in two weeks, and it's starting to weigh me down.

The henchman pulls the red curtain aside to reveal a spacious room bathed in a similar, dimmed lighting arrangement. Clouds of smoke hang over leather seats that face a row of poles on a raised stage. We step inside, my eyes darting left and right, scanning the room as I map the place out, sketching a possible escape route in case things get too hot. Young, naked girls writhe around poles, flashing middle-aged men with fake boobs. A bar is tucked away at the back, the room full of waitresses wearing nothing but bowties as they balance drinks on silver trays.

Julij pokes me with his elbow, pointing to the left, behind the dance floor. Thick, black, floor-length curtains hide, as I can easily guess, private rooms for those wanting to fuck either one of the pole dancers. A brothel under the banner of a strip club is standard in Vegas and any other major city.

"This way," the henchman says, leading us to the nearest booth occupied by three men.

Despite never meeting Mauricio in person, I have no trouble guessing who the boss is. He resembles mafia men from Prohibition times—white suit, dark shades, a cigar in hand. Resting one elbow on his knee, he leans toward the stage, almost drooling at the sight of naked ass. Signet rings mark his fingers, and a large cross with diamonds hangs from a thick chain around his neck. Oh… and let's not forget the hat. White with a black band.

Now, *he* does look like Al Capone. When compared to Mauricio, Nikolaj was merely a cheap tribute act.

"Dante Carrow," Mauricio says, the high-pitched voice out of place on a man of his overweight size. He shakes my hand, squeezing hard to establish seniority. Most bosses take time to introduce their main entourage, but Mauricio scrams his and my people away. They move to a nearby table, offering us a false sense of privacy. "What's your poison? Cognac? Whiskey? Bourbon?" He summons a waitress with a snap of his fingers.

The girl, her boobs bigger than my head, leans over the table, holding out a tray. I snatch a glass of bourbon and accept a cigar from Mauricio. Etiquette requires fifteen minutes of vague conversation before we get to business, so I start with the safest topic: I praise the club.

I don't get to finish the sentence before he cuts me off.

"How about we skip the pleasantries, Dante? I know why you're here. I know nobody has refused yet, and I know how much you offer."

My phone vibrates in my pocket, but I can't check who's trying to reach me. It would show a lack of respect, erasing the small chance I have to win Mauricio over, and my chance would go down the drain. "The price is negotiable."

"You're going about this all wrong. Instead of paying for protection, pay for murder. You're searching for the promoter yourself, but if you were to order a hit, pay, say, twice as much as Frankie wanted for Layla, you could lead most of the daredevils away from her."

My grip on the glass tightens of its own accord. "It won't work. Layla's the easier target. And Morte is mine."

Mauricio laughs, patting me on the shoulder. "Stop acting like a child. "*Morte is mine,*" he mocks. "What difference does it make who kills him? The main thing is that he'll be dead, right? The order will become insolvent, and you'll be able to bring Layla home."

A cold sweat slips down my spine as I watch Mauricio, searching his eyes for any sign that he knows where she is.

No, no way. That's impossible. Only me, Julij, Spades, and Nate know her exact location.

"No, I don't know where you hid her," he supplies before I can ask. "But I guess there's a reason why you drag this dimwit with you everywhere." He points at Julij and rises to his feet, urging me to follow. He gestures at his people to stay put before he takes me to his office at the back of the club. "Sit down, Dante. Julij's as clueless as his father was. If not for Frank, Nikolaj wouldn't have a thing. All he was good at was piggyback riding. If you don't stop focusing on one thing at a time, you'll share Frank's fate. Julij will take advantage of your inattention. He'll take your partners, your product, and your position." He takes a long puff of the cigar, leaning over the small coffee table between us. "Open your eyes, Dante. You're smart, you've been a part of this life for years, but ever since you met Layla, you make one mistake after another like a novice."

"How do you know so much about me?"

"Who did I work with all those years? Frankie was consumed with envy. He despised who you became because you became *better* than he could ever hope. You surpassed all expectations. Everything you touch turns to gold."

That's plausible. Frank's hatred started before we killed Dino. I didn't notice it then, but I connected the dots years later. Dino died because he trusted me more than he trusted Frankie, who was his second in command. Frank felt threatened. His position in the ranks hung by a thread. Degradation wasn't an option, and that's how the plan of taking over Chicago came to life.

Frankie and I were close back then. He had me wrapped around his finger the same way he had Layla not so long ago. At one point in our lives, we were both manipulated and taught to believe him and *in* him. To follow him blindly. It was his greatest gift: turning people around him into his puppets.

I needed several weeks of separation to emerge out of the haze. I saw through Frank's bullshit once Dino died, and I was locked in my house with nothing but my thoughts keeping me entertained for weeks.

It's a goddamn miracle Layla saw him for who he was when she did.

"Frank's been obsessed with you for six years, plotting elaborate revenge. His business was in decline, and partners started to turn away, but he didn't care. He wanted you. He wanted to leave you with nothing, not even a will to survive, and for that, he was willing to sacrifice his daughter."

"Are you suggesting that I'm following in his footsteps?"

"You're a racehorse in the fog. You're wandering a maze, feeling the walls instead of opening your eyes." He reaches for a bottle of cognac to refill our glasses. "Let me guess. You want to find Morte and force him to retract the hit. You'll wait for a few weeks, maybe months, kill those who don't get the message, and then bring Layla home to live a happily ever after. Am I close?"

I don't answer. I met the guy half an hour ago, and I have no intention of sharing my plan. "Nobody knows where Morte is. My people have been looking for him for a month now. If I can't find him, what makes you think anyone else will? Ordering a hit only conveys the message that I'm out of options and desperate. It'll prompt more killers to act, hoping to force a mistake on me so they can get to *her*."

A sad, pitiful smile crosses his lips. "Stop thinking about Layla for a moment. Stop worrying. I'm more than certain Anatolij will sooner kill half his people than let someone hurt her. He's a damn honorable guy."

I swallow hard, my hands damp. I really do make mistakes worthy of an amateur if Mauricio figured out where she is within half an hour. Julij shouldn't be here. He doesn't mean much in this world yet. There's no reason for his presence. I let him tag along because he helped transport Layla to Moscow. Because he's as determined to ensure her safety as I am.

"Relax. I don't start with the Russians. I have no intention of chasing Layla. Frank hit an all-time low when he ordered the hit. It's something I can't tolerate and would never participate in. I'm just trying to help you see that because of how you look at the case, you miss obvious things."

"Why are you helping me?"

"Let's say I'm getting sentimental in my old age. My grandson was born recently; my wife acts twenty years younger... I heard about the bounty on Layla, and I tried walking in your shoes. You're a clever guy and a great businessman. I regret that our paths didn't cross years ago. Things would look different now."

The short conversation is enough for Mauricio to make it onto the short list of people I respect for the kind of humans they are. If we met all those years ago, working with him would've been a breeze, but this is neither the time nor place to start a new business venture.

First things first.

"Thank you." I rise from the armchair and hold my hand for him to shake. This time, he doesn't squeeze hard—a nonverbal admission that I stand above him in this world.

"Get rid of Julij. Order the hit on Morte and find something to blackmail him with, just in case. And open your eyes," he says again, then embraces me like the authentic Italian he is before we leave his office.

Spades and Julij rise on cue. We pick up our guns before exiting the club, getting into a limousine parked outside. I pull out my phone to check who tried to reach me earlier. Instead of a missed call, there's an unread message from Layla.

I smile under my breath, looking at my star wearing a gold dress straight from the twenties. Feathers are pinned in her hair, and she wears a disarming smile that touches her gray eyes. A short question waits under the photo.

How do I look?

Like everything I need.

I dial the number to hear her voice. Mauricio's right, my ever-growing obsession destroys my ability to notice the big picture. I have to draw a line between us for a while to focus on what matters most right now. I don't think I can do that if we stay in touch.

"You look gorgeous," I say when she answers.

"I like it too. Twenties fashion suits me. I look pretty with feathers in my hair."

"You look pretty with a smile, baby. What time does the party start?"

"Late afternoon. It's only nine a.m. here. I wanted to show you the dress before you fall asleep."

"I'm glad you did. Dance until dawn and get used to it. You'll be on the dance floor all night long at our wedding."

Her light, happy chuckle titillates every nerve-ending in my body. "Can I count on my husband to dance with me too?"

The image of me standing at the altar never crossed my mind until I met Layla. I lived in the moment, not caring about what the future held. Then, Layla made an entrance... I wanted her to be mine right away, and a few weeks later, I wanted her to stay mine.

I don't enjoy dancing, but I'll make an exception for my wife. One dance, or five... maybe a dozen.

"I'll be the first one to dance with you. And the last. And some number in-between." I take a deep breath, convincing myself that we should stop talking for a while for her sake. She occupies my every conscious and unconscious thought, making it damn near impossible to protect her.

"Go on," she urges. "Get it out. What's wrong?"

As always, she senses the change in the atmosphere even though she's five thousand miles away. All it took was my one deep breath to kick-start her sixth sense.

"I won't call you for a few days, Star."

"Why? Did something happen?" A tingle of worry in her voice tenses the muscles on my back.

God, I fucking hate hearing her worried.

Relationships don't work this way, I'm sure. People don't feel the sort of extreme protectiveness I feel toward Layla, or else most men in the world would be certifiably insane. This isn't healthy, but I understand my own psychotic mind. We're both emotionally challenged in different ways.

"Everything's fine, but I need to switch off for a few days. I'll call you when the chaos is more manageable, but if anything happens, if—"

"I know. I'll call you. Do what you have to do. Don't worry about me. Maybe it's unreasonable, but I feel safe here."

She has no idea how desperately I try not to worry for just five fucking minutes. Long enough to catch my breath, to get a break from the overpowering, irrational feelings.

"You *are* safe. Stay close to Anatolij. He won't let a hair fall off your head."

She clicks her tongue. Although I can't see her, I have no trouble imagining what she looks like right now: pouty mouth, eyebrows pulled together, and probably one hand on her hip. Gorgeous. She's so fucking beautiful when she's annoyed.

"Funny you should say that. Julij has a different opinion on the matter."

My eyes narrow at the man in question who sits opposite me, watching Vegas out of the tinted windows. A dreamy, barely-there smile on his face clearly indicates who he's thinking about. Since he came back from Moscow, he acts more infatuated than before. Or maybe he just stopped hiding it. Either way, he's pissing me off.

"And what's that?" I ask.

"I spend a lot of time with Anatolij. Julij seems to think his uncle wants to sleep with me."

I can't help but laugh. God, keeping the truth away from Julij's ears is absolutely killing me. One sentence would dissolve his feelings in the blink of an eye, but I promised Anatolij to keep it a secret until he finds the courage to tell Layla.

"Julij's got a vivid imagination."

At the sound of his name, he looks up. "What?"

"That he does. I have to go. I'll wait for your call. If I can make it that long without talking to you."

The real question is whether I have it in me to stay away from her. "Have fun, baby."

"What was that about? What did she tell you about me?" Julij asks once I cut the call.

"I told you I'll tolerate it that you love her until you cross a line. Tone down with the jealousy, or I'll show you how much a broken jaw hurts."

He folds his arms over his chest, a knowing look on his face. "She told you..."

"You thought she wouldn't? You don't know her very well, do you? She won't risk jeopardizing the little trust I put in her so far."

Layla's been tiptoeing around me since I arrived in Texas. Always nervous about making one false move. She's slowly regaining her confidence, though. I can't wait to have the girl I fell in love with back, showing off her true colors.

"It's not about jealousy. It's about safety," Julij clips, seemingly pissed off that Layla hadn't kept their conversation private. "She's alone there. I just want her to be careful but don't twist it to your preference. She's not mine. I don't fucking care who she sleeps with."

Spades has no time to react.

Julij has no time to see my outrage coming.

It happens in a flash.

I lunge forward, grab him by the collar of his immaculate blue shirt, and smack his head against the window. "Layla's *mine*. She only sleeps with me."

I don't have to throw it out there, but in a way, I'm marking my territory. I've warned Julij not once and not twice. He should've listened instead of disrespecting my girl. There's no way in heaven or hell I'll let anyone say or suggest anything derogatory about her.

"That's strike one, Julij," Spades clips behind my back. "Do yourself a favor and keep your big mouth shut."

I feel his hand on my arm, pulling me back, and reluctantly let go of a wide-eyed Julij, who adjusts his shirt, eyes shooting daggers my way. This probably isn't how he imagined our business partnership. To date, all he gets out of our arrangement is a kicking. His patience is probably wearing thin by now. Too bad for him; the cards are in my hand. All he can do is nod along.

"It was your idea to send her over there. You supposedly trust Anatolij, and now you say he'd hurt her? Bullshit. You're in love, you're jealous, and you're getting on my nerves." I growl, staring him down, waiting for one false move, one more foul word out of his mouth.

It'd justify manslaughter.

At least in my eyes, it would. I'm on the verge of overloading. Julij might not want to give me a reason to use him as an outlet for my emotions. There's one thing that'd erase his feelings in a blink of an eye. One piece of information that'd turn his world upside down. He'd stop dreaming about Layla, fast.

I'm running out of reasons not to tell him. I want to see his face when he finds out. I want to see the sliver of hope he has for a relationship with my girl die a tragic death, but I *can't* tell him. Not yet. Not while Layla remains oblivious.

Fifteen minutes later, without another shitstorm, we arrive at the hotel. Julij, slightly pissed off and still sulking, storms toward the elevators, leaving me in the lobby with Spades.

"Why do you put up with it? You don't need him, Dante. You don't need Nikolaj's affiliates. We've been doing fine by ourselves. Cut him loose."

Yes, we have been doing fine. We sure don't need Julij, but in the face of the newly discovered information, I know he'll be a part of my life forever, no matter how I feel about it.

"He's not going anywhere. Keeping him close means turning a decent profit. How's Jackson doing with Morte?"

"No news yet." He slips a hundred in the waiter's pocket, earning us a far-removed table where a *reserved* plaque sits in the middle but is promptly taken away. "He'll find him. He just needs time, Dante."

"Yeah, I know."

Mauricio's words bounce around my head as I skim over the menu. *Find something to blackmail him with."* Knowing Morte's way of thinking and the effort he put into being untouchable, I didn't think twice about the reference to Sandra he slipped into our chat over the phone.

Maybe I should've.

She's the only woman he ever loved, the only one to break his heart. He lost a piece of his fucking soul when she left, which makes me wonder... Layla stabbed me in the back, but I forgave her. Even if I left her alone, finding out a few years later that she's in danger, I wouldn't turn a blind eye. Feelings don't go away. True love lingers at the back of our minds, hearts, and souls, numbed, suppressed, but always there, a bitter-sweet aftertaste of better times.

"Change of plans," I tell Spades, pulling my phone out of my pocket. "Forget Morte. We're looking for Sandra now."

"Sandra?"

"She's to Morte what Layla is to me."

CHAPTER TWENTY-THREE

Layla

"I'm sorry I'm late. Dante called." I join Anatolij in the dining room for breakfast.

"You're not at school, Layla. No need to apologize. Is everything alright?"

Who knows? Dante sure didn't sound alright...

As if it's not hard enough to be kept away from home, now I won't even hear his voice for God knows for how long. Anatolij's castle feels more like a prison every day. Even the ballet sessions no longer lift my mood. The weather outside the window doesn't help; a cold, snowy, beautiful picture keeps me inside because a short walk is enough to give me frostbite.

Last night, a raging blizzard kept me awake until the early hours. The wind played a haunting melody, slamming against the old, wooden windows as it raged outside while I lay in bed, watching the snow swirl in the air. Lack of sleep isn't helping me look at the bright side of things. Whatever that might be.

"I don't know... Dante doesn't tell me what he's up to, but something must be wrong because he called to say he won't be in touch for a few days."

"I'm sure it's nothing he can't take care of. Julij says Dante's clever, perceptive, and hell-bent on closing the hit to keep you safe. They both are."

"That makes one thing Julij's right about," I clip, the words bitter on my tongue.

Our recent conversation, the nerve of him implying what he did, boils my blood again. I've watched Anatolij closely since Julij left but found no proof to confirm Julij's words. Not one sentence or look I could fault him with. If anything, he grows on me day by day. The way he treats me has no sexual context, no lustful vibe. If anything, he acts paternal, like I'm a child that needs care, and Anatolij decided that he's equipped for the task.

"I sense annoyance," Anatolij drawls in his thick, colorful accent. "What did my nephew do to upset you?"

Regardless of how comfortable I feel around him, I won't explain that Julij voiced his absurd accusations not just to him but to me too. Under a layer of Anatolij's politeness and good manners hides an unforgiving, ruthless man whose patience I won't dare test.

"It doesn't matter. All that does is what Dante thinks."

"And what does he think?"

"That I'm safe with you."

The corners of his mouth curl. "As I said, he's clever."

That he is. Among an abundance of other things.

"I'm afraid you'll have no choice but to endure hours of listening to conversations held in Russian tonight. Don't worry, most of my guests speak perfect English. I'm sure you'll find a common topic with some of them."

The housekeeper enters the dining room with a pot of hot coffee. This time, she approaches me first. Anatolij's home closely resembles a soap opera set. The maids wear matching gray dresses with white aprons tied around their waists. Every single one is blonde and wears her hair in a granny bun. Security circles the perimeter, armed with long guns. Bouquets of fresh flowers are delivered weekly, and despite many rooms and corridors, the castle is always spotless.

"I took time to learn a few words," I say. The aroma of bitter coffee hits the back of my nose while the maid fills my cup slowly. "I won't be able to hold a conversation, but when you mentioned the ball, I thought it'd be nice if I could at least say, *zdravstvuyte, menya zovut Layla*, and *spasibo*."

Anatolij opens his mouth, but before any words leave his lips, peacefulness of the castle is shattered by gunfire. Blood drains from my face faster than Anatolij draws his gun from the holster by his belt. He's up on his feet, ready and focused within a second.

The maid almost jumps out of her shoes, spilling whatever was left in the coffee pot on my thighs. With a squeal and a strand of what must be apologies in Russian, she tugs my arm, eyes wide. Muffled screams reach our ears, cutting through the air, mixing with the sound of my pounding heart and the maid's pleas. Blood whooshes in my ears.

"Get down," Anatolij orders.

As if on autopilot, I slide under the table when he turns his back to us, not a trace of nerves in his posture. His cold-blooded focus fails to eradicate the fear spreading through my mind like a drop of ink in a bowl of water. Pulse throbs in my dry throat. Adrenaline temporarily numbs the burning skin of my thighs. Ten trembling fingers dig into my arm when the maid ducks under the table. I'm not sure if she wants to protect me or hide behind me. Either way, the castle is once again ominously still. Silence falls upon us. The only sound in the room comes from a large, old clock as it counts every nerve-wracking second.

Thirty-seven pass before footsteps echo in the corridor. The whole building has incredible acoustics. I've listened to Anatolij stroll down the castle's halls for two weeks, so I know it is him approaching the living room. His pace is off, though, not the unrushed pace he got me used to. More of an angry, heavy walk, but unmistakable, nonetheless. He enters the dining room, rounds the table, and crouches beside me and the maid who's still bruising my skin with her bony fingers and me.

"I'm sorry, Layla." He holds out his hand for me. "False alarm. One of my people didn't close the basement door properly. The soundproofing didn't work. There's a shooting range downstairs, next door to the ballroom."

A library I am yet to visit, a ballroom large enough for five-hundred guests, and now a shooting range. What else is hidden behind the many closed doors in this place?

"You didn't mention the shooting range." I grimace, scrambling out from under the table. Anesthesia in the form of adrenaline fades away, leaving my skin burning like hell.

Anatolij follows my line of sight to my soaked jeans. "You should take them off, Layla. Now. The sooner we apply a cool compress to the burns, the smaller the damage."

I shimmy out of the jeans, taking care of keeping my panties in place. Pain is stronger than shame, but I don't want to flash Anatolij by accident.

The maid rushes out of the room and comes back ten seconds later with a bowl of water and a towel. My cheeks warm up once I stand there, in just my t-shirt and a pair of black panties. Thank God I didn't opt-in for lace today.

"Sit." Anatolij gestures to the chair, wetting the towel. He kneels before me, his face five inches away from my panties, as he inspects the burns. "I can't see blisters. It will hurt for a while, but it will heal without scarring. A cold bath should help with the pain." He presses the make-shift cold compress to my thighs before meeting my gaze. "Can I carry you upstairs?"

"It's okay. I can walk."

"Yes, you can, but I doubt you want half of my people to see more of you than absolutely necessary."

"Good point."

He slides one arm under my knees, snakes the other around my back, and lifts me up with effortless ease. The maid covers my legs with a dry towel, tucking it in wherever possible so it won't slip off at the least convenient moment.

Dante would burst into flames if he walked in here right now. Despite showing no signs of jealousy toward Anatolij, his territoriality would surely rear its head. I try to ignore Anatolij's people gawking at us on our way upstairs. Thankfully, despite the raised eyebrows, no one dares to comment.

"I'm sorry my people scared you," Anatolij says, climbing the third flight of stairs.

"You'd think I'd be used to gunshots by now. I guess I was for a while, but then the shots no longer meant a hole in a paper target."

Even covered with the towel, my cheeks burn, matching the temperature of my thighs when Anatolij sits me on the bed in my room.

"You should take this off," he points at my jumper. "I'll get the bath ready."

This time, I don't hesitate before yanking the sweater off over my head. A black Cami top underneath keeps my modesty somehow intact. If it was Dante trying to submerge me in a cold bathtub, I'd argue until I'd turn blue in the face. I don't dare argue with Anatolij. The aura of authority surrounding him doesn't differ much from what Dante emanates, but it is different somehow. I nod along to everything he says.

"Let's get it over with," I mutter, crossing the room.

Anatolij holds my hand until I sit in the cool water, legs straight, hands on the edge of the tub. My breaths come in sharp gasps, goosebumps dot every inch of my skin, and my eyes fall shut, while I imagine that the water's not cold at all. Not that it's working. My body knows better.

"I'm fine," I assure when a worried look taints Anatolij's aristocratic features. "Too bad I won't dance tonight."

"Why do you think I told you to get in the tub? You'll dance. The maid will bring the first aid kit soon. Stay in the bath for ten minutes, then apply the cream." Two vertical wrinkles in his forehead deepen as he rises to his feet. "I must call Dante."

"Why? He doesn't have to know. He's got a lot on his mind, and you said I won't have a scar."

"I promised to call if anything happens. Something did."

"I think he meant something more important than a first-degree burn of..." my hand hovers over the burn to measure the extent of the damage, "...about eight percent of my body. If Dante decided he needs space, it means he's trying to focus. Please don't bother him. I don't want him to beat himself up later that he didn't do enough."

A shadow crosses Anatolij's face, and a slow glow of anger works through his body, tightening the muscles in his jaw. "You don't believe he'll close the hit?"

"I believe he'll stop at nothing, but... I don't expect a happy ending. He's just one man, Anatolij. One man against, God only knows how many. He can't win."

Mafia is no place for sentiments. Dante won't bribe everyone. My father orchestrated the hit, and if he put half the effort and brains into it as he put into manipulating me through the years, there's no way I'll come out alive. Frank was meticulous, always covered all bases, and prepared for a sudden wind change. The bounty on my head is plan B, and Frank's *B* plans never failed.

Anatolij crouches beside me again, his hands on the tub's edge. He looks like a man torn between right and wrong when he stares me down with light-gray eyes. I can't get over how different he is from Nikolaj. No common features, nothing that'd portray they were related.

"Dante's not alone," he says. "He has his men, there's Julij who, not unlike Dante, will do all in his power to protect you. There are Dante's partners from Detroit and whoever else he works with. He already bribed a few of the major bosses. This won't happen overnight, baby girl, but it *will* happen. Dante won't rest until you're safe."

A small, forced smile curves my lips. Hope still smolders inside me, but I try not to let it burn bright. Being a realist got me through the life Frank gave me. I won't become an optimist at the last stretch.

"Julij wants to help, but not many bosses respect him yet. The V brothers from Detroit have no reason to protect me. They'll stand back when it gets too hot—"

"Don't forget me," he cuts in. "You're safe here. If everything else fails, you and Dante can move to Moscow."

"And what's your motive? Why have you invited me to stay here with you?"

A pained expression flashes across his face again. "I can think of a reason. I'll tell you about it one day, but today isn't that day." He crosses the room and lingers with his hand on the handle. "I think you better get out before you catch a cold."

"Don't call Dante. He doesn't need to know."

With an apologetic smile, he closes the bathroom door behind him.

A young man whose name slipped my attention talks about the joys of living in America. He moved to Los Angeles two years ago and can't praise the city enough. For almost ten minutes now, he's been listing his favorite Lakers players since the early fifties. I wouldn't be surprised if LeBron's poster hangs above his bed. He probably kisses it goodnight too.

Bored describes my mental state perfectly, which is why I finish the second glass of champagne, despite arriving in the ballroom thirty minutes ago.

Anatolij introduced me to a dozen people before the basketball fanatic started his monologue, overly excited to chat to a *'fellow American'* here in Russia.

I scan the room, searching for a waiter, but instead of a floating silver tray, my eyes lock with Anatolij. He smiles over the sea of heads and shoulders. With practiced nonchalance, he raises his chin, pointing to my companion. I don't want to be rude, so I plaster a convincing smile on my face, one that always worked on Nikolaj, and return to scanning hundreds of guests in search of the Holy Grail.

Twelve waiters were employed to serve the guests, but as if sensing my desperation, they're all hiding. Enlightening conversations buzz in the air, accompanied by a string quartet playing a sad, monotonous melody. Two hundred kinds of perfumes mix with an equal number of colognes, but the sickening smell of white lilies overpowers the room.

The basketball fan is up to the nineties, gushing about Shaquille O'Neal, when a gentle hand touches my lower back.

I spin around, meeting the piercing gaze of gray eyes.

Anatolij hands me a glass of champagne, setting my empty flute back on a waiter's tray. "Would you mind if I stole Layla for a while?" he asks my companion.

"No, of course not. I'll find her later."

Anatolij nods, turning to me. "Waltz?"

"Only the basics."

He raises his hand, twirls his finger, and in an instant, the string quartet starts playing a waltz. Anatolij offers me his arm while the crowd of people part to create a circle in the middle of the dance floor.

"You look beautiful," he whispers in my hair before he spins me around, bows slightly, and we start dancing.

A heavenly female voice reverberates in the room. I turn to see a dark-haired woman standing in front of a microphone on the stage. She wasn't there five minutes ago.

I'm the only one looking at her while all eyes in the room are trained on Anatolij and me. Ballet is my true love, but during the many fancy parties organized by Frank, I had to learn the basics of Waltz, Tango, and Foxtrot.

As a little girl in tulle pink dresses, I danced, standing on the shoes of older men. Later, I hid in the corner of the room so no one would ask me to dance. Being there was bad enough. Especially that Frank insisted on my presence so he could put on a father-of-the-year act. Now, dancing with Anatolij, I'm a little thankful to my dad for teaching me the steps to the Waltz.

The melody is calm, Anatolij's moves perfect, and the words coming out of the singer's mouth make no sense. We swirl around the dance floor, my body light as a feather, my mind free of any problems.

I close my eyes briefly, enjoying the peacefulness, and smile when my imagination summons a vivid picture—Dante and I dancing at our wedding, surrounded by familiar faces. I hadn't dreamt of a fairy tale wedding before I met Dante, but since he proposed, I catch myself thinking about the flower arrangement, the venue, and my dream dress.

A minute later, more people join in, and soon enough, the dance floor is full of dark suits and colorful, sparkly dresses. Anatolij bows once the song ends, offering my hand to an older gentleman who waited for me to become available. I don't object. Not once for over an hour. I glide across the dance floor with different men until my feet start to ache.

I thank the last dancer, avoiding eye contact with anyone else, snatch a glass of champagne from one of the waiters, and slip out of the room unnoticed. I need a minute to catch my breath. Preferably away from the scent of lilies, that's making me dizzy. I climb three flights of stairs, marching down the corridor to my bedroom in search of the library Anatolij mentioned. I can't remember if he said it's on the left, right, or opposite my room, so I open the door on the left first.

Feeling the wall, I find the light switch and walk-in further when the lights come on. My eyebrows knot in the middle when I stare at the portrait on the opposite wall. Slowly, step by step, I walk forward, eyes on the woman painted on the canvas. Full lips, filigree posture, a smile that touches her baby-blue eyes... I can't peel my eyes off her, growing more confused by the second.

Every rational thought gets away before I can catch it.

I sit on the couch in the middle of the room, hiding my face in my hands. When will this end? I have enough to deal with, trying to accept the past and not worry about my grim-looking future. I'm also fed up with the present because, looking at the portrait, I realize there are still more riddles from the past to uncover.

Everywhere I turn, I stumble upon lies. Everywhere I turn, someone's trying to deceive me or hide information.

No one is honest.

My life is made up of a series of unfortunate events and accidentally spoken truths.

CHAPTER TWENTY-FOUR

Dante

I'm a wound-up toy. Mauricio was quite right—I needed to distance myself from Layla; look at the situation through the eyes of a passive observer, but such a strict cutoff from her tires me out both physically and mentally. As if it's not enough that I can't see or touch her, now I'm supposed to function without even hearing her voice?

Good fucking luck.

I was a fucking mess while Layla hid in Texas. Despite coping with unwanted separation better this time because at least I know where she is, safe and mine, not having her close is still torture.

Jesus Christ.

Whoever invented love should've been killed on the spot before he could spread the idea throughout humanity. Love is confusing. Overwhelming. Uncontrollable. A constant, energetic worry at the back of the mind. A rush of protectiveness that can make or break a man.

I'm still not sure if it's making or breaking *me*.

Love is messy. Fucking amazing too.

Layla's a little damaged thanks to Frankie, a damsel in distress. At first, she needed adoration, attention, and love. Now, she needs protection, and her *needing* is what has me running in circles, killing myself to fulfill those needs.

A fucking Knight in shining armor. No sword or horse in this fairy tale, though. A gun and a drug empire are all I got, but I snatched the princess anyway.

Instead of focusing on what eludes me, I wonder what she's doing. Is she having fun at the ball? She promised to call if anything happens, but I worry anyway... I'm fucking tired of worrying. Tired of thinking about her. Tired of the chaos she turned our lives into.

Granted—unknowingly, but still *chaos*.

I had it easy before she came along. Money, power, respect, women. What the fuck was wrong with that? Why did I have to fall in love with Tinker Bell? Sassy, feisty, troublemaker. My life would be much easier if I hadn't walked up to her that night in Delta. If I stayed locked in my office, none of this would be happening. No kill order, no worrying, no *feeling*.

I can safely say I wouldn't swap the chaos for one peaceful day. Despite all the shit that came along with her, I'm glad she stormed into my life and showed me there's more to it than money and power.

She's my more.

Still, I need space, peace, rest, and a reset, so after arriving back from Vegas early in the morning, I went straight to bed. Not a dreamless sleep, unfortunately, but six hours worked a treat to re-charge my batteries. Later in the afternoon, after a quick shower, I order food from Layla's favorite restaurant and sit in the living room with a bottle of cognac, trying to stop the express train of thoughts for a little while.

Jackson's hunt for Morte continues. He employed the best of the best hackers in the country to track the motherfucker. I knew it'd be difficult considering that Morte is well trained, a careful master of camouflage. I hoped to have a lead by now. The footage from the cameras at the hospital in Dallas wasn't helpful. Morte can't be seen entering or leaving the building. Fucking Houdini.

He came prepared. He knew where the cameras were and purposely avoided them all, making it painfully clear that getting a positive ID on Morte will be damn near impossible.

An hour later, after the first proper meal in three days, I polish the last three fingers of cognac from the bottle. "I can't go on without you" by Kaleo plays from the speakers around the house when the security alarm clicks once. My head hits the back of the couch as a jab of irritation spoils my drunken bliss. I'm barely touching base with reality right now and don't want to talk to Spades tonight unless he's here to relay good news for a change.

Hope bursts when instead of Spades, Grace enters the room, wrapped tightly in a long, military-green jacket.

"What are you doing here?" I frown, squinting against the bright lights she flipped on.

"I forgot my phone." She stops by the bar, eyeing the coffee table where the empty bottle of cognac stands in the company of a full one. "What's wrong?"

If not for double-vision making it hard to focus on her face, I'd say she looks worried. I try to tear myself from the couch to put out the cigarette but fail miserably. I throw it on the table instead, missing the ashtray by a mile. That'll burn a hole in the plush carpet Layla bought to keep her feet warm while we watch movies in the evenings.

Shit... I guess drinking isn't helping much. I'm still conscious, still thinking about her.

"Are you okay? I asked you what's wrong." Grace is suddenly right in front of me. She takes the glass out of my hand and touches her small, cold hand to my forehead.

"Make me a drink." I move away from her touch.

"Looks like you've had enough." She points at the empty bottle on the table. "Was it full?"

"Get me a drink, *please*."

Two wrinkles mark her forehead, and an exasperated huff follows. "Only if you tell me why you're on the best route to alcohol poisoning. What happened?"

Hanging my head low, I close my eyes to stop the room from spinning. One or two more drinks, and I'll be out. A dreamless state at last. A few hours of complete peace.

"Where's Dalton?"

"At my friend's house. He's staying there tonight. I had errands to run, and he fell asleep before I got back."

I smirk under my breath, lighting up another cigarette. Grace is no longer on the couch. How the hell did she get by me unnoticed? She's at the bar, a fresh bottle of cognac in hand.

"Have a drink with me. Go ahead. Make yourself a drink. You'll sleep in the guest bedroom, and come morning, you'll take care of my hangover. It will be huge, I assure you."

"I don't doubt it." She huffs out a laugh. "It's a miracle you're still able to articulate properly."

"Bacardi should be there somewhere." I wave my hand at the bar. "Layla loves mojito. Try it."

"I'll have a glass of wine if that's okay. I don't know how to make a mojito."

"Neither does Layla. She can't cook either. Or clean or iron a shirt, but I love her anyway. She's... she's flawless. Mine, so fucking mine. I can't function without her."

Grace grabs my hand to cuff my fingers around a glass of cognac. "Clearly. You're a mess." She plops down beside me, sipping on the wine, eyes closed, I think. It's hard to tell when there are currently three of her sitting beside me. "I envy her," she says quietly.

"All her life, people used her in the worst possible way, and now everyone wants to kill her. There's nothing to envy."

"You, silly. I envy her because she has *you*. The way you love her, how much you're willing to do for her..." She trails off and pulls the sleeve of her jumper lower. "She's only two years older than me. That's not much, but look, she already has her happily ever after. When this is all over, she'll live like a princess. Your princess. I hope she appreciates what she has."

The note of exasperation in her voice comes as a surprise. I hadn't paid much attention to Grace since Layla came back, but it looks like I should have.

"You don't like her." And I don't like knowing this.

"It's not like that. I just don't like being here when you're not around. Layla's not a nice person."

Objection forms in my mind but fails to become audible. Grace has a point. Layla's not a nice person. She's rude, bossy, and only respects people she likes, of which there aren't many. Then again, I don't fucking care. How can I? Layla doesn't need to be likable. I'd take the honest, no-bullshit attitude of hers over fake smiles every time.

"If you went through half as much shit as she did in your life, you wouldn't be nice either. She's cautious. It's not easy to break through her walls, but deep down, she's a good girl."

"Oh... yes, I heard," Grace mumbles, cheeks pink. My mind takes me an extraordinarily long time to grasp that she's referring to me calling Layla a good girl while we fucked in here while Grace involuntarily eavesdropped from the kitchen. "I'm not saying she's not a good person, but I prefer *you*. Keep your promise and tell me why you're drinking alone."

"I'm trying to distance myself from her for a while."

"From Layla? I don't understand."

"That makes two of us. I told her I won't call her for a while. I thought it'll help me focus on the problems here, but instead of thinking about her less, I think of her more," I wave the glass in front of her face. "I'm drinking to stop thinking."

"Is it working?"

"No."

Not one fucking bit.

"You know..." Grace stares at the glass in her hand. "I've never seen a man as in love as you are."

A frown and a hand gesture urging her to keep going is my only answer.

"She's the first person you look at when you walk into the house. The first you speak to." She steals a sideways glance at me, ghosting her index finger over the rim of the wine glass. "Not once and not twice, you walked right past me, not a word, not a glance until you kiss her."

She's not wrong. When the time comes to get home, all I can focus on is Layla. Seeing her, kissing her, touching her is all I wait for. What the hell has she done to me? People don't change. Or so I've been told my whole life.

Bullshit.

Layla brought a different side of me to life. A side I have a love-hate relationship with. *Feeling* is great, but it's getting out of hand. There has to be a way to put a cap on love. A way to stop the feelings from overpowering a man. A way to love just the right amount.

It'd be good to find balance before I go mental.

"You can stand right in front of her, and I won't notice."

"Exactly. You're very intense. Do you even know how deep she sits under your skin?"

A bitter laugh escapes my lips. "Too deep."

"I can't disagree. Why, though? I don't understand it. You are two different people in one body." She pulls her legs under her bum, curiosity clearly visible on her thin, pretty face, a soft glow of pink heating her cheeks. "When she's not around, you're quite scary."

"Scary?"

"Yes. Intimidating. Commanding, sometimes callous... but when Layla's around, you're even scarier. You're territorial. I watch every word I say to Layla because God help anyone who disrespects her."

I groan, annoyed at the involuntary reaction the mere *thought* triggers—my body tenses, fists clench, jaw ticks.

A moment of inattention is what got me here. One moment of letting my guard down when the curiosity of the girl dressed in red sauntering across the dancefloor of my club got the better of me.

Grace eyes the framed pictures of Layla hanging on the walls. From the corner of my eye, I see her lips, all three sets of them, form a thin smile.

"She's pretty. I'll give her that. High cheekbones, full lips, big eyes. You'll have beautiful kids."

An invisible hand grips my heart at the thought of Layla round with my baby. A throaty laugh that morphs into a groan follows. I'm borderline psycho whenever I think Layla's in danger.

Maybe it would be safer not to imagine her pregnant.

I pinch another cigarette between my teeth. Too lazy at this point to hold it in my hand, I settle for keeping it in my mouth and inhaling and exhaling on cue. With every next drag, I lose more and more reality, slipping deeper into the state of mind-numbing drunkenness. Almost two bottles of cognac work a treat. My mind finally waves a white flag, cutting me off from my girl.

Reset.

No thoughts. No feelings. I'm suspended in the moment, half-conscious of what's happening around me. My eyelids became too heavy, head slumps to my shoulder, raising and falling in sync with my short, shallow breaths.

Bliss. Pure, uninterrupted bliss.

A warm body presses into me, climbing onto my lap. My hands move, but I don't think I'm the one moving them. I feel the smooth texture of skin under my fingertips while my lips, grasped by different lips, cooperate, struggling to kiss. Small hands knot at my neck. A warm mouth deepens the kiss. Sweet sighs bounce in my overworked mind as the petite body clings to my chest. For a moment, I give into her efforts. For a moment, confused, blinded, I think this is okay.

It's only when my brain, among a plethora of information, fires up the fourth sense that I realize the perfume lingering in the air doesn't match Layla.

My eyes fly open, focusing on the picture before me. Three girls are there, so I blink and squint until they become one. With the little strength left in me, I push away the girl who definitely isn't my star.

CHAPTER TWENTY-FIVE

Dante

Grace lost her job the next morning. The minute I woke up from a dreamless sleep, her stunt replayed in my head. I jumped out of bed with a skull-piercing headache that threatened to bring me to my knees. As expected, I found Grace in the kitchen, preparing breakfast. Thirty seconds later, silent tears streamed down her young face.

I gave her all she could ask for: work with great pay, a rent-free, all-expenses-paid apartment, and kindergarten for Dalton. Today, I took it away.

She should've thought twice before trying to fuck with me. Pun intended. Had she not heard that you don't bite the hand that feeds you?

By the time I finish with Grace, locate a stash of painkillers, and freshen up, it's already past noon. With a cup of black coffee, I sit in the living room, ready for whatever this day brings. I grab my phone to call Jackson but stop short of dialing his number. Thirty-six missed calls, a dozen voicemails, and a few text messages wait on the screen. All from Anatolij.

Bile rises in my throat first before muscles turn to fucking steel. My hands no longer shake from the lack of electrolytes in my system as I dial his number.

"Finally," he answers, his tone relieved. Not a hint of unease. That's half the battle won. "Is everything okay? I've been trying to reach you all day."

"What happened?"

"Nothing. I mean, something, but Layla's okay."

"*What.* Happened?" I repeat, throwing myself against the couch. "Your definition of *okay* may be much different to mine, Anatolij."

"She's not hurt. Safe and sound as promised, but... I think you should come over" He exhales down the phone, an incensed puff of air. "She found her mother's portrait in my office last night. I think it's a good time for explanations. It'd be better if you were here for this conversation. I'm sure it won't be an easy conversation."

No, it won't. It may be the most challenging conversation he'll ever hold. There's also a fifty percent chance his truth will be the most devastating news Layla ever hears. I'm still unsure what goes inside her head where her parents are concerned. She hardly ever talks about them.

"Are you going to tell her the truth?" I ask.

"Of course. I've been waiting for an opportunity for a long time. I just hoped to wait until after you closed the hit. You should be here for her, Dante. This is a delicate matter. From what I gathered so far, Layla's quite temperamental."

"Quite?" I chuckle. Not the best idea considering it worsens my headache. "That's a polite understatement. Layla's a stick of small dynamite, short fuse, loud bang, but that's about it. She's stronger than you give her credit for, cut from a different cloth than all of us."

"Strong only on the outside. She'll need you here."

"You want me to come over and hold her hand while she screams your castle down, or are you hoping I'll take your side and calm her down? Layla has the right to know. She also has the right to hate you for keeping this a secret so long."

Hate is too big of a word. Layla's not capable of hatred. She couldn't even hate Frank, and he deserved it like no other.

"I know it's too late for such declarations, but if I knew what her life would—"

"You're right. It's too late for *if only I knew.*" I rub my face, glancing at the suitcase I failed to unpack after arriving from Vegas. "I have a few things to take care of before I can come over. Can you hold off the conversation for another day?"

"Yes. I think I can avoid her until you fly over."

Anatolij Aristow. The biggest fish in Russia. The man behind the biggest scams in Europe. The man who commands an entire goddamn army, dictates the rules, and deals exclusively with Russian Oligarchs.

And he's afraid of a *nineteen*-year-old girl.

"I'll see you tomorrow," I say and cut the call when the sound of a large engine revving outside floods the house. The car that can only be a Dodge stops on the gravel. No more than ten seconds later, the door bursts open.

"I've got her!" Jackson booms, running inside with Rookie close behind. "I've got Sandra." He snaps a handful of pictures on the coffee table. "And it gets better."

I glance at the polaroids, feeling a huge weight fall off my shoulders to hit the floor with a loud thud.

"When were those taken?" I stare at a photo of Sandra by the trunk of a white SUV with a *boy*. A child. A six or seven-year-old child with black hair and a face that leaves no doubt as to who his father is.

"Today. They're in Ohio."

I drop onto the couch, squeezing the back of my neck. Jesus fucking Christ. What the hell happened to my moral compass? The one that guided me in the right direction throughout the years. No more than six months ago, the prospect of kidnapping a child would've made me sick.

Now?

Now there's no mercy left in my fucked-up mind.

The journey to Ohio took four hours. The true optimist I became not long ago, I booked a flight to Moscow for six a.m. tomorrow morning, expecting no problems on the road to successfully blackmailing Morte into calling off the hit.

"Is this it?" Nate leans out of the back seat, looking closer at the farmhouse Spades pulled up in front of.

It's not much—an ugly white house with wooden shutters on the windows and a messy front garden overgrown with weeds. A large barn stands to the left, and the same SUV I saw in the pictures Jackson brought is parked out of the way by an old but still operational well. The neighbor's house is about a mile away, hidden behind a small hill, so only a part of the roof is visible in the distance.

"C'mon, let's get this over with." Spades heads out of the car with a frown on his forehead.

He's not overly happy about the whole kidnapping a child idea. Neither am I, but it's a means to an end. It's not like we'll hurt the kid. We'll keep him entertained until his Daddy starts playing ball. Spades doesn't accept my reasoning, though. His niece is Morte's son's age, making the job that much harder for him to stomach.

"Took you long enough."

We hear, and all three of us turn to find Sandra standing in the barn doorway, a riding crop in one hand and a black helmet in the other.

"I expected you here weeks ago." She admits, starting toward us, seemingly unfazed by our arrival. "Forgot about my existence, didn't you?" Her eyes lock on me as she strolls across the gravel in a casual step.

"I thought you left Morte to stay away from the Mafia, but it looks like you're still in the know," I say, holding my hand out, letting Spades and Nate know not to reach for their guns yet. If there's a chance we can settle this peacefully, I'll take it.

"Once you enter that life, you're bound to it forever, Dante. I keep tabs on Morte because I don't want him near my son. When he ordered the kill on Frankie's girl, I knew I'd have to face my past."

"She's *my* girl. Not Frankie's. I'll grant your wish. Give Morte a reason to follow my orders, and I'll make sure you and your son won't ever have to worry about him showing here."

She stops a few feet away, with no fear in her brown eyes. "Do you know why I left him? I didn't want to risk my son's safety by staying. Morte would never opt-in for a normal, peaceful life. Right now, you know best what lines your kind is willing to cross to get what you want. You're here to take Aiden and blackmail Morte into cooperating."

"Desperate times. If you hope you can appeal to my humanity, don't hold your breath, Sandra. There's no humanity left in me, but... you already knew that, right?"

For a moment, I was sure she wanted to cooperate. She should. There'd be no need to take the kid or hear a mother cry, but Sandra made a mistake trying to pull the wool over my eyes. She got in too deep with her lies.

"Yes," she admits, folding her arms over her chest. "And do you know Morte is very much aware of Aiden's existence yet wants nothing to do with him?"

Another mistake. Another lie. If that was true, she wouldn't keep tabs on his whereabouts.

"You had a choice." I trade glances with Spades, who immediately aims his gun at her head. "You could've helped me out of your own good will, or you could've lied, hoping I'd change my mind, and leave empty-handed." Spades flips the safety. The sound turns Sandra's face chalk white. "You chose wrong," I continue. "I'll give you a chance to redeem yourself. I strongly believe that a child should have a mother, so you get to choose again."

"I'll do it," she clips, not a moment of hesitation, her voice defeated. Maybe she's not as dumb as I have her pegged for. "You want me to tell Morte about Aiden, right?"

"Nate, find the kid," I say over my shoulder. Sandra's face falls a little bit more. "Tell him we're going for a ride."

"Don't touch him!" She steps forward, but the gun aimed at her head changes her mind. "Please, don't hurt him."

The scared, pleading note in her voice is all I wanted to hear. She needs to sound genuinely distressed, or Morte won't take this seriously. I pull my phone out, watching Sandra's wide eyes dart between me and the house behind my back.

"Dante Carrow," he answers with the same mocking tone he did last time. "To what do I owe the pleasure?"

"How could you be so stupid?" I fire the words he spoke to me right back at him. "You can be threatened and blackmailed because you were once in *love*."

Silence falls upon us. He needs time to process my words, but I doubt he finds much sense in them yet. "If you think I'll call off the hit to keep her safe, you're delusional." Uncertainty rings in his voice as if he knows I'm not that stupid. "You can kill her. I don't fucking care, Dante."

I chuckle, drunk on the power associated with being the one in control. Morte is at my mercy. Unknowingly to him, but he is. He will do as I say. I've dreamt of this moment since Julij told me there's a bounty on Layla's head. I didn't know who played the role of the promoter at that point, but I wanted to hear him beg.

"Did you ever wonder why Sandra left?"

Back when they were together, Morte was as smitten as I am now. He was ready to throw the world at her feet.

"I know why she left. She didn't want to be with a mafia man. She's a heartless bitch, Dante. I don't give a flying fuck what happens to her now. Put one bullet through her heart for me while you're at it."

"You really should've dug a little deeper." I turn to face the house. Nate emerges outside with Aiden by his side and a small suitcase in hand. "He looks just like you."

I pass the phone to Sandra, who strains her neck, looking over Spades' shoulder. There really isn't much humanity left in my black heart, and whatever's there is reserved for Layla.

Sandra's tearful gaze follows Nate's every move as she presses the phone to her ear. "Hello?"

Spades is rooted to the ground, a gun aimed between Sandra's eyes. He's perfectly still like a wax figure, refusing to make a move or glance behind him. Today marks the second time since we started working together when he's fulfilling my orders against his will. I can see he's struggling to keep his opinions unvoiced. Normally, he wouldn't hold back. He has no problem speaking his mind or calling me out when he thinks I'm going too far, but this time Layla's at the heart of this charade, and he knows there's no force on earth able to stop me from keeping her safe.

"You've got a son," Sandra squeals into the phone as silent tears escape her glossy eyes to trail down her pale cheeks. "His name is Aiden. He's six. Dante..." her voice breaks, the dam bursts, and a high-pitched wail cuts the air. "Whatever he wants, just do it, okay? Please, he—"

Nate starts the engine, and I think Sandra understands she's not going for a ride with us. I pull out a small syringe from my jacket pocket, stab her in the neck and fill her bloodstream with a powerful sedative courtesy of Dr. Carlton Carrow. It's supposed to knock her out for an hour to let us drive away in peace. Her body turns limp within a few seconds. I snake an arm around her back, holding her flush to my side, and retrieve the phone from her weakening grasp

"Sandra!" Morte yells in my ear. The sheer panic in his voice is music to my ears.

"She can't hear you. She's unconscious and will be for an hour or so. Before you start wondering if I'm lying..." I send him one of the snapshots Jackson showed me earlier. "Here's your proof. You know what to do. Once you're done, you'll find me in Moscow."

"Fuck!" He screams down the line. "He's, my *son*! You don't touch a man's family, Dante! This is way out of line!"

"I seem to remember you recently disregarded that rule. Did you honestly expect me to play fair? No holds barred, Morte. Be glad I'm letting his mother live. You wouldn't want such trauma for your son, would you?"

"Fine! Alright, I'm calling off the hit, but if anything happens to my son, I swear to—"

"You're in no position to make threats. Get. To. Work."

It's official.

To the long list of sins, I can boldly add *kidnapping*.

CHAPTER TWENTY-SIX

Layla

A thick cardigan and a long coat keep me relatively warm as I wander the garden at the back of the castle. Snow crunches under my feet, and frost bites at my skin. The snow stopped last night, but the freezing temperature keeps the white fluff from melting. I brush it off from a bench tucked between two huge, old oak trees and sit, breathing heavily into my hands.

I should've put on a pair of gloves.

Two days have passed since I found Jess's portrait in Anatolij's office. Questions shift swiftly through my brain, poisoning every thought. I'm getting no answers, though. Anatolij's nowhere around. In fact, I haven't seen him since the ball. He skipped all the meals yesterday and didn't come downstairs for breakfast this morning. I'm not even sure if he's in the castle. He's avoiding me; that much is clear, but he can't stay away forever. At some point, he will have no choice but to come out of hiding and answer my questions.

Unfortunately, patience isn't one of my virtues. Tired of waiting and frustrated, I decided to get some fresh air to clear my head. Instead, more absurd ideas bloom in my mind while I sit on the bench under the oak trees.

Were they lovers back then? Maybe they stayed in touch throughout the years? Were they sneaking around behind Frank's back? Jess had no problem fucking the Cuban workers, so cheating with Anatolij would be a plausible explanation if not for three major flaws.

One: Anatolij's powerful, handsome, rich, and sophisticated. All my mother craves. Why would she stay with Frank if she could have a much better version of him?

Two: Frank was perceptive. There's no way Jess could keep an affair that spanned over many years a secret. He knew she was cheating on him with the help but turned a blind eye to those escapades because he wasn't a saint either, but I doubt he'd allow his wife to lead a double life for years.

Three: Jess is pretty, and... that's about it. I can't imagine someone as intelligent as Anatolij taking an interest in my less-than-bright mother.

I wanted to call her and demand a few answers, but Dante made me promise not to tell Jess where I'm hiding. Mentioning Anatolij will give her a pretty good idea. She's daft, but not daft enough not to figure out where I am. Still, my finger hovers over her name in my contacts list occasionally. Dante's handsome face flashes before my eyes every time to stop me from dialing. I can't risk my safety to satisfy my curiosity.

On the other hand, I no longer feel safe in Moscow. If Anatolij offered to hide me here only because of his affiliation with my mother, he might not take the task of keeping me out of harm's way too seriously.

I rub my face with both hands. When will the secrets and lies stop? I want a normal, peaceful life with Dante. Or at least as normal as the life of a mafia boss and his future bride can be. Dante's the only person who puts me above all else. The one who loves me unconditionally. The one who never lies. I need him. His peace, presence, and determination. He'd chase the problems away with one kiss on my forehead.

A sad, bitter laugh slips out of my mouth. I did nothing to deserve him or make him fall in love with me. I did everything to make him hate me and nothing to get him back.

And now, I sit in the fancy garden outside the imposing castle doing nothing *again*. I'm not trying to save my own skin. I'm not even trying to force the truth out of Anatolij. No, I just sit on a bench, shivering with cold, wallowing in self-pity, close to tears.

I hate what I've become. A stupid, silly princess missing a shoe, biting into a poisoned apple, and waiting for the prince to kiss me back to life.

What a joke.

There was a time when I had to fend for myself; when I fought for respect and love. A time when I didn't let anyone walk all over me. A time not so long ago.

Then Dante came along, offering what I never had. He surrounded me with attention, admiration, and affection.

He locked me in that stupid tower.

He stole my shoe.

He broke me.

Took away my ability to fight my own battles.

Am I really *that* girl? I hate that girl. I can't be her.

I jump to my feet, sick and tired of feeling helpless. Dante's not here to help me force the truth out of Anatolij, so it's right about damn time I take matters into my own hands. Besides, up until we met, I did damn well on my own. I survived years with Frank and never once needed a chaperone.

Confrontation used to be my driving force.

A swirl of snow breaches the castle when I barge inside. Lew stands by the stairs with another man. Their stops abruptly when I storm past them, taking two steps at a time as I climb the stairs. Determination pumps in my veins, silencing the quiet voice in my head ordering me to stop and reconsider. The voice sounds a lot like Dante.

I shake my head, pushing away the *what-ifs*. The door to my bedroom slams shut behind me, and I pull out two suitcases from under the bed and start throwing all my belongings inside. If this won't force Anatolij to come out of hiding, nothing will. Dante trusted him with my safety. I'm not about to jeopardize it by leaving Moscow, but I need to get Anatolij's attention somehow. This, however childish, is my best shot.

No more than ten minutes later, the sound of a suitcase falling down the stairs rumbles in the empty corridors. It's too heavy for me to carry. Lew glances around the corner, eyebrows drawn together for a second before meeting his hairline. He jumps to the side, avoiding the second flying piece of luggage, then reemerges when it hits the floor with a thud.

"What doing?" he asks, his English nowhere near intermediate level.

I save my breath, descending the stairs in the accompaniment of my heeled boots, clicking loudly. The answer seems to hit Lew across the face. His expression changes to wide eyes and parted lips as he shoves his hand into his pocket, looking for his phone.

All the while, he takes one step back for every one of mine taken forward until his back hits the door. He's a brute of a man with bulky muscles on top of muscles, but I doubt he'll manhandle me if I try to squeeze past him.

A few seconds pass before two other guards stop on either side of him, walling the door with their oversized bodies. By the look of them, they must think I'm mentally compromised if I think I'll leave this place. We'll see who's right.

Two more seconds pass, and the rule Anatolij imposed on his men when I arrived goes to hell. Lew yells into the small microphone on his cell in Russian, throwing his hands about.

I step off the last step, haul the luggage onto its wheels and pull them behind me, starting in the opposite direction, toward the living room. French doors there will lead me straight into the garden. If only people would stop materializing in my path, that is. Two of Anatolij's employees appear before me, stealth like ninjas despite their gorilla-like shape. Another one sneaks up on me from behind to snatch the suitcases out of my hands.

I turn back to the two standing in my way. Both bent at their knees, with their hands outstretched to the sides, ready to catch me if I make a run for it. That's not my intention. I'm a guest here, not a prisoner. I can leave whenever I want, and I'm sure Anatolij wouldn't dare disagree.

"Waiting," Lew clips, glaring at me as he froths a little at the corners of his mouth.

Tapping my foot on the concrete floor, I *wait* for their boss to appear. He does, not even two minutes later.

"Good afternoon," He joins our little gathering.

"Good indeed," I say, an unmistakable hint of mockery in my voice. "I'm going back home. Do you mind?"

"I'd consider it unwise." He dismisses Lew with a wave of his hands, gesturing toward the living room.

I don't move. Something in his stance tells me his focus is solely on keeping me in the castle and not on answering my questions. "My flight leaves in two hours, and you know how long passport control took when we arrived. I'd rather not be late."

"Dante won't be pleased if you leave, Layla."

No, he probably won't. "What makes you think he doesn't know I'm leaving?"

"I spoke to him last night. Besides, he would never agree to you boarding a plane by yourself."

Things just keep getting better and better. Dante won't call me but found time for Anatolij? That's... ugh! I stomp my foot again. "He'll deal with it. I'll take his anger over your lies any day of the week."

"If you leave, you'll be risking your life. You're safe here. That should be your top priority right now."

"The trouble is, I don't feel safe anymore. You had two days to explain why my mother's portrait hangs in your office. You chose not to, and so I choose to leave."

He comes closer, slowly as if approaching a wounded animal. Too many conflicting emotions whirl in his gray eyes to guess which one dominates. "I never lied to you, and I'm not about to start tonight. I will explain. I wanted to explain when you arrived here, but I thought it'd be better if Dante were here."

A subtle suggestion in his words turns my stomach. "What does Dante have to do with this?"

"I thought you'd find the news less stressful if he'd be with you when we talk. He thought so too."

"He knows?"

Instead of being annoyed, I'm reassured. There's no reason to worry if Dante knows what this is about and hasn't changed his mind about sending me here.

Anatolij glances at his watch, then back at me. "Come on, let's have a drink." He extends his hand, waiting for me to take it. "If you still want to go back home once we're done talking, I'll personally deliver you back to Dante."

Mission accomplished.

Instead of taking his hand, I enter the living room, hang my coat on the back of an oversized wingback chair by the fireplace, and sit down, leaning closer to the fire.

Anatolij joins me with two glasses of Port. I'm not a fan of red, but Port tastes like everything that's right with this world. The atmosphere turns heavy once he sits in the chair opposite mine. His shoulders look unnaturally tense. Nonchalance and a bit of arrogance are the pillars of his personality. Fear is the last thing anyone could accuse him of, yet sitting three feet away from me, he looks anxious.

"When my brother moved to America twenty years ago, he took me with him." His tone is spiked with hesitance as if he'd never shared this piece of information with anyone before. "He opened a restaurant in Chicago and hired your mother as a waitress. She was fifteen. The most amazing woman I have ever met. Intelligent, beautiful, joyful."

I cock an eyebrow, calling him out on the blatant lie. "Intelligent? Are you sure you're talking about Jess? She's infantile, shallow, and self-righteous."

Anatolij snorts softly. "She is now, but she wasn't back then. She was ambitious. I loved that about her."

A cold sweat slips down my back. *I loved that about her* is all my mind can focus on. My assumptions were correct—they had an affair. One question remains. How long did it last? Or better yet, is it still happening?

"She was full of passion. She worked two jobs, was at the top of her class, and had her future planned to the smallest detail."

Whoever he's describing sounds nothing like the woman who pretended to raise me. "I'm having a hard time believing my mother ever thought about something other than what color lipstick suits her outfit."

"She might be vain now, but it wasn't always the case. Even now, I think she still has that spark. She just buried it deep to please Frank. He always was her only weakness." His expression turns severe. "I can honestly say I have no idea what she saw in him. We met the day Jess started working at the restaurant. He was uncouth, big-headed. He only cared about money and respect."

That I have no problem believing. Frank hadn't changed one bit over the years. Until he died, my father had close to zero good qualities. He was one big *flaw*. A living, breathing proof that evil had a face.

Anatolij downs his port and refills the glass as if there's no way he can tell me the whole story without liquid courage.

"I guess I know where this is going." I relax in the chair. "You were in love with her, but she chose Frank."

He nods, his eyes sad, hinting that the feelings never went away. Otherwise, Jess's portrait wouldn't be in his office, where he can see her every day. "I loved her, Layla. She was my little dream. I tried my best to separate her from Frank's influence. I was sure I succeeded. I was sure she chose *me*. Frank disappeared out of her life, and we started dating."

"How long were you dating?"

"Only a few weeks." He clenches his fist. His jaw ticks as his eyes snap to meet mine, a whole sea of regret in his gray irises. "What you need to know right now is that I'm sorry."

"Just say what needs to be said, Anatolij. I guess this is not the end of the revelations, so just say it. Did Frank find out about you? Why did you leave her?"

Anatolij sits up, his spine straight as an arrow. "She left me for him, but... she came back one night, crying." He pauses for a deep calming breath, draining the second glass of port with trembling hands. He's always an oasis of calmness. This sudden nervousness looks out of place on a man of his importance. "She was pregnant but had no idea which of us was the father."

Confusion hits me first, right before my heart rate soars. Hundreds of wet centipedes with icy feet crawl under my skin. Childhood memories flash before my eyes, reminding me of the life I was given by a man who took his revenge on my mother for her betrayal.

"She wasn't sure which of us was the father until you were born," he continues, his words distant as if spoken through a sheet of thick glass. "There was no need for paternity tests. Your blood type was enough..."

B negative. One of the rarest blood types in the world. Both Frank and Jess are A positive, but... "I inherited my blood type from my grandmother."

"You can only inherit your blood type from your parents, Layla. Frank and Jess are both A positive. You can't be a B type from two A type parents... I'm B negative too, baby girl."

Individual words fail to penetrate my psyche. They stretch, blending into a long, incomprehensible, distorted sound. My lungs stop pumping enough oxygen. I'm breathing too fast, too shallow. Black spots appear before my eyes, and everything mutes as if I'm in a vacuum. All I can focus on are the memories. Every disappointed look on Franks' face. Every time he screamed. Every time he considered me his enemy. Every time I felt worthless.

"Stop acting like a spoilt brat."

"Don't cry; crying is for sissies."

"I don't want to hear it."

"Go to your room."

"Don't touch me."

"You're just like your mother. Useless."

"Don't come crying to me."

"Get out of my face."

"I don't care."

"It's your problem. Deal with it."

"Don't count on me."

"You're on your own."

His words play in my mind on repeat, echoing in the deepest recesses of my soul, each memory as painful as a cigarette burn. I blamed myself for years, convinced I wasn't good enough or smart enough to deserve his love. No matter how hard I tried, I was never good enough.

Now, I know why. Frank couldn't love me.

He couldn't stand me because I wasn't his daughter.

I was a burden. A constant reminder of Jess's affair. A constant reminder of how close he was to losing her. Maybe that's why he grew to despise her as much as he despised me...

All my life, I looked at Frank and saw the eighth wonder of the world. I spent nineteen years perfecting my personality to please him, but no matter who I became or how I acted, he put me down time and time again. Instead of giving up,

I worked harder. I craved the day when he'd be proud to call me his daughter. He couldn't... He couldn't be the father I needed because he wasn't my father.

My mind races to its limits and panic pulls on my throat like tight ropes. I'm choking, struggling to resurface from the pile of unwanted memories. My mind strips me of defense mechanisms and self-worth.

"Layla."

A familiar voice knocks through my walls. My head snaps in the direction of the door. Only then do I realize that Anatolij crouches before me, his face pale, eyes wide, frightened. I snap out of the lethargy with two creases on my forehead.

"Breathe, Star," Dante says, and at the same time, I feel the phone Anatolij presses to my ear.

He squeezes my hand, letting out a shaky breath. "Talk to him. I'll give you a moment." He makes sure I have a tight grip on the phone before he marches out of the living room.

"Hey," I say to Dante as a cool drop falls from my nose to my lips, my face wet with tears. I didn't realize I was crying.

"You scared me, baby. What happened? Anatolij said he couldn't get through to you."

"You knew." My voice breaks, but the accusation rings clearly. "You knew that he's my father, and you didn't tell me."

"I know. I'm sorry. I should've told you, but he wanted to do so himself. I promised not to say anything."

"Will you be okay?" Anatolij appears in the doorway with three strangers and Lew behind his back. "I have a meeting to attend. It won't take long. We'll talk more when I'm done."

"I'm not going anywhere if that's what you're asking."

A tight nod is his only answer before he leads his guests away, leaving Lew to stand guard outside the living room door. Looks like he doesn't believe me not to run after all.

"Layla," Dante says. "How are you feeling?"

I shrug, aware he can't see it. "Angry. Confused. Sad..."

"Sad?"

A small smile curves my lips. He doesn't mind my anger. He wouldn't mind if I screamed or took my frustration and confusion out on him, but *sadness*? He can't cope with that. It physically hurts him to know I'm upset.

"I'll be okay. I just need time. I have so many questions."

"I'm sure Anatolij will be more than happy to answer them all. He cares about you very much. Let him prove it."

For the last three weeks, he did his utmost to get to know me, and in that short time, he learned more than Frank did during nineteen years. Anatolij deserves a chance to explain why he wasn't present in my life. Why he abandoned my mother and me. Why he didn't fight harder.

"I love you, baby," Dante says. "I'll see you very soon."

The sound of an engine murmuring in the background has me checking the time. It's two in the afternoon here, which means... "Where are you going at four o'clock in the morning? And how soon is *soon*?"

A soft chuckle is his first answer. "Good girl. So perceptive. How does fifteen hours sound?"

A full-blown smile stretches my face. "Like the best thing I heard since you told me I'll be Mrs. Carrow."

From the corner of my eye, I notice movement in the corridor. Anatolij didn't lie when he said the meeting wouldn't take long. I don't think five minutes have passed yet, but the three strange men are already leaving. One of them looks at me with a small smile. A peculiar feeling passes through me. There's nothing friendly about his smile.

I don't have time for a reaction.

I don't even have time to blink.

He draws a gun, aims it at me, and pulls the trigger. Pain fails to register with me right away while the sound of more gunshots rings in my ears, mixing with Dante's screams until the phone slips out of my hand.

I double over, pressing my hands against the gaping, bleeding wound on my chest.

CHAPTER TWENTY-SEVEN

Dante

The sound of a gunshot pierces my ears. I'd recognize it everywhere and at any time, whether standing in the same room, a hundred meters away, or listening to it over the phone. I can't fucking breathe when my conversation with Layla is interrupted by a gun going off in the background. One isolated shot first, then more, closer together.

I distinguish between pistols and machine guns while I scream, begging Layla to say something. She doesn't. Before the shots stop, the connection breaks, and I can't get through again. Anatolij's not picking up either.

Fifteen minutes pass.

I have a hard time comprehending how on earth I haven't lost my wits yet. With my heart on my shoulder, I push the black thoughts aside. My teeth threaten to break any second as I clench my jaw hard, searching for a rational explanation.

Maybe the sound came from the TV?

I'm lying to myself.

It wasn't on the TV. It was a real gun.

One of the many hitmen found Layla...

I block the possible scenarios pushing at me from every direction and lock them away so as not to drive myself crazy before Anatolij answers his phone.

Somehow, I know she got hit. I can fucking feel it. Just as I can feel that she's alive. There's no other option.

She can't die now.

Not when the hit is a few hours from being closed. Not when I'm about to bring her back home.

She *can't* die.

"Call Julij." Spades grips the wheel with all his might, speeding down the interstate toward the airport. "Maybe he can get in touch with one of Anatolij's men."

At least one of us is thinking straight.

With every passing second, my composure shatters more. Anatolij would've picked up the phone by now if nothing serious happened. But he's not answering...

"What's wrong?" Julij clips in my ear, his voice rough. The early hour must've triggered all kinds of alarm bells in his head.

"Something happened in Moscow. I was on the phone with

Layla when the shooting started. They're not answering their phones. I need Lew's number."

"Fuck. I'll check what's going on. I'll call you back."

I smash the back of my head against the headrest when he cuts the call before he gives me Lew's number. I want to know what happened firsthand, but he's not answering when I redial, probably already on the phone to Moscow.

Spades keeps his eyes trained on the road as if he's afraid he'll trigger an outburst if he looks at me. I'm sure he doesn't trust me to stay this calm for much longer and prefers not to be the reason why I'll snap. Whenever I do, a gun ends up in my hand, and I empty the barrel into the sky.

I'm itching to do it now, but a rational part of me locks the rage bubbling up somewhere at the back of my mind. It'll come in handy when I have Morte in front of me. He'll be the outlet for all the wrath coursing through my veins. In the end, this is his fucking fault. All of it. If he hadn't agreed to help Frank, none of this would be happening right now.

Julij's conversation with Lew takes almost ten minutes. My body turns cold when he rings back. One deep breath is all I need to prepare for the news I'm not ready to hear; for the words I never want to hear because hearing that the only person I love is hurt exceeds my capabilities.

Once again, with considerable surprise, I realize I can withstand much more than I ever deemed possible; that regardless of how bad things get, I'll find a way to push forward.

"You need to get to Moscow, Dante," Julij says, sending my mind into a frenzy. "Layla got hit. It's bad. They took her to the hospital. She's on the operating table as we speak."

Any courage I hoped to have in the face of *this* piece of information fades into nothing. I double over in the seat, and for the second time in my life, I feel fucking helpless.

"The bullet went through and out. Missed the heart but hit the lung. Lew doesn't know much; the doctors won't tell him more than that. Anatolij's unconscious. Lew accidentally shot him when taking care of the hitmen."

"What exactly happened?" I hang my head low at the sudden onset of nausea.

"Three French men arrived. For quite some time, they've been trying to get in business with Anatolij. He's not keen on them, so he refused point-blank. Lew said they were on their way out when one of them drew his gun. It looked like a last-minute decision. A spur of the moment. He took the shot, and the other two were unprepared."

I fall silent, waiting for at least a minuscule amount of courage to fill my body so I can ask another question... "Will she be okay?"

"She will." He answers immediately but doesn't sound so sure. "She has to, right? The bullet missed the heart. That's the main thing. Anatolij will get the best medical care money can buy. Don't fucking doubt her."

"She's tough," I admit.

"Yeah, she's tough. She'll be okay, but she needs you. Get to Moscow as soon as you can."

"I'm on my way to the airport right now."

"Good. I'll get on the next flight out from New York. I'll see you when I get there."

It doesn't bother me that he wants to see her too. I don't care about anything other than Layla making it out alive. She has to. She has no right to leave me. Not now that she agreed to marry me. Not after all the shit, we went through. Not when we're so fucking close to peace.

If there's any justice in the world, then she'll be just fine. And that's what I pray for. That's what I beg of God, the

Devil, providence, fate, and everything that springs to mind. The rational part of my brain knows praying won't do much more than calm my conscience, so I reach for the phone again to call the one person whose medical skills I trust endlessly. There's not enough time for him to fly out with me, but he can board the next flight at ten a.m.

"Who should I keep alive this time?" Carlton chirps, fresh as a daisy. Muffled sounds in the background suggest he's at the hospital. "Dante? What happened?"

"It's Layla... she got hit. They're operating."

"Which hospital?"

"She's not in Chicago. She's in Moscow. The next flight leaves at ten. Can you make it?"

"Of course."

Not one question or complaint. Not a second of hesitation. He didn't even give me a chance to say *thank you* before he cut the call.

CHAPTER TWENTY-EIGHT

Layla

Not one of Anatolij's pawns waits to pick me up from the airport in Moscow. Julij's there, sitting by the arrivals gate, staring at the screen of his phone, a suitcase beside him.

"How did you get here before me?" I ask.

He peers up. The look on his face matches what I'm going through inside. Bloodshot, puffy eyes, and a pale face; a true testament to his feelings... I couldn't care less.

Nothing matters except Layla. I want to see her, be with her, and I want her to look at me with those beautiful, big, gray eyes of hers.

"I landed half an hour ago. Don't forget it's a direct flight from New York. You had a change-over in Warsaw, wasn't it?"

"Yeah. How's Layla?"

"Stable," he pushes all air down his nose and tucks the phone away, getting to his feet. "She was in surgery for almost four hours. She's still unconscious. I spoke to Anatolij. I've never heard him so shaken up before, Dante. He's taking this really hard. Try not to kill the guy, alright?"

Julij still has no idea my soon-to-be-wife and the love of his life is, in fact, his cousin. This is neither the time nor place to drop that kind of a bomb on him.

"I'm sure he did more than he could to keep her safe, Julij. I don't blame him. How is he doing?"

"That's not what I expected, but I'm glad you see it that way. I don't know how he's doing. He says he's fine."

We leave the building and hop into the car Julij rented. Neither of us speaks as he navigates the maze of Moscow's streets. Less than half an hour later, we walk through the long hospital corridors side-by-side, climbing several flights of stairs and passing hundreds of small rooms on our way to the private suite in the intensive care unit.

My step falters as we reach room number six-hundred and twenty-two. I'm afraid to go inside. I'm afraid I'll break down. I'm afraid I'll lose my shit when I see the most important person in my life unconscious in a hospital bed. I close my eyes briefly, inhaling a deep breath. The door swings open, pushed by both of my hands, my eyes on the floor for the first two seconds. The potent, irritating smell of disinfectant hits the back of my nose. The hum of life-support machines fills the air: heart monitor, pulse oximeter, mechanical ventilator. That last one turns my stomach. I let my eyes roam over the bed, starting with the white sheets, then climbing up slowly to Layla's face.

Her light, pale skin tone blends into the sheets but she looks calm. Peaceful. If not for the patient monitors around the bed, I could easily believe she's asleep, not unconscious. Her blood pressure is low. Her heartbeats are slower than I remember her heart beating three weeks ago under my fingertips.

Multiple IVs drip through long, plastic tubes and into the veins on her hands. A part of the dressing covering the gunshot wound on her chest peeks from underneath the bedsheet.

On elastic legs, I walk further inside the room one step at a time. The door behind my back opens with a quiet creak. I don't need to look over my shoulder to know it's Julij.

He sucks in a harsh breath, equally as distraught by the sight of Layla as I am. I lean over her and press a gentle kiss on her forehead. She's warm, but her lips are almost blue. Long eyelashes cast small shadows on her bony cheeks. Even now, she's so fucking beautiful I'm not sure why she's with me. She could make any man beg. I sit in the chair beside the bed when Julij stops at the foot, eyes on the mechanical ventilator helping my star breathe.

"I'll go find Anatolij. Maybe he can tell us more about what the hell happened."

"I want to be there when you talk," I say.

With a curt nod, he leaves, taking care to close the door behind him quietly as if he's afraid he'll wake Layla.

"I'm here," I whisper, ghosting my lips along her knuckles. "Your turn, baby. Don't you dare leave me now." I swallow the lump clogging my throat and rest my forehead on her hand, eyes closed. "I love you so much. I'll take you home. You'll be just fine."

Time stands still and moves forward at warp speed. An hour goes by before a quiet knock brings me out of the haze I found myself in, staring at Layla, willing the dark scenarios to stop tormenting my tired mind. This isn't the time for *what-ifs*. This is the time to believe. The time to make sure she's well cared for and monitored from every angle.

Julij's pushes his head in the door. "Got a minute?"

"Yeah." I kiss Layla's temple first, then follow him out.

Anatolij waits in the bright corridor, a fresh dressing on his neck. The aura of superiority I got used to is absent now, his face an open book. The guilt-ridden expression is close to what I expected, but the fear tainting his steel-gray eyes isn't. He's not afraid of me, though. He's afraid to lose Layla hours after telling her she's his daughter.

"Dante, I'm—"

I stop him, raising my hand. Apologies won't help the situation. They're also unnecessary. "Don't apologize. You think I don't know you'd have taken that bullet for her if you could? I do, Anatolij. All I want to know now is the prognosis."

"She'll be okay. I don't doubt it for one second. The surgery went according to plan. She's got the best doctors money can buy looking after her."

No, she doesn't. Not for about five more hours. "The best doctor is on his way. Once he arrives, whatever he says, goes. Can you make sure the hospital staff knows he'll be in charge? He'll call all the shots."

Before he answers, a blaring noise starts behind Layla's door. Among the alarm noise, the air is pierced with a flatlining heart monitor...

Heart-bursting terror consumes me whole, filling my lungs with ice-cold vapor. Blood freezes in my veins. I throw myself at the door, bursting inside the room like a wrecking ball.

Hundreds of cold hands squeeze my throat. The image becomes blurry when I register the long, green line on one of the monitors. She's dead. Her heart's not beating.

Julij and Anatolij grab me by the shoulders, yanking me back and out of the room to make space for several doctors who rush past me to Layla's bed. The door slams shut in our faces as soon as we're out in the corridor.

My legs fail to hold my weight. I stumble back and slide down the wall throwing an arm over my face, my body nothing but a shell. In the magnitude of emotions too painful to bear, my mind isolates the sound of the flat-lining heart monitor. It's all I hear while I'm silently falling apart. I'm blinded by emotions, by rage and pain incomparable to anything I've ever lived through. No fucking words exist to describe this; no words to verbalize the agony or the fury. It seeks an escape route out of my body. I pull on my hair, but the physical sting doesn't numb the anarchy seizing my mind.

Before I met Layla, I wanted power. When she entered my life, I wanted her. When I fell in love, I wanted a future with her at my side. Now, I'm losing my way; my goal in life. My goddamn purpose.

My imagination summons memories from a few months ago. I see Layla in a red dress as she walked through Delta with enough confidence to rival my own. The whole evening comes back to haunt me; Layla's gestures, smiles, and every time my heart skipped a beat when she looked at me. I remember the crushing desire that washed over me when we kissed for the first time.

I cup her face and catch her lips with mine.

Fuck... she tastes like everything that's right with this world. Like sunshine, rainbows, and candy. Adrenaline throbs in my limbs, the sensation comparable to the first time I pulled the trigger. I slip my tongue inside the silk of her mouth, deepening the kiss. The touch of small hands on my neck ignites every nerve ending in my body.

This isn't sweet and tender. Not how I imagined it'd be. Not how I wanted her first kiss to be, but there's fuck all I can do about the burning need that consumes us both. The floral scent of her skin, the sweetness of her lips, and the quiet sigh that escapes her strips me of all inhibitions.

She grips a handful of my jacket, pressing herself to my chest, there's enough power in her kiss to light up downtown.

The cool evening air fills with the sound of blaring horns but I can't stop. I don't want to stop. Fulfilling her wish is the most gratifying moment of my twenty-eight years. Merciless desire starts in the pit of my stomach when her fingertips ghost across my jaw and with that delicate touch, the kiss evolves... slows... deepens.

And I want more. So much more.

Pieces of all the best moments flicker in my mind, inflicting more pain—her laughter; her warm, naked body covered by a mist of sweat; every smile; every *I love you.* I never told her how much she means to me or that I'd do anything for her.

"I'll be fine. I've got you, and I'm not leaving you here alone. There's a line of men waiting to take my place. No way in hell I'll let that happen."

She chuckles as she drapes her hands over my neck. "There's no one I'd rather be with. You make me the happiest I've ever been. I mean it, Dante. I love you so much. I really love you. More than you can imagine."

"I know, Star," I press my lips to her forehead.

For the first time in my life, tears sting my eyes. I hold my head, rocking back and forth like an orphan.

"Don't ever leave me again," I whisper, resting my forehead on hers, eyes closed. "Never leave me, baby."

"I promise." She steals another kiss.

"You promised," I whisper. "You fucking *promised...*"

I'd rather get a bullet than go through this, whatever it is. Mourning? Agony? Both and more. If I hadn't agreed to send her away, she'd be okay. She'd be safe.

Everything ceases to exist. Without her, there's nothing.

I'm nothing.

The terrifying sound echoes down the corridor and resonates all over my body, constantly announcing that Layla's heart stopped beating.

CHAPTER TWENTY-NINE

Dante

The Earth starts spinning again when wide-eyed Julij slaps me across the face with all his might. I'm not sure how he managed to lift me off the floor and up to my feet or where his strength came from, but it worked.

I jerk myself out of the lethargy, the sheer insanity.

"She's back," he says, snapping his fingers in my face to ensure I'm not just looking at him but seeing him too.

"Layla's alive. She's still here."

I blink a few times, noticing a doctor behind Julij's back. His eyes are trained on us, his expression impenetrable as he waits for me to pull myself together.

I have a hard time doing so.

My body can't keep up with my heart and mind. A few seconds ago, I was damn near catatonic, but now the good kind of adrenaline zaps me back to life. Hope returns along with determination.

I clear my throat, making room for words, moistening the dryness. "What the fuck happened?"

The doctor glances between Anatolij and me, his back straight. He draws his eyebrows together, utterly puzzled. I bet if he weren't scared of us, he'd shrug to say he has no fucking clue. For his sake, it's better that he *is* scared.

No one in their right mind, knowing who Anatolij is and what kind of damage he can inflict on a person, would dare to enrage him while his only child is on the other side of the door, putting up a hell of a fight with the fucking Reaper himself.

"Layla is very weak," he says.

"We know that," Anatolij snaps. Not unlike me, he has no patience left.

Guilt still taints his features. I think he wants to redeem himself somehow. Maybe he doesn't believe I really don't blame him. There's nothing I would've done differently if I were there last night.

"We thought it may be a clot, but we can't find it. I'm afraid her body is simply giving up. She's too weak."

She's not fucking weak. She's the strongest person I know. "What's the next step? What will you do now?"

"Unfortunately, not much. We did everything we could. Now we can only wait and see if she'll stabilize. It all depends on whether her organs pick up and start working, whether she's strong enough to pull through."

"She's strong," I repeat for the hundredth time. No one can doubt it. "She's strong. She'll be fine."

The doctor nods, pity in his eyes. He bows slightly before marching away in the opposite direction. Julij wants to say something, but I don't feel like talking. I raise my hand to stop him from trying, then enter Layla's room and close the door. She needs peace. I need her. Watching her calm face, I hold her hand, hoping that the worst is behind us, that things will only get better now. She has her whole life ahead of her. She's not even twenty yet but endured more than most do during a lifetime. She deserves peace, and I will make sure she gets it.

I sit in the chair by her bed, her hand in mine, my lips gliding along her knuckles. "When you get out of here, I won't ever let you out of my sight again. I won't risk losing you, Star. I'll reorganize my work. I'll change the way the business operates. I'll leave it all behind if that's what you want just don't give up. I need you. You promised you wouldn't leave me again."

There's not a thing I won't do if it means Layla will get better. Faith has never been a part of my life, but right now, I'm the most believing atheist God has ever seen. I sit motionless for what seems like hours. My eyes dart between her and the machines surrounding the bed. My heart sinks every time the pause between two heartbeats seems longer than before.

Around noon, a soft knock precedes the door opening slowly. "You should rest," Anatolij says, stopping at the foot of the bed. "Shower, dinner, nap. You're more than welcome at my house any time you want."

"I'm not going anywhere."

At some point, I'll have to leave her to catch a few hours of sleep so I can charge my batteries. Layla needs me to stay sane. I won't be much use if I'm exhausted or starving myself. But I won't move until Carlton arrives at the hospital. He's the only person I trust to keep Layla alive while I take a break.

"Spades, Vince, and some of my men called," Julij says, peeking into the room before letting himself in, eyes on Layla. "Morte closed the order. The news is spreading rather fast."

"We can expect him in Moscow anytime now. I have his son. He didn't know he had one, so he's determined to do as I say. His ex is under Nate's supervision too. Morte's supposed to meet me here once he calls off the hit."

"His ex? Why didn't you gut the whore when the order came out?!" Julij snaps.

Under normal circumstances, I would've snarled at him, but the circumstances are far from normal. I don't intend to waste my breath or shred my tongue on bickering with Julij. Besides, his emotional reaction is, in part, understandable.

"She ran away years ago. I almost forgot she existed." I look at Anatolij. "I hope you won't mind if I invite Morte to your house. I have something to tell him."

"Not at all. I'll send my men to the airport. They'll let us know once he lands."

CHAPTER THIRTY

Dante

Three cups of coffee and three hours later, I'm still at Layla's bed, watching the monitors as I try to decipher the charts. I even attempted to check her dressing as delicately as my calloused hands allowed.

Layla won't mind adding another scar to her ever-growing collection, but I will die a little under an avalanche of remorse every time I'll look at it.

With another cup of shitty, lukewarm coffee from the vending machine, I return to her room, and minutes later the door opens again. Lew stands in the doorway, his hand outstretched to show Carlton the way inside as if he can't cross a fucking threshold without a map.

He drops a small travel bag on the floor by the wall, eyes focused on the many monitors around the room. "How is she?" he asks Layla's notes already in his hands. Two vertical lines on his forehead tell me he doesn't understand much of the Russian scribbles.

"Her heart stopped. The doctor here says she's too weak."

"He's not wrong," he murmurs, glaring at her chart. "She's weak. She lost a lot of blood. Couple it with anesthesia, a blood transfusion, all the meds, and..." He pauses, eyebrows drawn together. He saunters back to check the notes, and it looks like his mind is doing two hundred miles an hour. "No blood-thinning meds? Why?"

"Fuck if I know, Carlton. Do I look like a doctor? This is beyond my fucking comprehension. All of it."

Good thing he knows me well enough not to take offense over my snappish tone. We grew up together, so Carlton's on a first-name basis with my commanding nature.

"Wait here," I say. "I'll get the doctor."

I leave the room to come back five minutes later with the attending, Julij, and Anatolij. Carlton's in his element, unplugging Layla from the monitors.

"Tell him I need access to radiology," he snaps, wheeling the bed toward the door.

"I speak English," the doctor retorts, crossing his hands over his chest. "We did an echo after the cardiac arrest. We haven't found a clot."

"It *is* a clot. Her heart will stop again. It's just a matter of time. Why didn't you give her any blood-thinning meds?"

"She didn't need them. There is no clot. I know how to do my job. An angiograph will strain her heart that much more." His eyes jump between Anatolij and me. "She might die during the procedure."

Carlton scoffs, shaking his head a firm no, eyes boring into mine as he taps his foot on the floor, urging me to hurry up and take care of the admin side of things.

"Like I said before. Whatever Carlton says, goes."

The doctor huffs, face red as he glares at Anatolij. "I will not be held accountable if something goes wrong." He turns to Layla's bed and helps Carlton unhook the IV bags. "The radiology is three floors down."

"Stay here," Carlton tells me when I move to follow. "Believe me when I say you don't want to watch this. It'll take a while. Go grab a coffee. I'll find you when I'm done. Or better yet, get some sleep. You look like shit."

"Have you seen you lately?"

He elbows my ribs. "It'll take a while to prep her and do the procedure. Once that's out of the way, I'll still need to get rid of the clot, so you're looking at a good few hours wait."

Anatolij grips my shoulder. "He's right. You should rest. We'll go back to my house."

Sitting around in the waiting room for the better part of the night won't do me any good. Carlton will call with updates, so I bob my head, kiss Layla, and step aside. They push her bed down the corridor into an elevator.

Now that Carlton's here, the incessant whooshing in my brain subsides. She'll be okay. There's no other option. She's too important to die. Her life won't end today or any time soon.

I'll die first as a punishment for years of sins. Years of extortion, racketeering, and murders. The scams, ruthlessness, and arrogance. They say a bad thing never dies... I hope, at least in part, that's true because I look forward to a long, happy life with Layla.

Exhaustion hits me square in the gut when we leave the hospital, where a black limousine waits outside. Half an hour later, I collapse on a large bed in the room Layla had slept in for the past few weeks. Snow-white sheets, soaked in the sweet smell of her skin, lull me into a false sense of security. With the phone set to the loudest setting, I let myself sleep.

I'm jolted upright by an incoming call. A quick glance at an antique clock on the wall confirms I was flat out for six hours. Wide awake, muscles harder than steel, I slide my thumb across the screen.

"She's fine," Carlton says, smart enough to put my mind at ease in the first second. "It was a clot. I almost can't blame the doctor here for not spotting it. We did the surgery, and her vitals improved massively. She's still unconscious, but I'll gradually reduce the meds now."

I get up, sleep the very last thing on my mind. With good news comes new strength, a new dose of courage. "Does that mean she'll be okay?"

He chuckles lightly. "Did you dare to doubt my skills? Of course, she'll be okay. Forty-eight hours from now, you'll be able to take her home."

I clench my fist, then bite on my knuckles, my heart ramming against my ribs. "Thank you. I owe you *everything*, Carlton. I'll be there soon."

"You owe me nothing. Don't rush. It'll take a couple of hours before she wakes up." He cuts the call.

The castle is dark and quiet twenty minutes later when I exit Layla's room after a quick shower. My footsteps ricochet off the stone walls, booming down the staircase. A glint of light shimmers in the living room, halting me on my way out the front door.

"I thought you'd be asleep," I say, finding Julij at the table, a half-full glass of whiskey in his hand.

He lifts his drunken head, unfocused gaze on my face, fire burning in his usually cold, blue eyes.

"What's wrong?"

He downs the rest of the drink. "She's my *cousin*," he clips, pulling a cigarette out of the packet. Two seconds later, a cloud of gray smoke fans my face. "You fucking *knew*. You knew all this time, and you let me fall deeper in love with a girl I can't ever hope to be with."

"You never should've hoped." The satisfaction I expect to get out of this moment doesn't arrive. He's so heartbroken I actually feel sorry for him. "Layla's mine. She's been mine for a long time now. You had no right to think she could be yours."

"I'd never act on it while she's with you!"

"But you were waiting for us to fall apart so you could swoop in and make her fall for you, right?"

Anatolij enters the room wearing the same suit he wore the previous evening. "I think you had enough, Julij. Go. Sleep it off."

"Don't tell me what to do!" He takes a few unsteady steps in my direction. "You won at life, Dante. Don't you dare fuck it up. I take care of my family. You can be goddamn sure you'll end up six feet under if you hurt her."

Sensible, smart words.

Not what I expected. Especially not in the state he's in right now. He loves Layla almost as much as I do. I expected nothing short of a row, but not for the first time, Julij proves there's more to him than his father's legacy. I can see our friendship growing stronger over the years and lasting a lifetime.

"I assume you're awake because Carlton called," Anatolij says. "How is Layla?"

"He removed the clot. She's fine. More than fine, actually. Carlton says she'll be good to go home in two days."

"She's an Aristow after all. A fighter," Julij mumbles, stumbling out of the room.

"You go ahead. I'll freshen up and follow you to the hospital," Anatolij says as his phone starts ringing.

And before he answers, mine's ringing too...

"I'm at the airport in Moscow," Morte says, his voice strained. He probably walked through fucking hell and back.

That makes two of us. We're on the same boat. Both worried sick, prepared for the worst, ready to unleash our demons on one another. "Someone's waiting for you. He'll bring you straight to me."

"The order is closed," he offers quietly. "I did everything you asked, Dante. I want my son."

"We'll talk when you get here."

Deep down, I know Morte was Frank's tool; he merely did a favor to an old friend, but the satisfaction with which he carried out the task thus far turned him into an accomplice. He has to pay for his sins. Everyone does in the end. Morte will settle his debt much sooner than he anticipated.

We both have our fair share to answer for. Karma is out to get me, but today isn't that day. Today is judgment day. Today is revenge day. Today is the last day of my life as a man with no boundaries.

Tomorrow, a new chapter of my life will begin. No more living on the edge or looking danger in the eye. No more dealing with shit personally. No more putting myself on the line. Layla and I will be dead ten times over before my accounts dry out. Enough people work for me to do the work while I step back, coordinating from behind the scenes.

Layla deserves a bit of normality. And normality she'll get even if it means revaluating life as I know it.

Anatolij sits at the table, drumming his fingers on the armrest of his chair. I rang Carlton to tell him about the hold-up while Anatolij woke up one of the maids to serve us breakfast.

I can't stomach more than a piece of plain toast, but two cups of black coffee go down without a hitch while we wait for the son-of-a-bitch I once considered a friend.

"I take it you had confirmation that he retracted the hit?"

"Yes." I pinch a Marlboro between my teeth. "From more than one source."

"How long before everyone finds out?"

There's no guessing. Although because the same person issued and retracted the bounty, it'll take half the time than it would if I killed Morte, hoping for word of mouth alone to work its magic. Morte must've issued the retraction through the same channels he put this whole farce into motion in the first place to reach the same people.

"I'll keep the security running for a few months just to be safe, but I doubt we'll deal with many more killers. News travels fast among the likes of us. By the time we reach Chicago, ninety-nine percent of those interested will know Layla's no longer a feasible target."

Forty minutes go by before Lew arrives with the man who stopped the war between Frank and me from ending the night Layla put a bullet in her father's heart.

Morte enters the room. Sagged shoulders and a mask of indifference he wears is a front designed to avert my attention from the dark circles surrounding his eyes. From trembling hands, he keeps out of view. He's not the one to willingly showcase his weaknesses or admit defeat, but today, I hold his son in the palm of my hand.

He might be reckless, but he's not stupid enough to make one foul move. He knows my hand will ball into a tight fist, obliterating what he cares for.

All he can do now is hope I'll show mercy.

The thing is... I don't feel merciful.

The sound of the flat-lining heart monitor lingers at the back of my head, an endless reminder of how close I was to losing Layla, elevating my rage to blind fury.

"Sit down." I point at the seat opposite me.

He shakes his head, rooted to the ground. "I just want my son, Dante. Where is he?"

"Dead."

Four letters.

One word packed with more power than an H-bomb.

His world splinters apart before my eyes. He rocks on his feet, unable to hold himself up, and falls to his knees. Thick tears trail down his cheeks, his mind a cage. A fucking prison with no doors or windows. No way out.

I know. I lived through the insanity a few hours ago. I sank into the maddening trap at a snap of fingers, blinded with indescribable anguish.

Morte can't say a word. He can't scream. He can't do anything. Panic, regret, and an overpowering emptiness tear his heart, soul, and mind apart.

Catatonic, paralyzing fear.

No amount of physical pain I could inflict on the fucker would compare to the torture he's experiencing right now. If I chose to beat him to death, he'd have breaks from pain. Short, sure, but breaks, nonetheless. Every time my elbow would fall back before administering another blow—a break. A second to catch a breath.

There's no escaping from the madness consuming him whole as he kneels on the floor, tearing his hair out.

Anatolij, Lew, and I listen to his senseless, heartbreaking sobs for one hundred and ninety-seven seconds. That's how long Layla was clinically dead yesterday. Three minutes and seventeen seconds, which may well have been a lifetime.

The watch on my wrist tells me the seconds are up. I pull my gold revolver from the holster and get up on my feet, the gun aimed at his head. "Aiden's alive and safe in Chicago."

His eyes snap to me so fast I swear he almost broke his neck. Hope glows in the black, soulless eyes. With a strain, he rises to his feet, face wet, eyes tearful as he stares into the barrel with fresh terror. "Why...? Why tell me he's dead?"

"Layla's heart stopped yesterday because one of the hitmen found her here. He took the shot. The bullet missed her heart by a hair's breadth... for three minutes and seventeen seconds, I thought she was dead. The longest one hundred and ninety-seven seconds in my life and now yours. I wanted you to know what the pain of losing what you love feels like before you die."

I don't wait for an answer. There's no point in prolonging his misery. No point in talking or listening to pleas. Whatever he has to say, whatever bullshit excuse or deal he came up with on the long-haul flight here *isn't* good enough; isn't worth losing time I can spend by Layla's side.

I'm sure deep down, he knew he came here to die. When my index finger slides onto the trigger, a glimmer of relief flashes in his eyes. Relief, which can only be interpreted one way. He's grateful I chose to kill him over his son.

EPILOGUE
SIX MONTHS LATER

Dante

"No," I say, arms folded over my chest, eyes on Jean, who mimics my stance. "That's not up for discussion."

She scoffs, blowing an unruly lock of red hair off her flushed face. "You're right. It's not. She's staying with Jess and Anatolij, and that's *not* up for discussion."

"Um, can I say some—"

"No!" Jean and I both snap at Layla.

"You're staying home, Star."

"She is *not*!" Jean cries.

This might take a while. Jean's adamant Layla should spend the night at her parent's house, so I won't see her all day tomorrow until Anatolij walks her down the aisle at four in the afternoon. I am, obviously, very much against this idiotic idea.

For six months since we came home from Moscow, we spent every night together. Even if I had to fly to Detroit, New York, Dallas, or anywhere, Layla came with me.

I'm not letting that girl more than three miles out of my reach, and even when she's at college or visiting with Jess and Anatolij, one of my men is always there, standing outside the building.

What's most surprising is that not only does she not mind, but she was the one who asked for a bodyguard. The bounty, shooting, and near-death experience took a toll on her. She still wakes up drenched in sweat sometimes, plagued by nightmares. The scar on her chest reminds us daily how close we were to *the end.*

Both of us.

As much as I try not to replay the dreadful days I spent at the hospital in Moscow or the sound of the flat-lining heart monitor, I do. My mind was made the second Layla's heart stopped beating, and my resolution hasn't changed with time. I'll follow her out of this fucking world if she checks out before me. I go where she goes. No exceptions.

"I think Jean's right," Layla says. Great, two against one. "It's just one night, and they say it's bad luck to see the bride before the wedding."

"See? She's staying with Anatolij and Jess." Jean grips the small travel bag she already packed for Layla.

I've got a love-hate relationship with Jean. We get along well until we don't, but I like the verbal scuffles just as much as I like when she's easy-going. Now that she moved to Chicago two months ago, she became the mama-bear to all my men's girls, fighting for their rights, which drives her man—Jackson, up the fucking wall.

He knew what he was getting into falling in love with Miss independent, so I don't feel one bit sorry for him.

"Fine, one night," I huff, checking my watch. "I'll bring her over in two hours. For now, you might want to make yourself scarce."

No way I'll let her out of the house for a whole night before I get my fill.

The only person not to speak one word for the past twenty minutes rises from the couch. "We better go." Jackson grabs Layla's suitcase and Jean's hand. "You're not the bride, so why the hell are you staying with—" The door closes behind them.

Layla smiles, already on her way upstairs. She knows what I want. What I crave more and more every day, if that's even possible. I catch up with her in the bedroom and pin her to the wall, one hand clasped around her throat, the other on her hip.

"I don't like this idea."

She rises on her toes to reach my lips, speaking against them. "I know how to make this more bearable." She slowly pops all buttons on my shirt, her warm fingers ghosting down my chest. "Can I do as I please, or would you rather take over?"

"I think you know the answer to that." I fucking devour her, slipping my tongue in the silk of her mouth, tasting and teasing. I move one hand to press my fingers against the swollen bud on the apex of her thighs, earning a soft moan in return. "Good girl." I yank the zip on her dress, tugging so hard the fabric rips, then take off her bra and rip off her white panties. "On your knees for me."

She sinks. Not a moment's hesitation. She frees my stiff cock out of my boxer shorts, yanking my pants down. I step out of them, and Layla wraps her fingers around the base, confident, focused, and unmoving as she waits for further instructions.

"Open," I rasp, watching her lips fall apart. "Good girl. Make me come, baby."

She guides me into her hot mouth, and my eyes roll back into my head. She's delicate today, in a teasing mood as she only works the head of my cock. I watch her plump lips pump in sync with her small hand, and it drives me fucking wild. I grip her hair into a tight fist as the orgasm builds, bubbling to the surface like a boiling pot of milk.

"Fuck..." I pause when she takes me deeper, her cheeks hollow, eyes closed. "You're so good at this." A low growl leaves my lips, and it spurs her on.

She pumps faster, and the hold I have on her hair tightens, my hips bucking when she claws at my thighs, pulling me closer and deeper until the head of my cock hits the back of her throat, and I'm fucking done for.

"Out," I rasp, yanking my hips back, but she moves with me. "I'll come in your mouth if you don't let me go."

She sucks harder, holding onto my ass to keep me in place. I pin her head to the wall, pumping in and out of her mouth a few times before a powerful orgasm shatters my entire body, and muscles cramp with my release. Black spots flicker before my eyes, and I hold onto the wall for support, watching Layla swallow. A tiny trickle of cum slides from the corner of her lips. She looks up at me, cheeks pink. She's so fucking beautiful. I bend down, grip her under her arms and throw her on the bed.

"This is not how this was supposed to go down. I want to feel you come around my cock, Layla, so you're in for torture before I'm ready to go again." I cover her body with mine, twirling my tongue over her pebbled nipple.

It doesn't take long for the first orgasm to run through her body. Two, maybe three minutes of my lips on her clit and my fingers pumping in and out before she gasps, biting on my lip when I try to drink her moans.

We get to three before I'm ready, and the first deep, urgent thrust scoots Layla up the bed. I rest my weight on one elbow while the other hand holds onto her neck.

"Oh God," she breathes, the words like a breathless staccato when my thrusts gain pace and orgasm number four looms nearby.

I learned exactly where to push and probe to have Layla coming time and time again, and I sure use that skill to my advantage tonight. If I can get her exhausted beyond reason, she'll fall asleep and stay home tonight.

"It's too much, Dante, please, enough, I—"

"It's not too much. Don't hold back, Star. Let go."

Seven. Seven orgasms within two hours. Mission accomplished. She's so exhausted and mellow that her eyes fall shut on their own accord when I get out of bed.

"I know what you're doing," she mutters, cuddling one pillow to her chest. "Jean will be here within the hour if you don't take me to Anatolij's."

"Sleep, Star. I'll deal with Jean."

She smiles, eyes closed, and by the time I emerge from the bathroom with a washcloth, she's passed out.

The smell of freshly brewed coffee pulls me out of a peaceful, dreamless sleep—the kind I like best. I wash up and throw on a robe, heading downstairs.

"Good morning, sweetie," Jess chirps, rushing around the kitchen, setting cups of coffee in front of Jean and Anatolij.

Dante lost the fight with Jean last night, or rather, I forfeited when she screamed her head-off downstairs and woke me up less than half an hour after I nodded off.

"Good morning."

"Sleep well?" Jean hides a grin behind her cup.

"I would've slept better in my own bed."

She pulls a face, sticking out her tongue at me, then immediately straightens her spine when Anatolij walks into the kitchen. He bought this house a few days after I was released from the hospital in Moscow so he would have somewhere to stay when he visits. Still, not even three months later, he re-arranged his business in Moscow and moved to Chicago permanently when he and Jess got back together.

I'm happy for them, especially since my mother is changing back into the woman Anatolij described a few months ago, passionate and ambitious, no longer focused solely on her looks. It's all thanks to Anatolij, who, unlike Frank, nurtures Jess's qualities instead of fueling her flaws.

I've been spending a lot of time with both of my parents lately, working through my issues with Jess and getting to know Anatolij better. I'm not ready to call him Dad, and I might never be, but the bond we've formed over six months is more than I could've hoped for.

With a smile that might not leave my face for one second today, I take a cup of coffee from Jess.

"What are you grinning at?" Jean huffs.

I shrug, smiling wider. "Seven hours from now, I'll be Mrs. Carrow."

"If it was anyone else you wanted to marry so young, I'd strongly object," Jess says, resting her back against the cabinets. "But I won't because Dante is..."

"The right guy for me?" I laugh, expecting a cliché to come out of her no-longer-pink-and-glossy mouth

"I was going to say *scary*, but *right* works too. Jokes aside, this isn't the life I want for you, but Dante is the kind of a man I hoped you'd find. Take away his job, and he's all a mother wants for her daughter."

"What's so amazing about the guy?" Jean scoffs, shaking her head. "For the lack of more suitable candidates, I guess he'll have to do for now."

She'd fall ill if she admitted that Dante's her favorite person in the world. Most of the time, they bicker and argue, but they've become good friends during the past few months of her excessive visits to Chicago while she and Jackson couldn't stay apart for longer than a week at a time.

That might be why he proposed two months ago and whisked her out of Ivanhoe to live with him. They're not in a rush to get married, but the engagement ring on her finger meant Aunt Amanda couldn't oppose. Not that she's happy her daughter is dating a criminal.

The gravely interesting conversation is interrupted by Mr. Carrow himself when my phone vibrates on the counter. "Good morning," I say, pressing the phone to my ear. "Have you missed me already?"

"You have no idea," he breaths, sending a pleasant, tingling sensation down my spine. "Did you sleep well?"

A doorbell rings and Jess frowns, looking over my shoulder, down the hallway. "Are we expecting someone?"

"Yes, we are," Jean smiles. "I'll get it."

"Please don't tell me you're outside the house," I tell Dante, watching Jean rush past me to yank the door open.

"No, it's not me. Who is it?"

"It's Tyler and Rick." I smile at the boys, then frown when Jean snatches the phone out of my hand.

"Hey, lover boy. I hope you had your fix because you won't talk to her again for six hours." She pauses, listening to Dante as she chews on her lip. "That shit's getting old. Put your big-boy pants on." Another pause, accompanied by a cheeky smile. "I'll take care of it. Bye."

"Take care of what?"

I'm not allowed in on the secret, although judging by what happens during the next hours, I'd say Dante asked her to make today a stress-free day for me.

Too bad she almost turns gray, panicking that things aren't ready on time. She rushes around the house, shouting at the make–up artist and the hairdresser every five minutes, taking her role as my maid of honor a touch too seriously.

"We've only got an hour left, and you're not even dressed yet!" she cries, prodding my chest with her finger.

"Stop panicking. God, you'd think you're the bride. Better go and get me more coffee."

"How are you so calm! What if you're late for your own wedding?!"

"I'm pretty sure Dante will wait for me." I smile, feeling perfectly at ease and happy for the first time in my life.

Let's connect! Join my reader group and newsletter for exclusive news, content and giveaways

Instagram
Facebook
Reader Group

Printed in Great Britain
by Amazon

83205275R00181